ROUGH CUT

Also by Wendy Church

The Jesse O'Hara Series

MURDER ON THE SPANISH SEAS *
MURDER BEYOND THE PALE *
MURDER IN THE GREEK ISLES *

The Shadows of Chicago Mysteries

KNIFE SKILLS *
TUNNEL VISION *

* *available from Severn House*

ROUGH CUT

Wendy Church

First world edition published in Great Britain and the USA in 2026
by Severn House, an imprint of Canongate Books Ltd,
14 High Street, Edinburgh EH1 1TE.

severnhouse.com

Cover and jacket design by Piers Tilbury

British Library Cataloguing-in-Publication Data
A CIP catalogue record for this title is available from the British Library.

ISBN-13: 978-1-4483-1563-5 (cased)
ISBN-13: 978-1-4483-1895-7 (paper)
ISBN-13: 978-1-4483-1564-2 (e-book)

All Severn House titles are printed on acid-free paper.

Typeset by Palimpsest Book Production Ltd., Falkirk, Stirlingshire, Scotland.
Printed and bound in Great Britain by TJ Books, Padstow, Cornwall.

The manufacturer's authorised representative in the EU for product safety is Authorised Rep Compliance Ltd, 71 Lower Baggot Street, Dublin D02 P593 Ireland (arccompliance.com)

Praise for the Shadows of Chicago Mysteries

"A gripping read with an unusual plot, a quirky heroine, and plenty of bizarre twists"
Booklist on *Tunnel Vision*

"Dizzying . . . Audiences who wished the TV series *The Bear* had made room for Russian mobsters are in for a treat"
Kirkus Reviews Starred Review of *Knife Skills*

"A riveting, entertaining read that will appeal to fans of Janet Evanovich"
Booklist on *Knife Skills*

"With brisk pacing and dynamic characters, Church keeps readers enthralled"
Publishers Weekly on *Knife Skills*

About the author

Wendy Church, PhD, is the author of the Shadows of Chicago Mysteries. *Knife Skills*, the first in the series, received a Starred Review from *Kirkus Reviews*. Her debut novel, and the first in her Jesse O'Hara series, *Murder on the Spanish Seas*, was named by *Booklist* as a Top 10 Debut Mystery & Thriller of 2023. She lives in Seattle, Washington with her partner and several animals.

wendyschurch.com
@wendychurchwriter

For Lynnette Church, who will never see this, but supported my love of books from the beginning. Rest in peace, mom.

ONE

I hadn't been downtown at morning rush hour in a long time. Normally people would be streaming into the Loop to start their workday.

Instead, growing rivulets of humanity were moving toward the river. Some stopped to lean over the metal and stone barriers on the street above. Others poured down from the Riverwalk to the shallow steps at the shore. They were all looking at the water.

Every year on March 17th, the Chicago River was dyed bright kelly green to commemorate the holiday. Once, in 2016, they turned it "Cubbie Blue," in honor of the team's World Series championship.

Today it flowed like a bloody wound through the heart of the city, the rising sun revealing the naturally olive green water as deep crimson.

Too late for Halloween. Someone's idea of a joke?

I stepped around the growing crowds and crossed the Dearborn bridge. As I reached the other side I heard shouting.

Hundreds of fingers were pointing in the same direction. Snagged on an underwater fixture at the base of the State Street Bridge bobbed a body. Its arms lay flat on the water's surface, like wings, the head disappearing and resurfacing in rhythm with the gentle current.

I turned away and continued downtown. FBI Supervisory Special Agent Smith was waiting for me at the diner on Lake Street. He gave me a hard time when I was late, and I wanted to get it over with.

"Smith," I said, sitting down across from him in the booth. The last one in the back, of course. I left my coat on.

"Sagarine. Thanks for coming."

"Did I have a choice?"

"Do you want some coffee?" He waved to the waitress.

We stayed silent until she refilled his cup and poured one for me.

"How are things going?"

He didn't call me here to catch up on my life. "Just spill it. What is it you want me to do?"

"I need you to cook for an event."

When I didn't respond, he continued. "There's going to be a dinner party, a very exclusive dinner party, taking place on the *Enterprise*."

"Nikky Bullware cooks on that boat." I knew her fairly well; occasionally we slept together.

"She's not going to be able to make this event."

"How do you know that?"

He stared at me.

"OK . . . Can you tell me whose party it is?"

"It's Richard Nottingham's annual bash."

"Nottingham? The diamond guy?"

"Yes."

"Why is it so important that I cook for this particular party?"

"I'd rather not give you any more information right now. The most important thing is that you make the best meal of your life. Money is no object. And I really mean, no object. Do whatever it takes to impress them."

"What's wrong with Nikky?"

I'd been seeing her for six months. It wasn't serious; we were both busy with our careers, and neither of us were looking for a long-term relationship. But I liked her, and I had no interest in taking over her gig. And I had my own restaurant to run.

"Nothing. She's just being encouraged to say no to this event."

This sounded sketchy, but it wasn't like I could decline. In exchange for not arresting me a year ago for various transgressions, I was now on the hook to do favors for Smith and the FBI whenever he asked. And I had to agree to be a good girl from now on. Which, as far as he knew, I had been.

It wasn't a bad deal for me. I'd stayed out of jail, and had also gotten my restaurant out of it. The FBI thought it would provide a good front for my continued participation in their activities, and gave it to me after confiscating it from the previous owner, a Russian mob boss who they'd put away. With my help.

"When is this dinner party?"

"Next Saturday night."

Jesus. "Do you know how long it takes to plan and prep a meal like this? And they haven't even asked me yet."

"Don't worry, they will. Ms. Bullware will decline with very little time for them to find a replacement, and she's going to recommend you. I suggest you start preparing now."

"What about staff? Servers? Cooks? The bar?" I wish he'd given me more notice on this stuff.

"The boat has its own bar and staff, but you can augment that with whatever servers or cooks you want. Other than Maude, or anyone else associated with law enforcement."

No law enforcement. That meant criminals at the event. "Is this another Russian mob thing? The last time you made me do that I almost got killed. Several times."

"No mob. I don't expect anything dangerous to happen on the boat."

I didn't miss the fact that he'd said nothing dangerous "on the boat."

"Can I get a guest list?"

"I'll send it to you. In addition to Nottingham and his family will be a hundred or so very well connected, powerful, and wealthy people." He picked up his menu and opened it.

I stared at him while he pretended to peruse the food options. "That's all you're going to tell me?"

"Yes, for now. Can I buy you breakfast?"

"No thanks." I finished my coffee and stood up. "If I'm going to make the meal of my life I need to start getting ready now. It's not like I have a restaurant to run, too, or anything."

He looked up from his menu. "We'll meet the day after the dinner. I'll let you know where and when. And, obviously, don't tell anyone about this discussion."

I nodded distractedly and turned away.

"I mean it, Sagarine. Tell no one. That includes Maude."

I was a little surprised at that. The two of them had been seeing each other, off and on, for over a year, and I assumed they shared everything. But after the leaks they'd had in the Chicago PD it wasn't all that surprising he didn't want me sharing his operations with anyone.

Still, she was my roommate, and best friend. It would be hard to keep it from her.

"Sure, fine."

I left him sitting there with his menu and walked out. I headed for the Merchandise Mart L stop. Not the closest one, but I liked walking over the bridge.

By the time I made it back to Wacker Drive crime scene tape was blocking both ends of the State Street Bridge. Uniformed police and firefighters had replaced the onlookers on the steps. Two divers were in the water, bringing in the body.

I crossed the bridge to head back uptown. I didn't need to see the body. I already knew who it was.

It took just under an hour to get to my restaurant, Saga, in Chicago's northwest Portage Park neighborhood. I met with my sous chef Zoe to review the day's menu, then I went upstairs to plan for the cruise dinner.

Smith had sent me the guest list, and I spent the first two hours doing research on Nottingham and his friends. He'd been right, the guests were a who's who of the richest and most well-connected people in the city, as well as a fair number from outside of it.

Most of them represented businesses and countries important in the worldwide diamond supply and distribution chain: diamond moguls and ambassadors from diamond-producing counties, businessmen from Belgium and the United Arab Emirates, a few politicians in charge of regulations that affected the industry. I took careful notes of each guest, in particular Nottingham and his family. As one of the wealthiest in Chicago they were regularly in the news, although there was surprisingly little about Richard Nottingham.

Once I nailed down the menu I put together my shopping list. Time flew, and when I took a break, dinner service had started. I poked my head down the stairs to see if they needed any help.

Zoe was focused on the night's amuse-bouche. Everyone else was at their stations, calmly prepping the seven courses that made up the tasting menu. I went back upstairs and started calling my food vendors.

By the time I was done dinner service was over and I could hear them cleaning up in the kitchen. I checked in again with Zoe. We discussed the menus for the next week, and I let her know I wouldn't be around much but to call me if she needed something. When I finally left it was close to midnight.

It took another hour on the bus to get to our place in Andersonville. I used to be able to walk from the restaurant to our last place, an apartment in Portage Park, but we'd decided to buy our own house. I hadn't been thrilled about moving, but we'd found a good deal, and Maude insisted. After spending three days last year wandering around alone and almost dying in Chicago's tunnels, she was done living in a basement apartment.

What sealed the deal was that with Zoe running things at Saga I didn't need to go in every day. She was good, at both cooking and managing a kitchen, and would have her own restaurant at some point. For my sake I hoped it would be later rather than sooner.

I got off at the Argyle stop, the only train station in the city with a pagoda embellishment above the tracks, and walked to our place on Ashland. Situated between two taller buildings, our house had been sold as a duplex, with two kitchens, four bedrooms, and four bathrooms spread out over three floors. I had the bottom floor bedroom and bathroom and we shared the upstairs living room and kitchen, leaving me free to use the lower one for recipe testing.

As was often the case Maude was still up when I got home, sitting on the floor in the living room working on her computer. I grabbed a beer and joined her.

"Writing, or working?"

In her spare time she wrote novels, under the pen name Betty Phang. Some people called them porn; she referred to them as "female-centered pleasure books." Each one included a diagram with the relevant female anatomy in the back, complete with arrows, descriptions, and suggestions.

She'd written a bunch of them, with titles like *It Rhymes with Delores*, and *Jurassic Cock*, all published in paperback by a small house. She'd often give them out after dates, her book choice a reflection of what she thought about her date's romantic acumen.

"Working. They're putting me on another task force. Our first official meeting is tomorrow."

Maude liked her job as an analyst, and was good at it, so it wasn't a surprise that the PD put her on as many projects as possible. This despite the fact that she didn't look the part, and put up with regular, albeit good-natured, ribbing about her spiked blonde hair and goth-themed makeup, wardrobe, and jewelry.

"You don't sound too happy about it. What's this one for?"

She normally didn't mind being assigned to the task forces the department set up, even though the work on the teams was in addition to everyone's regular duties, and meant working weekends, and canceling paid leave or vacations. She loved what she did, and it provided a solid outlet for her prodigious intellect.

"Did you hear about the river?"

"What about it?"

"Someone turned it red last night."

"Oh, yeah. I saw it this morning."

"This morning?" She looked up from her computer. "What were you doing downtown?"

Oops. "Checking out a fish vendor." I hated lying to her, and was terrible at it. Smith would need to bring her in on his operation as soon as possible.

"A little dye in the river rates a task force? Why do they have you working on pranks?" They usually saved her for the really important stuff.

"I know. It shouldn't. But it's the second one of these that's happened in the last two weeks."

"Second one of what?"

"Last Wednesday someone left a huge pile of meat in front of Wrigley."

"Meat?"

"Raw meat. Not-so-fresh raw meat. Dumped in the middle of the plaza, right underneath the sign."

"That's disgusting. Why do they think the river's related to the raw meat?"

"At both sites whoever did it left a string of numbers nearby. Big, white spray-painted numbers. There was a set left at Wrigley, and another one written across the State bridge."

She pulled up a picture on her computer, an up-close shot of the bridge. Across the metal supports was 007 245 679.

She switched pictures to one of Wrigley Field. On the hallowed sign, just under "Home of Chicago Cubs," was 987 654 223.

"Huh. Still, don't the police have better things to do than chase down vandals?" This seemed trivial compared to all of the other shit that went on in the city on a daily basis.

"We do. But this makes two of Chicago's iconic landmarks that have been desecrated in the last two weeks. The mayor wants it stopped right now. In his defense, it looks like whoever is doing it is escalating. There was a body this time."

Uh oh. "A body?"

"Yeah, in the river. It got caught up underneath the bridge."

"How do they know the body's related to the dye in the river?"

"It's quite a coincidence, don't you think? And besides, they think it might be a murder."

"Why do they think it's a murder?" I said, looking down.

"They're not sure, but the dead man was Frank Chimen. He's a big time drug dealer, and—" she looked up again. "Is there something you want to tell me?"

"Let's just say I'm pretty sure Frank Chimen didn't have anything to do with the river turning red."

"Goddammit," she mumbled, shaking her head. "Just what I need. What am I supposed to tell the rest of the team? That an 'unnamed informant' assured me that the body doesn't have anything to do with the rest of the scene?"

"Chimen was a pimp and a drug dealer, and he preyed on young girls. He was a dirtbag, but not the kind of dirtbag who would have anything to do with something as innocent as dyeing the river. I'm sure of it."

TWO

I spent the rest of the week getting ready for the dinner cruise, only going to the restaurant once to adjust the menu when one of our food vendors suffered a break-in and lost all of his inventory. Weird, people stealing raw food.

Smith had said to make the best meal of my life. I knew enough about cooking for the wealthy to know that serving great food wasn't going to be enough. People with this kind of money routinely experienced wildly expensive delicacies such as caviar, Kobe beef, and gold flakes. In order to wow this group I needed to give them something they didn't always get. And of course everything had to be perfect.

The morning of the event I went to Navy Pier early to board the *Enterprise* and start prepping. Just north of downtown, the 3,000-foot pier that jutted out into Lake Michigan was loaded with shops, restaurants, a Ferris wheel, and other attractions, and was usually crowded with people. But it was early, and cold, and most of the shops were closed, and I was able to experience it sans throngs of visitors. I walked to the end and sat on the bronze couch next to the Bob Newhart statue and looked out on the lake.

Many people weren't aware that at one time the Pier had been an operating naval aviator training installation; George Bush the First, among others, had done his training here at the beginning of World War Two. People also weren't aware that there were a number of crashed planes sitting on the bottom of Lake Michigan from less-than-successful training sessions. Two facts that I was sure were unrelated.

After a few minutes I boarded the *Enterprise* and headed straight for the galley.

It was a chef's dream. Larger than most restaurant kitchens, its polished metal surfaces and cabinets were spaciously arranged on spotless floors, surrounded by multiple prep, stove, oven, and processing stations, and lots of counter space. A quick glance suggested the pantry was well stocked, and the walk-in freezer was almost as big as the one at Saga.

There were worse things than being forced to cook in this kitchen with an unlimited budget.

My food vendors showed up soon after I did, and at noon my staff from Saga arrived. The *Enterprise* had its own kitchen and waitstaff, but I'd wanted a few of my own people.

Zoe couldn't get away on a Saturday, not these days. We'd been steadily receiving good press since I'd taken over the restaurant from its previous owner and revamped the menu. Pushing us over the top was a recent stellar review from one of the city's top food writers.

Saga Brings Warm Refinement to Chicago's Portage Park
By Maggie Hennessy

It takes more than excellent food to make a great restaurant. Unique, compelling, and formidable, Saga defines quiet greatness. Owner and chef Sagarine Pfister has created a restaurant experience that occupies a distinct intersection of exceptional cuisine and personal storytelling. The seven-course chef's menu at Saga is more than a meal; it's a journey that disarms, delights, and challenges in equal parts.

Unassuming from the outside and located humbly on the eastern edge of Portage Park, Saga's warmly lit, industrial space is softened by pendant lighting and rotating local art, the kitchen revealing in small snippets the low buzz of intensity at each sweep of the swinging doors. The spacious dining room is only partially separated from the cozy bar tucked in the back, offering its own mini climate to those stopping by for one of Saga's unique specialty drinks, a glass of wine from the extensive list, or locally sourced draft beers.

Chef Pfister, aka "Sags," is classically French trained, yet boldly wields molecular gastronomy performance art that is often mind-blowing and always delicious. The amuse-bouche of green ramp flan, topped with a small dollop of caviar that does its job waking up the palate, is followed by a deconstructed vichyssoise, playfully entitled “Not Your Mother’s Cold Soup.” A chilled, brightly green leek foam is poured tableside over small potato spheres coated in clarified butter and dusted with cilantro ash. Light and beautiful, the dish delivers perfection, and raises concern that the menu must be downhill from here.

The main course—“Fowl Play”—puts that worry to rest. Smoked duck breast resting on a cranberry reduction is served alongside a delicate duck-liver mousse sheathed in a translucent sphere of cherry consommé. The flavors blend into an inexplicably gentle cacophony of umami, tart, and sweet.

Dessert, too, is dramatic and flawless. “Treasure Garden” arrives as a sugar dome resting on chocolate mousse and persimmon gelée. Wielding a petite mallet cracks the dome, revealing edible rose petals and perfectly formed gel pearls.

The other courses can be left to the reader’s imagination, as while Saga’s menu changes biweekly, describing them here would spoil the surprise for anyone who might be going there this week. Suffice it to say that each course seems to surpass the previous, and none missed a single beat.

Service at Saga is both clinically perfect and graciously warm. Approachable staff lack the officiousness often displayed by haute-cuisine waiters, and move you gently along the meal, sharing not just the ingredients, but the story of each dish. Like the food, the wine pairings are perfect, yet unpretentious, never sacrificing flavor and appearance for grandiose affectation.

Saga is adventurous and comforting, excellent and humble, personal and perfect.

Rating: Five stars plus.

We were now booked up five to six weeks in advance, and I'd had to hire extra waitstaff and line cooks. But it meant that there was no way Zoe could get away on a Saturday.

I did manage to grab Elliott from the kitchen, our bartender Courtney, my outstanding pastry chef Declan, and our newest staff member, Michael.

Michael was Maude's brother. He'd disappeared twenty years ago as a child, and his family thought he was dead. But he'd turned up last year after living on the streets for most of his life, and when Maude found him he was working for one of the fentanyl-pushing gangs in the city. She'd helped him get off the streets and out of the gang, and now he was living with their parents in Avondale.

He was a good kid, and I'd offered him a dishwashing job at Saga. Before long he'd shown his affinity for cooking, and was now one of our main prep chefs. He didn't talk much, but he was detailed and focused, and his work was outstanding.

I gave the team a summary of the menu and the evening's schedule and we went to work. At four o'clock the staff from the *Enterprise* joined us, and we all worked quietly for the rest of the afternoon, the cooks putting together the food, the bar staff setting up the alcohol, the servers laying out the dining room, and me moving among them to answer questions and help where needed.

At seven on the dot the diners began to board. Mostly men, in expensive-looking dark suits and ties. A few were joined by glamorous women, all of whom were adorned with diamond earrings, diamond necklaces, or both.

The dining area filled up quickly. I hadn't wanted to be too fussy with pre-dinner service, so we'd put together minimal tray offerings. Waitstaff circulated among the guests with platters of simple smoked fish bites and my green ramp flan served in spoons, along with small skewers of Ibérico ham and the aromatic and incredibly juicy Yubari King melon.

The tray service was augmented by caviar stations positioned around the room. While the main bar was crewed by the *Enterprise*'s bar staff, Courtney greeted each guest at the door with a glass of Louis Roederer Cristal Brut.

She'd been thrilled when I'd told her about the event. "Seriously? No fucking budget?"

"Seriously."

I knew she'd go all-out, and wasn't surprised to see her start with the Louis Roederer, a bottle of this vintage generally costing in the high four-figure range.

At seven thirty the low murmur of conversation stopped. Heads turned as Richard Nottingham stepped through the dining room's double doors.

He towered above his conspicuous security detail, the four of them arranged around him like a Roman phalanx. His perfectly styled white hair matched the white of his shirt, which lay underneath a tailored silk suit that stood out in a room full of tailored suits. I'd done my research on Nottingham and his family, and had seen pictures of him, but they didn't capture his piercing blue eyes, or how his high cheekbones seemed to pull his face up from his thin, tight lips.

He looked just like what he was: the wealthy and powerful owner of a diamond empire, and one of the world's leading diamantaires. The people in the room discretely jockeyed to move close to him.

Courtney left for the kitchen, returning shortly with a tray holding a single cup of tea. English breakfast tea, with cream, a dash of salt, and a little butter. She offered it to Nottingham, whose eyebrows went up slightly as he took it. I got the sense this was an extreme expression of emotion from him, and was glad I'd done my research.

His security team were wearing matching black turtlenecks and brown suits. Most of them had dispersed to points around the room, their heads on slow swivels, their faces blank. Mason Cooper, the leader, had reportedly been with the family for years. He stood closest to Nottingham, and as he moved through the room Mason stayed with him, as if they were attached by a string, never drifting more than a couple of feet away. Like the others he was clean shaven, his only distinguishing feature his curly reddish-blond hair cut so close to the scalp it looked like it hurt.

Now that Nottingham was here the boat pulled away from

the dock. The people in the room quickly broke into discussion groups, the largest circled around Nottingham.

He'd lost his wife years ago and never remarried. Standing next to him was his oldest son, Alan, who looked like a younger, happier version of his dad. He was smiling broadly, and in his Daniel Craig-version James Bond suit looked like the heir apparent to the Nottingham empire.

Close at Alan's side was his wife, Celeste. Similar to the other women in the room she was dressed to kill, and covered in diamonds that set off flawless makeup and styled hair that was swept up off of her neck. Her off-the-shoulder black cocktail dress fit her body perfectly, and almost but not quite garish diamond pendants hung from each ear. A sparkling necklace transformed the room's ambient illumination into tiny points of perfect light that somehow managed not to take away at all from the fact that she was drop-dead gorgeous.

Her brilliant smile matched her husband's, the two of them the archetype of a happy perfect marriage of perfect happy people.

Somewhere on the boat were Nottingham's daughter and youngest son, but I was too busy to look for them. I'd wanted to start the evening off with a bang, something that signaled this wasn't going to be a typical dinner. It was time.

I pulled Michael away from his prep station and went to the walk-in freezer. We carefully wheeled my surprise out of the kitchen and into the dining room, placing it next to the bar.

I drew off the covering cloth, revealing a near-perfect replica of Chicago's Jewelers Row, carved out of ice.

My ice guy, Jake, had spent an entire week working on nothing but this. Eight feet wide and five feet high, the recreation of Jewelers Row was meticulously detailed, down to the Wacker Drive that ran across the front of the entrance to the shops. In the center was Nottingham's own store, the largest one in the jeweler's complex, Carat and Crown.

Diamonds of various sizes were carved in and among the scene's elements, the largest of which, at almost a foot across, rested majestically at the top.

I'd paid an exorbitant amount for Jake to put this together. Some of the cost was the rush nature of the job, but some because he'd paid a diamond cutter to help with the ice diamonds. They were all carefully carved not only to resemble real stones, but to include facets that would reflect light.

LED lights were discretely distributed at the base of the sculpture. When I plugged them in the scene burst to life, the light perfectly catching and amplifying the layered facets of the diamonds.

The conversation around the room stopped. Everyone's eyes were on Courtney as she walked to the sculpture with a bottle of Watenshi, Japanese Angel gin, in one hand, and Cinzano 1757 Vermouth di Torino Extra Dry in the other. She poured them into two openings at the top.

The two liquid streams flowed inside the sculpture via separate tunnels. In the center they merged into a single chute that emptied from an exit at the bottom, and into a martini glass that she held beneath it.

She dropped a Castelvetrano olive into the glass, and then raised the perfectly chilled martini to the crowd.

After a long moment, the ambassador from Gabon walked forward and took the glass. He sipped it and smiled.

Muted golf clapping arose from around the room, a relatively raucous response from a crowd like this. Many of them were making their way to the sculpture for their own martinis.

Mission accomplished.

I snuck a quick look at Nottingham. He and Alan had already gone back to his discussion with their group. It would take more than a spectacular ice sculpture martini station to impress him.

As I headed back to the kitchen I spotted Nottingham's other two kids. Martin, his youngest, was standing off to the side of the main family group, an empty champagne glass dangling from two fingers.

Most of the tabloid reporting on the family had been about Martin. He was famous for wild parties, drugs, and alcohol fueled debauch-fests, and had narrowly avoided jail time on multiple occasions. Tonight he was wearing the same no-doubt-five-figure suit as his father and brother, but his shirt was already starting to untuck on one side, and his tie hung slack. Bangs from an unruly mop of brown hair almost completely covered bruised brown eyes. His full lips, in stark contrast to his brother, were set in a scowl, all of it somehow contributing to a sloppy handsomeness.

Next to Martin was the daughter. Anastasia. "Tasia" to her friends and family, she stood out as the only woman in pants. Black silk pants, matched with a black mandarin-collared blazer that was held together by a single button. As far as I could tell there was no shirt underneath.

Unlike Martin she took after her father. She was as tall as me, close to five ten, with striking blue eyes framed by thick lashes. Her simply styled black hair dropped to just below her shoulders.

No diamonds for her, her only adornment a silver locket hanging from a thin chain around her neck.

In a room full of beautiful people it was hard to take my eyes off of her.

While I was watching them Martin disappeared into the hallway that led to the bathroom. Likely to put more coke up his nose; I'd noticed a dusting of white powder on his nostrils. Tasia's eyes followed him.

We'd been told to serve dinner promptly at eight thirty and it was getting close to that. I went back to the kitchen to add the final touches to the meal while the *Enterprise*'s staff arranged the main room for dinner, moving the tables from the sides of the room into the center and getting people seated.

At eight thirty on the dot the servers walked out to the dining area with the first course.

Smith had said I needed to make the best meal of my life, but making a great meal meant more than just using expensive ingredients.

People cherished food that provided positive flavor memories. My theme for the night was dishes tailored to the individual guests, with variations of comfort food from each of their home countries.

The caviar stands around the room had been accompanied by fried potato cakes, an Australian favorite. I started the sit-down portion of the dinner with appetizers of Matemekwane, the popular Botswanan dumpling, and blue-fin tuna carpaccio. These were followed by dishes that displayed luxury ingredients used in bulk, including black truffle noodles, white truffle soup, a few simple green salads, and Kobe beef served three ways. The cheese plate featured Belgium's award winning Baliehof Houtlandse Asche kaas, and everything was accompanied by Courtney's perfectly matched wines.

As always, Declan knocked the dessert course out of the park. Australian lamingtons, South African malva pudding, and Canadian butter tarts were served family style. There were exclamations of surprise and delight when the large platters were placed on the tables, and I watched as hands eagerly reached for pieces of familiar confections.

Success, at least if Nottingham rated this meal by the happiness of his guests. He ate little, and his flat expression never changed.

After dessert the staff moved the tables aside and the talking groups re-formed, this time mostly smaller ones of two or three.

It was quiet, the boisterous conversations at and before dinner replaced by intense—in a few cases, heated—discussions conducted in hushed tones. Big business was happening here.

I stood next to Courtney near the bar, pulling the tie out of my hair and shaking it out. "Quite the perfect family. Wealthy, beautiful, and gracious. Except for Martin. But even perfect families tend to have one black sheep. And he still knows how to behave at one of his dad's events."

"You think?" she murmured, looking at Celeste.

"You think not?"

"Well, for one thing, that one has a serious drinking problem."

"What are you talking about?" I'd only seen Celeste with water in her hand, other than when she'd tried one of the ice sculpture martinis.

Courtney snorted. "That's straight vodka. She's been mainlining it all night."

"You're kidding." Celeste didn't look the least bit drunk. She'd spent the evening by her husband's side, smiling and nodding appreciatively, making gracious small talk with other guests. The perfect spouse to the heir apparent.

"And I don't know if you noticed, but I think there's some kind of rift. Tasia and Martin didn't speak to the other family members all night. They didn't even go near them."

"They're just trying to stay out of the way while their dad and Alan do business."

"Maybe. But look at the big guy," she said, nodding at Nottingham. "I mean, I get it, he's the big serious man, but how can you go a whole night and not crack a single smile? How can he be that unhappy? He's got everything, and he looks like someone just took away his favorite toy."

The muted drone of conversation in the room was abruptly joined by another sound. A sizzling hiss, and a small tinkling crackle.

"Oh my God," one of the women gasped.

Martin had pulled a chair over next to the ice sculpture and was standing on it. His pants were unzipped, and he was holding his penis in his hands. A steady stream of urine was splattering on the large central diamond on the sculpture, now rapidly deforming under the warm spray.

My first instinct was to laugh. The sculpture was expensive and beautiful, but its useful life was near over. I couldn't think of a better way to say goodbye to a piece of temporary art.

Nottingham didn't share my delight in his youngest son's artistic comment. He gave a small nod to Mason, who in turn waved his hand at one of the other security staff, who fast-walked to the ice sculpture and put his hand on Martin's arm.

Mason shook his head, then strode over to the sculpture. He moved like a big cat, his footsteps barely making a sound as he crossed the floor. He brushed the first security man aside and roughly pulled Martin off the chair.

Which turned out to be a mistake, as he wasn't quite done urinating. The last of his spray made a short semicircle as he was spun around, some of it landing on Mason, and some on the South African ambassador and his wife who'd been standing nearby.

"Take it easy!" hissed Tasia, as Mason dragged Martin toward the door by the arm. She followed them outside, on the way throwing a dark glance at her father.

"Yep. A perfect family," said Courtney.

THREE

True to his word, Smith called me the next morning, way too early, to set up our meet. At least this time I didn't have to go all the way downtown.

It was a straight shot down Clark Street on the 22 bus. After enduring a crowded, hot, and humid twenty or so minutes, I stepped out into the freezing cold and joined him in line at the Wieners Circle.

We didn't say anything until we'd gotten our food, along with the requisite insults and famously surly service, and then got in to his SUV.

I wasn't sure why he bothered meeting secretly. Between the pristine black paint job and blacked out windows, his car screamed "law enforcement."

"Here, use this," he said, handing me a napkin. "I don't want crumbs all over my seats."

To his credit he waited for my information until we'd finished eating arguably the best hot dogs in the world. No small distinction in a city famous for them.

"How did it go?"

"Fine, I think."

"'Fine'? Do you think you wowed them?"

"I did my best. The guests seemed happy."

"What about the family?"

"Celeste was definitely excited. Although that might have had something to do with her blood-alcohol level."

"She was drunk?"

"Not that anyone could tell. But she put away a week's worth of booze."

"Huh. What about Richard Nottingham? The rest of the family?"

"Hard to tell. Apparently his superpower is maintaining the same expression at all times. Alan and Celeste worked the room, between them I think they managed to chat up everyone. There's some kind of rift. Neither Anastasia—Tasia—nor Martin spoke to any of the other members of the family the entire night. They're a pair; the only time they weren't next to each other was during his trips to the bathroom to coke up, and his ice sculpture performance art."

In response to Smith's puzzled look, I added, "He capped off the night by urinating on the $25,000 ice sculpture."

"You're kidding."

"No. It was kind of funny. But daddy didn't think so. His security guys dragged him outside."

"So, what's your impression of the family?"

"Typical billionaires, I guess. An impossibly rich patriarch, with a perfectly handsome and gracious Ken-doll son being groomed to take over the family estate, with a perfectly gracious, beautiful, albeit possibly alcoholic, wife. The youngest son is clearly the black sheep. I didn't get much of a take on Tasia, other than she seems to be in some kind of caretaker's role for Martin. And she's really hot."

He nodded. "That's our take, too, other than we weren't aware of Celeste's drinking problem. There is some kind of family rift, between Tasia and Martin and their father, although no one seems to know what it's about. But it's been going on for years."

"Are you going to tell me what's with all the interest in this family?"

"You're going to work for them."

"I'm sure they already have a private chef."

"They do. The job is as their event chef."

"Don't they already have one of those, too?"

"They did, but they lost him a couple of weeks ago. A family emergency of indefinite duration."

I had no doubt the FBI was responsible for the family emergency. "OK. Now are you going to tell me what the hell is going on?"

"The dinner on the boat was your audition. We know they've already asked Ms. Bullware to replace their event chef, and she's turned them down. It's natural they'll turn to you."

"In case you haven't noticed, I already have a job. I'm running a restaurant, remember?"

This was technically true, although lately I'd been getting a little bored. Zoe handled almost everything at Saga at this point, and I'd started to look around for something else to do. But I didn't want to tell Smith that. He needed to believe he was inconveniencing me.

"You can still do that. You won't be living at their estate; they have a live-in cook for daily meals. The event chef is dedicated to, you know, events. They host a dinner at their home about every two weeks."

"There's no way I can do what I just did on that boat every two weeks, Smith."

"No, no," he said, raising his hands. "Not like the thing on the boat. That's an annual event. The home things are never more than thirty people or so. Mostly small business dinners, or sometimes family parties like birthdays, or anniversaries. Occasionally holiday events. You'd basically be on call to them."

I leaned back against the window, shaking my head. "I don't care. I'm not doing this until you tell me what's going on. I presume you didn't go to all this trouble to expand my professional horizons."

He stuffed his napkin in the paper bag and crumpled it up, placing it in a small trash receptacle behind his seat. Then he looked around, out of the side and back windows, before speaking.

"Do you know what a sleeper cell is?"

"A sleeper cell? You mean, like spies?" I'd seen *The Americans*, and vaguely recalled reading something about sleeper agents in the US getting caught. They'd been in the US for years, married with kids, and were living normal lives in places like Montclair, New Jersey.

He nodded. "Let me tell you a story. In 1943, a young couple named Vasiliy and Mila Kholodov lived in Yakutsk, the northeastern part of the Soviet Union. It was the height of World War Two, the Germans were invading, and Vasiliy was called to the front, to Stalingrad. He never came back.

"Mila was pregnant when he left. She gave birth eight months later with their first and only child. A son, named Alexei.

"Mila died in childbirth. Alexei was placed into one of the Soviet Union's orphanages, along with millions of other war orphans. Around the time Alexei would have been eleven years old, a kimberlite vein was discovered in the Yakutia region in Siberia. A second vein was discovered a year later, the Mir mine."

"Kimberlite?"

"Kimberlite veins are where raw diamonds are found. These discoveries marked the beginning of what is now Russia's preeminent status as the world's leading diamond producer. They are the largest supplier of diamonds, and 98 percent of their diamonds come from mines in the Yakutia region.

"The company that bought the rights to and started mining the veins was Alarosa. Like a lot of war orphans, Alexei was sent to work in the Mir mine for them, initially doing menial jobs. But he was a tireless worker, and demonstrated a real knack for the business. By the time he was twenty he'd moved his way up, and had gained experience in every phase of the diamond-mining and production process.

"In the early sixties Alarosa signed a contract with De Beers, the monopoly that controlled worldwide diamond distribution. Alarosa sent Alexei to college to groom him for a leadership position in their rapidly growing company. He was to take formal training in economics, and learn languages, an important skill for someone expected to work on the international stage.

"They placed him at Plekhanov Russian University of Economics, where he excelled. While he was there his performance attracted the attention of the Russian security service. The KGB, as it was known then.

"At the time the KGB was aggressively searching for talent for the spy program. Alexei was obviously very smart, and had shown an affinity for languages. Against the wishes of Alarosa, the KGB stole him away and put him through their own school, the Red Banner Institute of the Ministry of State Security. The school for spies.

"After completing the program he was given a new name, and a new legend. Alexei Kholodov ceased to exist. He was sent to England, to attend Oxford. While he was there he met and married Amanda Stanley. In 1975 they moved to the United States, where he got a job in Chicago's Jewelers Center. He worked his way up, and eventually took over for Max Miller, an unmarried man, who when he died left all of his money to Alexei. He used it to buy his first diamond mine in Canada, which turned out to be extremely productive, and ended up being an enormously profitable investment. During this time he fathered three children."

"Let me guess. Richard Nottingham is Alexei Kholodov. And he's been a sleeper agent, an inactive one, for decades?"

"Yes."

"You're telling me Nottingham is a Soviet sleeper agent?"

He nodded. "Yes. An inactive one. Until now."

"He's really Russian?" I hadn't detected even a hint of an accent, which was a surprise, as I'd spent a lot of time around Russians in the last couple of years.

"Yes, although barely, at this point. As far as we know he's never been back to Russia, and has no Russian ties, not even in the diamond industry. For all intents and purposes he's an Englishman who emigrated to the US to pursue his business dreams."

"If he has no ties to Russia, why would he want to spy for them? He's one of the world's most successful capitalists. He lives a perfect life." Even if he doesn't act like it.

"We're not sure about his motivation. But we believe he's funneling money to them."

"So why not pick him up for that?"

He shook his head. "Giving money away isn't illegal. And besides, I said we believe he's funneling money to them, but we don't know how. We're following all of his accounts, and there's no significant movement in any of them indicating transfers back to Russia, even through middlemen."

"How do you know all of this? And even if everything you're saying is true, Nottingham's a little long in the tooth for this, isn't he? Dude's gotta be pushing eighty."

"He is. But these are different times. Historically the Soviet Union, and now Russia, have embedded their spies into their diplomatic corps. It's never been secret; everyone knows that Russian diplomats do their diplomatic jobs during the day and their spying at night. But, since the Ukraine invasion, countries are expelling Russian diplomats en masse. As of right now, over five hundred of them have been thrown out of various embassies around the world.

"It's seriously weakened Russia's intelligence efforts and created an untenable situation for Putin, who is himself a KGB veteran. They're turning to their sleeper agents, in some cases scraping the bottom of the proverbial barrel, to conduct their clandestine operations."

I didn't like where this was going, and I had a million questions. But just one big one.

"What is it you want me to do?"

"We've had low-level surveillance on Nottingham for years, since he was identified in the sleeper files. Meaning that we didn't pay much attention to him, unless and until we were notified of a trigger event that he'd been activated.

"We got the trigger event. Two months ago, we caught Nottingham meeting in person with Grigory Rykov, who we know to be a GRU operator."

"GRU?"

"Russian military intelligence."

He pulled a folder from between the seats and pulled a picture out of it, handing it to me. "This is Rykov."

Short and thick, Rykov stared out from the image with dead eyes and a thick, Stalin-esque mustache.

"He's worked primarily in Europe; as far as we know this is his first appearance in the US. He's a bad actor. A very bad one. We've tried to keep a close eye on him since he entered the country. After the meeting with Rykov, Nottingham stepped up his personal security, and installed anti-listening devices at his estate. His home is now impervious to electronic surveillance."

"Why is Rykov so important?"

"He's one of Russia's go-to guys for large projects. We know he's been getting large infusions of cash over the last two years, most recently six months ago, which is a sign that he has something big planned. We believe the money is coming from Nottingham."

He looked away. "And he's, uh, their main man for wet work."

"'Wet' work? 'Wet,' as in blood?"

"Yes."

"Cut to the chase, Smith."

"We believe Rykov's gearing up for a terrorist attack in the city. Our analysts expect it will happen sometime in the next few weeks, and will cause significant loss of life."

No wonder he hadn't filled me in on this earlier. If he had I'd be running for the hills. "You haven't answered my question. What is it you want me to do?"

"We need more information on Nottingham."

"Information? What kind of information?"

"Anything, everything. His schedule, his activities, his meetings, anything we can get to augment our other data-gathering efforts. And we want to know who else is involved. His family? His security team? It's not clear to us if any of them are working with him and Rykov on this, or even if they know what Nottingham's doing. We're not even sure that any of them know he's Russian."

"Don't you have agents for this? And can't you bug his place? Use informers?"

"His security team is tight, and he never goes anywhere without at least one of them, usually Mason Cooper. And as I said, his house and phones now have state-of-the-art anti-surveillance technology. We can't penetrate it. The only way we can get closer to him is to put someone in his house. That's where you come in."

"The last time you put me in someone's house to spy on them I almost got killed." I shuddered thinking about Anatoly Morzov's basement torture room, and its gleaming metal devices.

"It won't be like that. We're not having you place any bugs. He'd find them, anyway."

"I'm not a fucking spy. And you told me," I said, pointing my finger at him, "when we made our deal, that all I'd have to do is run some pop-up restaurants."

"Look, I'm not asking you to do anything but keep your eyes open and report back. That's it. We have other arms of this investigation. We're tracking his money, we're setting up StingRay cell capture stations at his usual haunts, we're following him and Rykov. What we need you to do is just this one piece. It will be a low lift, and you get to cook for one of the wealthiest families in the city. It's a win-win."

I sincerely doubted I'd be doing any "winning" on this. "So what would I be looking for?"

"First and foremost, I'd like to know any time you see him with Rykov. As I said, we're tracking him, but we're not able to keep tabs on him 24/7, and we want to make sure we're not missing anything. I doubt he'll show up at Nottingham's estate, but if he does I want to know. Normally Rykov wouldn't dare do that, he'd keep a distance from the agent. But these are new times, and all bets are off. With all of the sanctions, Russia's operating differently now. We also need you to see what you can learn about the family, and Nottingham's security team—whether or not any of them seem to be aware of Nottingham's background, and anything that indicates they may be involved in whatever he and Rykov are planning."

He leaned back and spread his hands. "Really, Sagarine, all you have to do is cook for the family every now and then, and as I said, keep your eyes open, and report back. We're just trying to cover our bases. Having someone in the house is just one piece of what we have in place."

"I don't care. I'm not an agent, or a spy, or whatever. I almost got killed last time. All I'm good at is cooking." We both knew there was something else I was good at, but Smith didn't bother pointing it out.

"I know you're not an agent. That's why I waited so long before I got you involved. But I don't have a choice. We know they're planning something terrible, soon, and it's all hands on deck now."

I folded my arms across my chest and stared at him.

He looked away from me, out the windshield. "How would you feel if they launched a dirty bomb, in your city, and knew you did nothing to stop it?"

"You really think it's going to be something like that? A nuclear bomb?"

"Yes. Russia's go-to methods for assassinations are poisons and radiation. The GRU has used both, as recently as last year, to kill dissidents abroad. It's not a leap to think they'd use them on a larger scale."

He leaned toward me, his eyes locked on mine. "Homeland has this threat rated as 'elevated.' The only reason it's not rated as 'imminent' is because we don't know where or exactly when it's going to happen."

Dammit. It wasn't like I had a choice. I was on the hook to Smith for as long as he needed me. The least that would happen if I refused would be that they would take away my restaurant. I'd worked too long and too hard to have that happen.

And he was right, I wouldn't be able to live with myself if I didn't help stop an attack on the city.

"Fine. What am I supposed to do?"

"Nothing, yet. Just wait to hear from the family. The meal you gave them on the boat was your audition. If it was good enough you'll get an interview."

"And if they don't contact me?"

"Then you're off the hook. But I wouldn't count on it. Just go home and wait."

He reached into the console between the seats and pulled out a phone.

"This is yours, make sure to keep it on—"

"I know the drill. Keep it on me at all times." I hated his damn spy phones. Somehow he always managed to configure them with the ringtone set at "maximum irritation." I handed back the picture of Rykov.

"No, you keep it. You need to memorize his face so you can know if you see him."

He turned the key to start the engine, then looked pointedly at my door. "I'd give you a ride home, but I don't want anyone seeing us together near your place."

Sure. "Hang on. I have a few conditions of my own."

"It doesn't work that way."

"It does now. First: you need to tell Maude what's going on. Soon. I can't live with her and keep this a secret."

He shrugged. "OK. We were going to bring the Chicago PD in on this soon, anyway."

"Second: at the first sign of trouble, I'm out of there. His security team doesn't look like they're messing around."

"Of course. I don't expect anything to happen to you. We truly only need you to cook for them and just provide any information you gather while you're with the family."

"Third: Saga needs a new bar. Something in copper would be nice."

He shook his head and started the car. "This is no laughing matter. There's going to be an attack, soon. And if we don't do our job, a lot of people are going to die."

FOUR

Smith was right, I received a call just before six that night with a request to go downtown the next day for an interview with the Nottinghams.

It meant they liked my food, so I wasn't entirely disappointed. And I wouldn't mind seeing Tasia Nottingham again.

I didn't know who'd be doing the interview, but I hoped it wouldn't be Richard. I couldn't imagine sitting across from that face for any length of time.

At eight fifty-five the next morning I stood on Wabash at the south end of the Loop, in front of Carat and Crown. They'd told me to wait out front, and someone would come and get me.

A Chicago landmark for over a century, Chicago's Jewelers Row included the Mallers Building, home to close to two hundred jewelers, and a number of jewelry stores on either side of it, of which Carat and Crown was the largest.

At nine a.m. sharp the doors opened. A small man in a suit waved at me. "Miss Pfister?"

I nodded and he led me into the store. We walked past the gem and jewelry displays, to behind the long glass counter and through a door in the back.

I'd only been to Jewelers Row once, years ago with my mom. I'd followed her as she wound through the labyrinthine hallways and past the businesses, looking through the glass windows to the working areas in the back, trying to get a look at the mysterious men huddled over tables full of equipment and precious stones. But we'd never been in Nottingham's store. Mom had been looking for bargains.

We walked through the back door and into a large work room. Metal racks lined the walls, surrounding six tables that were crowded with tools. The men at each table—they were all men—had their heads down, and were poring over gems on workspaces that were brightly illuminated by individual lamps. No one talked, the only sounds in the room our footsteps and occasional high-pitched hammering.

I'd never seen a jeweler work with stones. The act of taking a dull piece of rock and turning it into a shiny, faceted jewel seemed arcane, and impossible. But I wasn't able to catch more than a glimpse of their work. My escort walked briskly through the tables and to another door in the back.

He knocked softly, then opened it and stood back, gesturing me in. He closed it behind me.

A gleaming wooden desk embellished with sturdy carved legs rested on thick carpet. Red velvet curtains framed a window, the walls covered with silver-framed paintings, all featuring diamonds.

I was surprised and a little relieved to see Celeste behind the desk. It must have shown on my face.

"Were you expecting Richard? He doesn't get involved with house issues." She smiled, and gestured to the lone chair in front of the desk across from her. "Please, sit down."

I expected her to look tired, or at least a little dragged out, given how much she'd had to drink just thirty-six hours ago. Most people would be on life support.

But she looked as fresh as she did when she'd first arrived on the boat, her skin clear and smooth, her eyes white, her makeup perfect. The only difference was she was wearing a suit instead of a cocktail dress, and the dazzling event diamonds she'd worn before had been replaced by less ostentatious, but no doubt still very expensive, diamond stud earrings and a matching necklace and bracelet set.

"Can I get you some coffee, Miss Pfister? And may I call you Sagarine?"

"Sure, yes."

She stood up and poured me a cup from a machine near the desk and set it in front of me, then sat back down.

She took a sip from her own cup. "Do you know why you're here?"

"The guy on the phone said you needed a chef?"

"That was Ellis. An event chef, yes. The family was very

impressed by your meal on the *Enterprise*. Richard in particular was pleased."

I wondered how she could tell. "Thank you."

"And that ice sculpture, that was a piece of art, Martin's antics notwithstanding. This is the kind of thing we're looking for with our family events."

She looked down at an open folder laying on her desk.

"You're the chef and owner of Saga? The restaurant in Portage Park?"

"Yes."

"How old are you?"

"Twenty-nine."

"That's a bit young, isn't it, to have your own restaurant? And I see you don't have investors. You bought it outright?"

I shouldn't be surprised they'd done their homework, but it presented a problem. Smith had said he didn't want any law enforcement involved, and I guessed that mentioning the FBI's role in getting me the restaurant wouldn't be the right thing to do here. Or maybe she already knew?

"The previous owner died, and his partner was in the mob. The restaurant was confiscated, and I was able to pick it up for well under market price."

Technically true, if incomplete.

She surprised me and didn't dig any further, changing the subject. "Running a restaurant must be a full-time job, yes?"

"It was at first. But I have a good crew, and a great sous, so I don't need to be there all the time. I'm looking for something to do on top of running the restaurant, something interesting. And I love doing events."

All true, and fairly complete.

She closed the folder and took another long sip of her coffee. "We have smaller events at the house at least once a month, and every now and then a larger one, like the *Enterprise* dinner, as well as a few holiday parties. Occasionally there are trips involved."

She stood up and came around from behind the desk. She sat on the edge of it in front of me, leaning down, her ample cleavage inches from my face.

"This is not a full-time job, but it can involve a lot of time away, sometimes on short notice. Is there, uh, anyone who might care if you're away for periods of time?"

Her perfume was making me gag, and I could smell alcohol on her breath. Her coffee had a little something extra in it.

Jesus. Nine in the morning.

"No."

She nodded. Her eyes dropped down. Was she checking me out?

They returned to my face. Did I just imagine that?

"Your eyes are very unusual. I don't think I've ever seen gray eyes."

"It's a mutation."

Still staring into my eyes, she said, "The Nottinghams are one of the most powerful and wealthy families, not just in this country, but in the world. Our reputation is something we guard closely. Richard is a stickler that all employees and contractors are required to sign a non-disclosure agreement. Would this be a problem for you?"

"Not at all," I said, doing everything I could to breathe through my mouth and not obviously lean back.

"And along those lines, is there anything about you that might bring disrepute onto the family, were we to employ you? Please keep in mind that we will be doing a thorough background check. If there is anything in your history that if known could tarnish the family's reputation, now would be the time to share that."

Gosh, where to start?

"No."

"Good. Do you have any questions for me?"

"When would I start?"

She laughed and stood up, then walked back around behind the desk. "I take it you're interested?"

"Definitely."

"We'll be in touch." She pushed a button on the desk and took another long sip of her booze coffee. "Stephen will show you out."

Stephen opened the door and we walked back out. When

we got to the street I looked at my watch. The interview had lasted less than ten minutes.

Maybe she'd decided right away I wasn't a fit? Or maybe it was normal for one of their interviews; they already knew I could cook, and plan an event. And they'd be doing background checks.

Depending on what they turned up this could be over before it started.

I decided I'd be OK with that. I wasn't eager to take a job where I'd be getting hit on all the time. Celeste was nice looking, but definitely not my type. And regardless of what Smith had said about it being a simple "observe and report" thing, it sounded like it could turn dangerous. I'd had enough of that to last me a lifetime.

From downtown I went straight to the restaurant to check in. If I got this gig with the Nottinghams I'd be spending a lot of time away.

As expected Zoe had everything under control. I poked around for a few minutes then left.

When I got home Maude was sitting at the kitchen table in front of her laptop. Across from her was Linda, her buddy from the PD.

They'd been spending a lot of time together in the last year, ever since Linda had helped Maude find Michael. Not only had they found him, but their mostly unpaid overtime efforts resulted in the PD taking down a new gang that was provoking a bloody turf war in the city. For that Linda had earned a ticket out of police purgatory.

Early on in her career she'd been a rising star in the force, demonstrating intelligence and initiative, including taking and succeeding at several vice and narcotics undercover assignments. She'd been destined for great things.

Then, through no fault of her own, she'd been shot. The bullet had entered her hip, and while they'd been able to remove it and restore most of the function to her leg, the limp remained. The powers that be wanted her to retire, but she'd stuck around, doggedly succeeding at every thankless job they gave her, which included increasingly terrible assignments like community complaints or the perpetually underfunded tech support. And eventually a stint in the dreaded evidence room.

She'd taken everything they'd thrown at her and done a great job, even earning her sergeant's stripes. After her work with Maude she'd applied for a detective position, and they'd had no choice but to give it to her. Detective wasn't as physically demanding as patrol, and they couldn't justify disqualifying her because of a limp.

"Hey." I greeted both of them with a wave. "To what do we owe the pleasure?"

"Linda's on the Red Rogue task force with me," said Maude, looking at her monitor.

"Red Rogue? Really?"

"Don't look at me, I didn't come up with it."

"Congratulations," I said to Linda.

"Thanks." She smiled.

Linda looked great. She was in her late thirties but could be mistaken for someone younger. She was extremely fit, and her hazel eyes were always on alert, her only apparent imperfection the limp that she tried hard to hide.

"Is it nice to be out of the basement?"

Her last job had been at the evidence desk, a counter in front of a cage in the PD headquarters' windowless basement.

"You can't imagine."

"How does Bill feel about your promotion, and all of those extra hours you have to put in?"

I'd been around Maude long enough to know that police detectives didn't punch a clock. Investigations took as long as they took, and there was no paid overtime.

"He's fine. He likes the extra income. And he's working more now, too, since the plants were turned over to the private sector. But he's still got time to take his trips to Vegas. And next weekend my niece is coming in, he'll spend it with her even if I'm not around. He loves being an uncle."

She pushed an eight-by-eleven color photo toward me from a file on the table. "There's been another one."

An enormous mound of fish was piled on a sidewalk up

against a building, blood leaking onto the cement and draining into the gutter. Spray-painted on the wall above the pile was 547 980 231.

"Fish?"

She nodded. "Dumped next to the Monadnock Building."

Damn. Defiling the Monadnock Building was an especially heinous act. A historic landmark over one hundred years old, it was beloved by Chicagoans who cherished the city's architectural history. This building in particular was unique, at the same time one of the oldest load-bearing brick buildings in the world, and one of the symbols of the modern skyscraper.

"Have you figured out yet what the numbers mean?"

"We don't know for sure," said Maude, "but we think it's a code."

"A code for what?"

"We don't know that either."

I picked up the photo and looked at it more closely.

"Nine digits? Are they phone numbers, or social security numbers?"

"They could be, but they're not. We've checked. I'm working on it." She pointed to her computer screen. "I picked up some cryptanalysis software from a . . . uh . . . friend."

"One of your friends on the dark web?"

"You didn't hear me say that."

I looked at the bewildering array of letters and numbers on the screen. "How do you even know where to start?"

"I run the numbers through a list of common ciphers. When the software thinks it has one that transforms the initial set of numbers into something meaningful, I get a notification. These aren't telephone numbers, or social security numbers. And we've looked at pager numbers. They're old-school, but they're currently the cipher of choice for drug dealers."

"Wait . . . is it a code, or a cipher?"

"It could be both. Ciphers are about substitution. A letter might represent a number, or the other way around. A simple cipher might be that every number corresponds to a letter. Codes, on the other hand, transfer meaning. A word, or a phrase, means something other than what it appears. So, an example of a code might be that a particular word, like 'bench,' means an entire phrase, like, 'meet me in Millennium Park at the usual place.'"

"That sounds impossible to figure out."

"It might be. But you'd be surprised. The software we have now can try out millions of guesses in seconds. It's brute force, and not at all elegant, but it's effective."

Her eyes sparkled; she loved this shit. "Most ciphers are made to hide numbers—phone numbers, addresses, amounts of money, or phony accounting, like in illegal business transactions. This one is different; it's sets of numbers we believe are hiding a word, or words. So the default starting point is to assume that each number is a letter. Then we'll move on to more complicated tools like frequency analysis. But that's going to be hard."

It already sounded hard. "Why?"

"Frequency analysis works by knowing what letters are used most frequently in common speech. We don't have enough characters here to work with for that. At least, not yet. If more of these turn up it will be easier."

"Well, at least you've got time to figure it out. It's not like anyone's dying from this."

"Well, there might be," said Linda. "There was a body in the river the same day it was turned red."

I glanced at Maude. She shook her head. Apparently she hadn't been completely successful convincing the team that the dead body found in the river was a really poorly timed coincidence, and not related to the dye.

"They think it was an opioid overdose. Most likely fentanyl."

"No surprise there. Wasn't the dead guy a drug dealer?"

"The amount was more than you'd expect with an accidental overdose, especially for a guy who dealt the stuff. In any case someone else is looking into that. I'm investigating the dye."

I was glad Linda wasn't looking at the body. She'd only just recently been promoted to detective, but she was smart, and tenacious.

"Not the meat? Or the fish?"

"We're assuming it's the same person, or group, who's behind all three events. We figure we have the best shot of tracking them down through the river dye. Whoever turned the river red had to come up with a formulation that would not only lead to that exact blood-red color, but once put into the water would spread rapidly, and then persist for almost twenty-four hours. Something like that had to be made in a lab, and then it had to be distributed in the water overnight, quickly and quietly.

"All of that would have taken significant resources, and a fairly sophisticated operation. Dumping meat could be done by almost anyone."

That made sense. Chicago, aka "Packingtown" and "Porkopolis," had at one time been the country's epicenter for meatpacking and distribution. Those days were long gone, but it was still a meat-centric city, and trying to track down meat scraps would be hopeless, no matter the amount. It was the same with fish. There were at least a hundred restaurants that regularly served fish in the city limits, and numerous fish-processing operations.

"Has, uh, Smith said anything to you?" I asked Maude.

"About what?"

"About what he's working on?"

"No. You know he doesn't talk about his projects, unless I'm on the team. Operational security and all that. Besides, we have better things to do," she said, grinning.

She'd told me that the two of them had fantastic sex. I couldn't see it. Smith seemed like a buttoned-up stick-in-the-mud, but according to Maude he was a beast in bed. And she would know. After their first date she'd given him *Panty Raiders of the Lost Ark*, one of her books that she gave out only to top-notch dates.

She cared for him, a lot, although so far had rebuffed his efforts to make their relationship more permanent. She was perfectly happy with how things were, and to-date had ignored his hints about getting married.

"Why, is something going on that I should know about?"

"No, not yet."

"He's got you working on something, doesn't he?"

She knew all of the details about my ongoing obligation to Smith. But I didn't want to say anything until he talked to her. And definitely not in front of Linda. Maude totally trusted her, so I did, too, but I'd taken Smith's warning to heart.

I was saved from having to answer by my phone buzzing in my pocket.

"Hello?"

"Ms. Pfister? This is Celeste. I wanted to let you know personally that you've got the job."

Shit. "Great."

That didn't take long. I wondered how thorough of a background check they'd done.

"Please be at the estate at ten a.m. tomorrow morning. I'm looking forward to seeing you."

"Uh, me too. Thank you."

She hung up.

"Good news?" asked Linda.

Probably not.

FIVE

Celeste hadn't given me an address for the Nottingham estate. She'd assumed I knew where it was.

Of course she was right. Everyone knew where it was.

It took me a little under an hour on the bus, changing twice, before I got to the Edgebrook neighborhood. More of a northern suburb than a typical Chicago neighborhood, there were no three-flats or bungalows in this community. Edgebrook lots were larger than anywhere else in the city, and contained exclusively single-family homes.

It was easy to find the estate, it took up an entire block next to the forest preserve, with an entrance blocked by a massive gate. Framed by Stonehenge-sized gateposts set tightly in between tall hedgerows and trees, the black metal of the gates was topped with spikes that didn't look like they were there for show.

There was no speaker box or buzzer.

Now what?

I stood there, looking around, and was startled to hear "Please step back."

I looked for the voice and spotted a discrete metal box sitting on top of one of the posts.

After I took a few steps back the gates started to move, creaking open slowly toward the main road.

Once they stopped I walked through. I was barely inside when I heard them close behind me.

The house was nowhere in sight. I walked down the winding, unblemished black asphalt until it turned. Once I was around the bend I was able to see the house.

Three stories of white-trimmed red brick, accented by square cupolas at the corners, the Nottingham mansion sat majestically in the center of a carefully manicured lawn. The driveway ended at a small circle, with a flowing fountain in the center that emptied into a cement pond. Orange and white fish swam lazily in circles. I wondered what they did when it froze.

The lawn that surrounded the house was broken up by slim bush-lined gravel paths that disappeared around both corners. I could see the edge of a small detached building on one side.

No other houses or structures were visible from here, the large trees that lined the driveway also shielding the estate from pesky neighbors or paparazzi.

White columns framed the wide front stoop, up a few shallow steps to an overly large wooden door with an ornate carved metal knocker.

As I approached the door it opened.

"Please come in, Miss Pfister."

A tall, slender man in a dark suit and tie answered the door. His perfectly coiffed short dark hair displayed just the right amount of gel.

He gestured me into the house and closed the heavy door behind us.

The first thing I noticed was that the house was cold. Not as cold as outside, but unlike most places this time of year I wasn't greeted with a warm waft of air when I stepped in.

The second thing that stood out was one of Nottingham's security team standing like a statue just inside the doorway. He was looking out the front window, toward the driveway.

"This way, please." He led us to a long hallway, past a staircase and toward the east side of the house.

I hadn't been in a lot of mansions, but this was about what I expected. Sweeping spiral staircases, very high ceilings, and wood floors that were probably made out of some endangered species were softly lit by inconspicuous recessed lighting and a few decorative lamps. We walked through a large sitting room and then down another hallway.

He stopped in front of a door and knocked.

"Yes?"

"Miss Pfister is here, ma'am."

"Please show her in."

He opened the door and waved me in, then started to close it behind me.

"You can wait here, Ellis. We'll just be a moment. I'd like you to give Ms. Pfister a tour of the house before we meet."

"Yes ma'am." He nodded and stood next to the wall.

We were in an office, and unlike the one at the Carat and Crown it was clear it was Celeste's.

Lighter in color and more delicate in design, the desk, chairs, and tables rested on thick velvet carpet, everything accented by flowers arranged in every available nook and corner.

Conspicuous in the room was a lush couch set against one of the walls. It faced a well-stocked bar on the opposite wall.

"Hello, Sagarine. Welcome to Nottingham Estate. Ellis will give you a tour, and then we'll talk over our first event. But before you do anything, I need you to sign these forms."

She leaned down over the desk, her generous cleavage almost pouring out of a low-cut sweater. She opened a manila folder, inside of which was a small stack of stapled papers.

She held up a pen, but didn't extend it, forcing me to take a step closer to her to take it from her hands. I was hit again with her distinctive aroma of perfume and booze.

"This is the non-disclosure agreement. Among other things, by signing it you agree to not share anything you learn about the family with anyone, and in particular, the media. As you can imagine they are relentless in trying to dig up dirt on the family. Not that we have any." She smiled.

"There are severe ramifications of breaking this agreement. I suggest you read it over and be certain you are willing to abide by the provisions. After you've read it you can sign here," she said, pointing to a line at the bottom of the last page. It was one of several pages of numbered and sub-numbered sections, everything in size-four font. "It's fairly boilerplate," she said mildly, seemingly contradicting what she'd said earlier.

I did a cursory flip through the pages, and then signed. I usually didn't sign anything without reading it carefully, but I was doing this for Smith, and assumed any rights I signed away would be moot after they'd nailed Nottingham for whatever it was they thought he was involved in.

I also wanted to limit my proximity to Celeste, whose perfume was starting to make me gag.

"Wonderful. After your tour you will meet me back here and I'll give you your first assignment."

Ellis and I stepped out of the room. "Please follow me," he said in a bored voice that suggested he'd done this a million times.

We started in the kitchen, predictably good-sized, with lots of counter space, a large refrigerator, the requisite eight-burner Viking gas stove, and an adjacent pantry room, also large and well stocked.

A small, balding man was standing next to one of the counters, putting together a tray of food. Cubes of cheese in a small mound, a rack of petite meat ribs, a disk of flatbread, and an empty glass.

"This is Percy, he is the house chef."

"Hi. I guess we're going to be working together."

He offered a desultory nod. "I doubt it. I'm the only one who does Mr. Nottingham's meals, and I cook the private family dinners. You'll have nothing to do with that."

Guarding his turf. Got it.

In the back of the kitchen was a door that led downstairs to a hallway where there were doors to a wine cellar that was as big as my previous apartment, and another one to the walk-in refrigerator. After I came out of the refrigerator I continued around the corner to a longer part of the hallway and another set of doors. Standing against the wall by the closest one was one of the security team. He glared at me.

Ellis touched my arm. "That area of the house is off limits."

I waited for further information but he turned and led me back upstairs. From there he showed me around the family living area, only slightly less formal than the main living room, and also sporting a marble fireplace, and then to a modest dining room that seemed too small to host the kind of parties I expected the Nottinghams to have.

We crossed to the other side of the house, passing another spiral staircase, and to a short hallway that opened to a much larger and more formal dining room.

This was more like it. It would comfortably seat fifty for a sit-down dinner, and twice that for informal cocktail events. High ceilinged, like most of the rest of the house, an elaborate chandelier hung down in the center. The space was bright, courtesy of an entire wall of mullioned windows.

"This is where the home dining events are held. You will spend most of your time here when you are outside of the kitchen."

The strong implication being that I wasn't to have the run of the house. It was confirmed when we left the room and walked back past the stairs.

"Those are the family quarters," he said, nodding to the stairs. "All of the stairways and the rooms upstairs are off limits to staff. As is this entire wing." He waved his hand toward the far side of the living room, off of which were two more hallways.

He led me around the forbidden zone and past the kitchen to a set of glass double doors that opened to the backyard. We stepped out onto a stone patio, by itself larger than the floor plan of my house.

The backyard looked like something out of a painting. The manicured lawn stretched almost as far as I could see, framed like the driveway by a tall, impenetrable line of spanning oak and evergreen pine trees. Elaborately designed metal benches were positioned on the edges of the patio and along the gravel path that extended most of the way down the yard, ending at a single large oak. Rectangular square flowerboxes, surprisingly colorful for this time of year, were placed at regular intervals around the patio and at various places along the gravel paths.

Close to the side of the house was a narrow set of stone stairs that led down to a separate entrance to the basement. One of the security team members was standing at the top, his head moving in a slow pivot as he scanned the yard. I wondered what he was watching for. As far as I could see there was no gate to the backyard, or even a break in the trees.

Two of the gravel paths fingered out from the patio to small cottages situated on either side of the yard. We crunched down a path to one of them, and Ellis pulled out a key to open the door.

It was a studio apartment. Relatively spartan compared to the main house, but well appointed, with a queen-size bed against one wall, a living area with a comfortable-looking couch, a few chairs, and a large TV taking up a wall on one side, and a fully equipped kitchen on the other. The bathroom was presumably past the lone door on the back wall.

"This is yours."

"Mine?"

"Yes, for when you need to stay overnight." He handed me the key.

I hadn't realized that had been part of the deal. "Why would I need to stay overnight?"

He shrugged. "Occasionally the dinners go late."

I followed him back out and he walked toward the main house. "What's the other building?" I asked, looking at the other cottage across the path. It was almost identical to mine, other than that the blinds were drawn.

"Mr. Nottingham stays there. It is also off limits to staff."

"Mr. Nottingham?"

"The youngest Mr. Nottingham."

Huh. So Martin didn't stay in the main house. For that matter, where was everyone? The whole place was dead silent.

And, so far, at least two thirds of the house was off limits. This would put a serious crimp in my ability to observe the family. Too bad I wasn't here to keep tabs on the security team; I'd counted at least nine of them, conspicuously stationed around the house and grounds like malevolent statues.

"Where is everyone?"

He ignored my question and led us back to Celeste's study, which was a good thing, as I wasn't sure I'd be able to find it on my own.

She was sitting on the couch, leaning back against one of the pillows. "Thank you Ellis."

He left, closing the door behind him.

She patted the seat next to her. I sat down, making an effort to sit as far away from her as I could, which was challenging, as she was taking up the middle of the couch.

She turned to me, causing her knees to press up against my thigh. “I assume Ellis showed you your quarters? In the event that you might need to stay overnight?”

“Yes.” Oh . . . Jesus. Was this why they gave me the cottage?

“Good.” She opened the folder on her lap. “The first event for which we will need you to cook is tomorrow night.”

Tomorrow night? No wonder they’d hired me so quickly.

She must have read my face, because she added, “It’s just a small dinner, thirty people. Here are all of the relevant details.” She closed and handed me the folder. “Percy will help you as you require. In the folder is a number to call if you need transportation, or help bringing things to the house. We have several drivers on call. Please let me know if there is anything you need. Especially with the cottage. I like to make sure our staff are comfortable, and see to things personally.” She put her hand on my knee.

“Sure, OK.” I took the folder out of her hand and stood up, causing her hand to drop off. “Thanks. Is it OK if I take another look around the kitchen?”

“Of course, you’re free to go where you need. Other than the off-limits areas, and family quarters, of course. Unless you are invited by a member of the family,” she said, smiling.

Yikes. “Great. Thanks. See you tomorrow.”

I tried not to run out of the room. Once I was out I walked back down the hallway. When I got to the T in the hallway I heard footsteps.

It was Tasia.

“Hey,” I said.

She brushed past me like I wasn’t there, a scowl on her face.

I already knew she didn’t like her dad, and possibly Alan and Celeste, for reasons that weren’t clear. But she didn’t know enough about me yet to dislike me. Maybe she didn’t like anyone, other than Martin. Or maybe it was just one of those rich-people things, not mingling with the help.

Whatever. I went back to the kitchen to poke around, and familiarize myself with the appliances and layout, and the contents of the pantry and freezer. I wasn't surprised to find all of the appliances were top of the line, and the pantry and refrigerator were indeed extremely well stocked.

I was starting to get excited. Smith was right, this could be a win-win situation. The kitchen was big and well equipped enough that I could do whatever I needed to here; I wouldn't need to use Saga or my own kitchen for any prep work. That made things much simpler.

An awesome kitchen, and an unlimited budget . . . yeah, this would work out. And maybe Smith was wrong about Nottingham. If so I could see myself doing this for a while.

Percy was still in the kitchen, putting the finishing touches to the plate of food he'd been preparing. He reached into the refrigerator and pulled out a glass milk bottle.

Percy didn't look up and I didn't say anything. I was done here, and needed to get going on the dinner.

When I got to the foyer I expected someone to stop me. But other than the security guy still staring out the front window, no one was around. Apparently I was free to just leave.

I walked down the driveway, looking behind me at the two other security guards who were stationed at the edges of the house.

It was a relief to get around the bend in the driveway and be out of everyone's line of sight.

When I got back to the gate I realized that I didn't know how to make it open. I stood there for a few minutes, and just as I was getting ready to go back to the house, a long, dark limo pulled up outside of it.

The gates creaked open, and the car rolled through. Its windows were blacked out, the only visible person the driver.

I stepped aside, then slipped through the gate as it closed behind me.

SIX

The dinner party I was doing for the Nottinghams was for thirteen couples, plus Richard, Celeste, and Alan. Twenty-nine people. Apparently Tasia and Martin were off the hook for this one.

I looked over the material in the folder I'd gotten from Celeste. Despite her perpetual inebriation she seemed to be well organized; the information included everyone who was coming, the theme she wanted, and desired timing for appetizers and dinner. Also included was a credit card and phone numbers for the driver who would pick me up and take me where necessary to shop and bring whatever I needed to the house.

There wasn't much time for planning and prep, but I didn't need it. I assumed it was an unlimited budget, which made things easier. If it wasn't, they'd let me know afterward. But I wanted to shine for this first event at the estate, so would spare no expense.

I put together the menu when I got home and made a few calls. I could pick everything up tomorrow. I would have liked to wow them with some molecular gastronomy creations but there wasn't enough time.

The next morning I was up early, and after showering was pulling out my phone to call the Nottinghams' driver when I heard the irritating ring of Smith's spy phone coming from the bedroom. I'd already forgotten about it.

I dug it out from underneath a pile of clothes. "What is it, Smith? I'm getting ready to head out."

"We need to meet."

"I don't have time. I have to get going on a dinner for the Nottinghams." I actually had plenty of time, as I'd arranged to get to the kitchen early for a leisurely prep. But I didn't like his last-minute calls interrupting my schedule.

"Make time. Meet me at Rosehill, at our usual spot near the lagoon, in ten minutes."

Dammit. "Fine."

I threw on a coat and walked over to the cemetery, a five-minute walk from our house. More often than not Smith chose cemeteries for our secret meetings. I didn't know what his fascination was with the dead, but I didn't care enough to ask.

I found him at our usual spot, pacing behind the stone bench.

"What's up?"

"Keep your voice down," he hissed.

I looked around. There was no one within fifty yards of us.

"Have you been to the house?"

"The Nottinghams? Yes. I got the tour yesterday. And I'm supposed to be there now." I made a point to pull out my phone and check the time.

"Have you learned anything?"

"Yeah. Celeste is a serious alcoholic, and she's hitting on me at every opportunity. Tasia's a bitch, and you can't go twenty feet in or out of the house without being stared down by one of Nottingham's security goon squad. Most of the house is off limits to staff, and as far as I can tell no one spends any time there except Ellis, Percy, Celeste, and possibly Tasia. I do have my own little servant's cottage, for those days when I'm in the mood for a sleepover. There are two, Martin lives in the other one. Also, I'm not sure, but I'm a little concerned that late-night booty calls from the boss might be part of the job description."

He sighed. "You need to take this seriously."

"Jesus, I am. Give me a minute, won't you? I've only had the ten-cent tour of the house, and even that was just the parts of it I'm allowed to go in. And I don't know what you think I'm going to be able to do. It's not like they leave important secret documents laying around. You said yourself, the guy's stepped up his security. All you said you needed me to do was to keep my eyes open and let you know if I learn anything. I'm doing that."

"Things have changed. Rykov has just withdrawn a big chunk

of the money that's been flowing into his accounts over the last two years."

"So?"

"So, based on his previous operations, it means that whatever he's going to do will happen soon. Typically he amasses money over twelve to twenty-four months prior to the attacks, then spends the bulk of it in the month or so beforehand. He'll need to get his hands on more as he gets closer to the date of the action. We need proof that Nottingham's the one providing it. See if you can find any indication that Nottingham is sending money around."

"How in hell am I supposed to find evidence that it's from Nottingham? And I still don't understand why it's so important that you know that he's the source of the money."

"If we can show it's from Nottingham we can bring him in for questioning, then hold him."

"Why not just pick up Rykov? Or freeze his account?"

He nodded. "There are people who think that's the right move. But he hasn't done anything yet. If we pick him up now, they'll just replace him with someone else, and we'll lose any chance of keeping tabs on Nottingham. Once he knows we're watching him it will be impossible to track his movements. This is a golden opportunity, and we need to take advantage of it."

Great. It sounded like the FBI wasn't even sure what they should do.

"Keep your eyes peeled for documents, see if you can get inside his study, or wherever they keep financial papers."

"I told you, everything that has to do with him or the family is off limits. I have no idea where his study is, or even if he has one. The place is crawling with security, who by the way are extremely scary looking, and I haven't checked, but I'm pretty sure anything important is locked up. And wouldn't his financial documents be somewhere else? Like with his accountant, or at his store? And everything's going to be electronic, anyway."

"We have an informant at Carat and Crown, and we've already recruited Nottingham's accountant, who's fully cooperating. Nottingham likes hard copies. And nothing in the books we already have looks suspicious. There might be a different set of books, with different cash streams, one that his accountant doesn't know anything about."

Whatever. Smith must be really worried to ask me to look for the guy's financial stuff. Regardless of what he was saying, he knew the chances of me actually getting my hands on any documents were close to zero.

"Just do your best."

"Is that all, Smith? I've got an event to do."

He nodded stiffly and I walked away. When I got home I called the driver, and in twenty minutes was inside another limo. If it wasn't for Smith's constant agitation, I could get used to this.

We drove to Hagen's Fish Market, and then to my butcher for the meat. I hit the grocery store for the few things I needed to augment what was in the Nottinghams' pantry.

Dinner was to start at eight. I made it to the mansion by three to start prepping. Percy was nowhere in sight, so I unloaded everything and got to work. I hadn't counted on any help from him, anyway, and didn't mind doing my own prep.

Celeste had said there would be a few minutes of mingling before everyone was seated for dinner, and she'd specified a "cultured" theme for the meal, which I took to mean "rich-people chic," so I set up caviar stations at strategic places in the room. I'd used them for the event on the *Enterprise*, and while I didn't normally like to repeat dishes, caviar was a staple with this crowd, and they expected it. I did spruce the construction up a bit, replacing the standard blinis with slim rectangular single-serving waffle bites where the caviar could be spooned into one of the little square waffle depressions, next to another one filled with crème fraîche, and a third holding finely chopped chives. They were fun and extremely tasty.

The guests thought so, too; they all arrived on time and made quick work of the caviar during the brief mingling period. Fortunately the seated portion of the meal started before I ran out.

I started them out with a small shellfish assortment, including tempura-fried king crab, one oyster served Rockefeller style, and a simple but perfectly seared scallop. Guests then had their choice of Wagyu steaks or black cod, accompanied by truffle risotto and lobster champagne salad. We finished with one of Declan's masterpieces, a Chilean rose petal jam crêpe with saffron ice cream.

Once the sit-down portion of the evening was over the guests dispersed around the room in small groups. Nottingham made his way among them, managing to get each politician alone by him or herself for private conversations.

I'd seen no sign of Mason during the meal, nor Zach, the security team member who looked to be primarily responsible for Martin. It wasn't a huge surprise; this was a small group of politicians and their significant others looking to get financial support, not murderous commandos.

Given the small crowd I was able to spend more time around Celeste and Alan than I had on the *Enterprise*. She paid no attention to me during the meal, her beaming smile turned to Alan and whichever guest she was talking with at the moment. He was his usual plastic self, with his perfect suit and perfect smile. But now that I had a chance to hear some of his conversation, I realized that was the main thing he brought to the table.

Alan was an idiot. A perfectly turned out idiot, but an idiot, nonetheless.

His comments were stilted, like they'd been scripted, his laughter inappropriately timed, his comments empty, and I wondered how Nottingham felt about leaving his business in the hands of a moron. At least Alan had Celeste. Alcoholic and lecherous, for sure, but she was sharp, and was doing the heavy lifting on the conversations.

It was well after midnight and I'd cleared the table. At this point I was just refilling glasses with whatever priceless wine each guest was drinking, although by now many of them had switched to water. There were more than a few muffled yawns in the room. But no one would dare leave a Nottingham party early.

Nottingham was wearing down his guests. He was older

than anyone in the room, but he looked as fresh as he did when we'd started four hours ago.

This had to be a clue to his success. In addition to being exceptionally smart and well trained, he had the stamina of a sled dog.

Finally at one thirty Celeste thanked everyone and told them Ellis would get their coats. To a person they worked hard to not look relieved. The room emptied quickly.

I'd had more than enough time to pack up, and was getting ready to leave when Ellis poked his head into the kitchen.

"Mrs. Nottingham would like to see you."

"OK, I just need to—"

"Mrs. Nottingham would not like to wait."

"Right." I put down my bag and followed him down the hallway.

Celeste was in the study, pouring herself a drink from the bar. I imagined it had been a tough dinner for her, restricted for several hours to only champagne and wine. Still, she'd put away at least a gallon of wine over dinner, and if I hadn't seen it I wouldn't have believed it. Her eyes weren't the tiniest bit bloodshot, and there was no slur to her words.

"Would you like one?" She gestured at the bar.

"No, thanks."

"Are you sure? It's unlikely you've ever tried this." She held up a bottle that was covered in white fur, banded by several bracelets made out of shiny stones. Diamonds, no doubt.

"It's Billionaire Vodka. One of the most expensive bottles in existence. The vodka has been filtered through crushed diamonds."

I didn't really want to drink with her, but I was curious about how diamond-filtered vodka would taste. It wasn't like I'd be getting another chance to try it any time soon.

"Sure, thanks."

She poured and handed me a glass. We clinked and I drank.

I wasn't a huge vodka fan, but this was pretty good. Very smooth, clean tasting, a little sweet, and with almost no aftertaste.

"Not bad."

She laughed. "For a four-million-dollar bottle, yes, it's not bad."

"Four million dollars? For one bottle?"

"Yes," she chuckled, refilling her glass. "It was an anniversary gift from Alan."

I wondered if Alan had a clue about his wife's drinking problem. How could he not? Maybe he thought she'd slow down if she was drinking something that was worth hundreds of thousands of dollars a glass.

If so, he would have been disappointed. She put her next shot away like it was water. "That was a lovely meal, thank you. The next event will be this weekend." She picked up a folder from the desk and handed it to me. "It's Martin's annual alumni event. We usually use caterers for these, but he specifically requested you."

"OK." I finished my diamond vodka and set the glass on the bar.

She picked up the bottle. "Another?"

"No, thanks. I need to get going." I ignored her small pout. "I'll see you next weekend, I guess."

"Oh, no," she laughed. "I wouldn't be caught dead at one of his parties."

I doubted she'd been invited.

When I was out of the room I opened up Martin's event folder. One hundred of Yale's finest would be treated to food, drink, and festivities at the Rooftop Terrace in Millennium Park.

This was very cool. The Terrace was an open-air venue, perched on top of the three-story Park Grill building in Millennium Park. I'd always wanted to do something in that space. Celeste was hiring a band and bringing in someone else to do the decorations, take care of the equipment, and clean up. It looked like all I was responsible for was the food and alcohol. Perfect.

Other than the specter of a terrorist attack on the city, being the event chef for the Nottinghams was turning out to be an excellent gig.

I was still looking at the folder when I bumped into someone coming the other way. It was Tasia.

"Sorry," I said. "We have to stop meeting like this."

This time instead of walking past me she stopped.

"You're doing Martin's party next weekend."

"Yes, apparently."

"Don't screw it up."

"I don't plan to." This woman was hot, but was starting to irritate me.

"I mean it. Martin does this once a year. It's a big deal to him. It needs to be special." Her blue eyes flashed. "If you mess this up, you're done."

I doubted she had much say in the staff decisions; it seemed like Celeste's purview. But I bit back my reply. It wouldn't do any good to alienate her more than she already was.

"I'll do my best."

She gave a slight nod and continued down the hall.

Bitch.

I went to the kitchen and grabbed my bag, then went downstairs to the cellar to put away the last two unopened bottles of ridiculously expensive wine left over from dinner.

I reshelved the bottles, and as I turned to go back upstairs I heard a faint whirring sound from the other direction.

I took a few slow steps down the dimly lit hallway and turned the corner, expecting to see one of Nottingham's security thugs.

The hallway was empty. A beam of light spilled out of the door at the far end.

Ellis had said this section was off limits. But the door was open, and there was no security around. Whatever was going on couldn't be all that top secret. I walked quietly down the hallway to the open door and peaked in.

SEVEN

The room's floor was plain cement, on which lay a thin, faded rug. Recessed lighting in the ceiling illuminated large black and white photographs covering the walls. The image closest to the door was a mineshaft, the one next to it a pile of dull, barely translucent stones. The other images were of similar stones, each one in the sequence increasingly refined and brilliant.

The very last image was of a single diamond, multifaceted and beautiful, lit in such a way that light seemed to explode out of it.

"You're not supposed to be here."

Richard Nottingham was sitting at a sturdy metal table in the center of the room. His suit jacket hung on a hook next to the door, his tie was off and his sleeves were rolled up. He wasn't looking at me, staring intently instead at the end of a long nail he was holding in one hand underneath a bright desk lamp. He was using the other hand to hold an eyepiece, through which he peered at the end of the nail. Now that I was in the room I could hear the soft hum of ventilation.

A flat round plate in the center of the table started to spin, and the whirring drowned out the hum. He lowered the nail down, touching the tip of it to the plate.

I took a tentative step closer. Attached to the end of the nail was a diamond, now pressed against the spinning plate. Small pieces of dust flew away from it.

During dinner, and at every other moment I'd seen him since the first event on the *Enterprise*, his expression had been set in a pinched frown. Now he was relaxed, his lips loosely set, his forehead smooth.

He pressed the diamond against the plate for a few more seconds, then pulled it off and inspected it. He set the nail down on the desk and looked up at me.

"What are you doing here?"

His English accent was faint but notably aristocratic, and I had a hard time believing this guy had any Russian in him.

"Uh, just watching."

"Well do your watching somewhere else."

I took another step closer and looked down. On the table were stones, presumably diamonds, neatly arranged in several piles. A few dull and rounded, several heart-shaped, with precise, flat facets, and shining. Rectangular containers bordered the desk, some containing more of the nails, along with long tweezers, mallets, and small hammers, as well as a few other things I didn't recognize. The bright lamp was set to the side, its small spotlight focused on the wheel.

"What are you doing?"

"I'm polishing a diamond. Do I need to call security, or are you going to leave, Miss . . .?" His hand slid underneath the desk, I assumed for one of those emergency call buttons that would bring his security staff down to haul me out of here.

"Pfister. I'm the event chef. I'm sorry, I've never seen a diamond being made before. It's amazing . . . incredible, even; how you start with a dull rock, and turn it into that." I pointed at the photograph on the wall of the finished diamond.

His eyes followed mine to the photograph. "It *is* incredible." His hand came back from underneath the table.

"How would someone even know, the first time they found one of the dull stones, that it could turn into something so beautiful?"

"How indeed?" His mouth formed into the barest hint of a smile.

Against one of the walls was another small metal table, this one holding something that looked like a saw, and more tools. A gas cannister was on the floor next to the table, rubber tubing leading from it to a Bunsen burner.

"It must be complicated."

"It is. People think that diamonds just come out of the ground like that," he said, nodding to the picture of the finished diamond. "But they start out like this." He picked up one of the dull stones and held it up. "It takes patience and skill to turn it into this." He selected one of the finished heart-shaped stones from the table and held it up to the light, rotating it slightly in his fingers.

"How do you do that? I mean, even decide where to cut it, the first time? So it comes out like that?"

He chuckled. I'd never even seen him smile.

"It takes years of practice, close observation, and patience. Each stone has its own personality. Identifying what it could become is the most important step."

He held up one of the larger dull stones, and tilted his head. "Should this be one large diamond, or several smaller ones? Making a mistake at this stage means the mined stone never reaches its full promise. The most skilled diamantaires are able to ascertain right away a stone's potential."

I had no doubt he included himself in that group.

"Then the stone must be cleaved along specific lines, according to its crystalline structure. It is shaped and polished. The entire process can take days, or weeks, sometimes months, depending on the stone. At every stage, one small misstep can destroy it."

He was sitting up straight in his chair, his posture perfect. His voice had taken on an almost dreamy quality.

"It is the perfect marriage of art and science. The merger of basic material science with ultimate beauty."

He took the thin disk off of his machine and replaced it with another one, then continued polishing.

I watched in silence while he stopped and started the wheel numerous times, each time peering through the eyepiece at the diamond attached to the edge of the nail.

I was entranced, and wasn't sure how much time went by before I pulled out my phone to look at the time.

Shit. I needed to go.

"Bye. And, uh, thanks, for letting me watch."

He nodded absentmindedly. I turned to the door.

"Miss Pfister?"

"Yes?"

He looked up from his table. "Close the door on your way out. And don't ever come down here again."

So much for Mr. Touchy Feely. I guess our moment was over.

Still, it was interesting to see Nottingham in his element. He no doubt had the best diamond cutters in the industry working for him. But he loved it, so much so that he found a few hours after a long dinner party to go off and do it himself.

Maybe his youth wasn't as bleak as Smith had described. Maybe he had fond memories of working in the mines, learning about diamonds, gaining skill in the process of turning them into priceless gems. His life now was about business and money, but working with diamonds was his real passion, the one thing that made him content.

I could relate to that. It was how I felt about cooking.

I wondered again why Tasia and Martin hated him so much. I stepped out and started to close the door.

"What are you doing down here?"

Mason was standing in front of me. I hadn't heard a sound as he'd come down the stairs. His face was flushed, the red oozing into the roots of his shortly cut hair.

"Sorry, I was just, uh, putting things away in the cellar, and I heard a noise."

He took a step closer. "You were told that you were not to be in this area, weren't you?" His eyes bored into mine.

"Yeah, yes." I couldn't help but look away.

He grabbed my arm and knocked on the door, then pushed it open and stepped in, dragging me behind him.

"Mr. Nottingham. I'm sorry, did this woman disturb you?"

Nottingham set the nail with the diamond down on the desk and looked up.

"Briefly."

"I'm very sorry sir."

"It's fine, Mason. No harm done."

Mason turned and dragged me back out of the room, closing the door behind him.

He frogmarched me down the hallway to the other set of stairs, not taking his hands off of me until we were back up in the kitchen. He nodded to my coat and bag.

I picked them up, then he pulled me down the hallway and to the front door. I thought he would let me go, but he escorted me roughly all the way down the driveway to the gate. When we got there he released me with a firm shove.

"Don't ever go down there again. If I see you there, or in any of the other areas of the house that are off limits, you will be fired on the spot."

He turned around. In a few moments the gate opened.

I tried not to run out of it, and didn't stop to call for a ride until I was on the other side and well down the street.

EIGHT

The evening had gone late, and even then I had a hard time getting to sleep. The interaction with Mason left me jumpy. His reaction had been over the top, in response to what seemed like a minor transgression. Especially when Nottingham hadn't seemed to mind.

I'd turned off Smith's spy phone so I could sleep in the next day. I left it off until I woke up, took a shower, and went upstairs for my first cup of coffee. When I sat down at the table and finally turned it back on it rang within seconds.

"Where have you been?"

"Sleeping. I didn't get to bed until four last night."

"I don't care. You're supposed to always have it with you, and it always has to be on. Always. That's non-negotiable."

I mumbled assent.

"How did it go last night?"

"Fine. It was about thirty people, all politicians and their significant others." I gave him the list of names. "It went late, until after one."

"That's it?"

"What else do you want to know?"

"Anything. Everything. What was Nottingham's demeanor?"

"During dinner he was the same as always. He didn't say much, he usually lets other people do most of the talking. He did manage to have short private discussions with almost everyone. I didn't catch much of what they were saying, but from the body language it looked like negotiations."

"About what?"

"I don't know. I never got close enough to get any idea."

"Next time do something to get in on the conversations. They could be important."

"I'll try. But how convinced are you that he's your guy? I mean, I get that he's some kind of dormant agent, but are you sure he's getting ready to do something terrible?"

"Yes, we're sure. Why?"

I described finding Nottingham in the basement, and our private moment. "I don't know. He seemed kind of happy. Not like someone who's getting ready to torch a city. It's hard to explain . . . I guess he looked the way I feel when I'm cooking. Like I'm completely, totally in my element. Like hours can pass, and they feel like minutes. Why would a guy like that want to get involved in an attack on his own home?"

"Good question. I don't know. But it doesn't matter. Anything else?"

"Yeah. Mason caught me coming out of Nottingham's room in the basement and went ballistic. He threw me out of the house, and I thought he was going to fire me on the spot. It was pretty extreme, especially considering Nottingham didn't really seem to mind."

"That level of paranoia may be a sign that he's in on what Nottingham and Rykov are doing."

"I don't know . . . I think it might have had more to do with making a mistake. I think he's supposed to be down there all the time, and he got caught taking a break. I might have made him look bad."

"Maybe. Anything else?"

"No. Other than I'm doing Martin's alumni event this weekend."

"Do you know who's going to be there?"

"A hundred of his closest friends from Yale. Likely Tasia. Definitely not Celeste."

"Richard Nottingham?"

"I doubt it." I looked at my phone. "I gotta go, Smith."

We hung up, and a few moments later Maude came out of her room and raised her eyebrows. "You ready?"

"Yep." I stood up, then grabbed my coat and followed her out the door.

"Thanks for doing this," I said to her as we got into her

car. She never took time off when she was working a case. This was a big lift for her.

"No sweat."

She put the car in gear and pulled out of our garage. It wasn't anywhere near rush hour, so the traffic wasn't too bad, just a few minutes to I-90 until the Nagle exit in Norwood. Then we drove another ten minutes on surface streets until she pulled into the parking lot of the Face the Future Rehabilitation Center.

"You don't have to go in if you don't want to," I said, opening my door.

"Do you want me to?"

Desperately. "Only if you want to."

"I do."

The two of us walked into the lobby and signed in at the front desk, then waited.

This place wasn't bad, as far as rehab centers went. I'd been in enough by now to know. My sister Gigi had been in and out of them for years, starting in high school. My parents had paid for them, each time hopeful that she'd be able to kick her habit.

She'd left every one of them after no more than a few days, returning to the street and to drugs. Eventually our parents gave up, and stopped paying for them.

I couldn't give up on her. She was the only person in my family I gave a shit about. And what happened to her wasn't her fault.

Our parents had stood around, for years, while she was abused by my dad's brother. They ignored the signs, and ignored me telling them about it, until she was a wreck. When I was able to finally do something about it, it was too late. The damage was done. By the time she was ten years old there was nothing left of the sister I'd known growing up. She dropped out of school, and started drinking. Eventually she discovered heroin, which evolved into a fentanyl addiction, which was worse. To pay for it she started selling herself on the street.

I'd been doing what I could to help her; letting her crash at my place, giving her cash on occasion. Some people said I was enabling her, but I was doing whatever I could to keep the lines of communication open between us, in the hopes that one day she'd come back.

While I hated my parents for how her life had turned out, part of me blamed myself, too. I wish I had done more to help her, or at least done it sooner.

I could hardly stand to look at my parents now, and had to summon every speck of self-control to get in front of them this time to get them to pay for the rehab. They were reluctant, but relented, once I told them about her near death at the hands of her recent pimp. And now that her long-time dealer and pimp was out of the picture, she had a real chance.

After a few minutes Gigi met us at the front desk and gave us each a weak hug.

"Let's go outside," she murmured, pulling a pack of cigarettes out of her pocket.

The three of us walked out of the building and onto a path that ran around it. As soon as we left the building Gigi lit a cigarette. Her hands were steady.

"How are you doing?" My typical lame starting point.

"OK."

"Really?"

She nodded. She actually did look pretty good. Amazing what a few weeks off of opiates and booze will do to your complexion. Along with regular healthy meals, a bed to sleep in instead of cold cement on the street, and not hooking every night.

"Have you seen Mom and Dad?"

"Yeah. They came by last week."

"How did that go?"

"Oh, you know . . ."

She must have noticed my frown. "In the therapy, they talk about forgiveness. I'm working on that."

At least one of us was. She might have to do it as part of her healing, but I didn't. And I never would.

As usual she wasn't very chatty, and I didn't push it.

After cigarette number two she said, "Do you think . . ." she took a long drag, looking off into the sky.

"Do I think what?"

"I just can't imagine . . . you know . . . what it's going to be like when I'm out of here."

This was progress; I couldn't remember the last time I heard her talk about the future.

"Well for one thing, you have a place to stay. We have an extra bedroom with your name on it."

She looked at me, her eyes wide, and then at Maude, who nodded.

Maude and I had talked about this, and she'd readily agreed. When we were looking for a house we'd made a point to find one big enough to accommodate both Gigi and Michael, if either one of them ever needed it.

Gigi gave a small smile, a remnant of one that I hadn't seen in years.

We walked around the building, enough time for her to smoke another cigarette, and then went back inside.

"I've got a group meeting." She gave us each another feeble hug and walked to the back.

We watched her go. When she disappeared I leaned over the counter.

"Is Hannah here?"

"Yes, would you like me to call her?"

"Yes, please."

A few moments later Hannah joined us at the front. She was Gigi's case worker, and an ex-addict herself.

"How's she doing?" I was on Gigi's HIPAA, which allowed me access to her health status. My parents weren't, which annoyed them to no end.

"She's making progress. It's a process. She's made it through the most difficult physical part, the opiate withdrawal. Now comes the harder part. You're aware your sister's been in rehab before?"

"Yeah . . . five or six times."

"Then you know that for it to stick she needs to address the underlying conditions. The reasons she withdraws into drugs."

"That's a good euphemism, 'underlying condition.' So how does one recover from a dirtbag uncle abusing you for most of your childhood?"

"It's not easy, and it's going to take time. Gigi is in a trauma-focused therapy group of people with similar backgrounds. As she gets closer to discharge we'll focus on dealing with triggers."

"Do you think she'll stick it out this time?"

She paused. "I don't know. It would help if she could confront her abuser. We've found that victims are more successful healing when they have their day in court."

"That's going to be a problem. He's dead," I said flatly.

"Oh. Well, we'll find other ways to help her find closure."

I liked her attitude. And I was optimistic; Gigi had already been here longer than any other of her stays in rehab.

"Do you know, has anyone else come to see her?"

"Your parents have been here a couple of times. She refuses to meet with them."

"Is that it? No one else? No men?"

"Men? No. Just you and your parents."

I exhaled softly. Two of the previous times she'd been in rehab her pimps had come and encouraged her to leave. It didn't take much; sneaking in one hit of whatever drug she'd been using was enough to set off the strong pull of her addiction.

I thanked Hannah, and we left.

We were back on the freeway before either of us spoke. "You OK?" asked Maude.

"Fine. It always takes me back, seeing her. What that animal did to her."

Maude was in a unique position to know how I felt. She'd lost her brother at a young age, too. She'd gotten him back, after twenty years, more or less intact. But those lost years could never be recovered.

"Do you mind dropping me off at Navy Pier? I'm helping

Nikky do a thing today." I'd jumped at the chance to give her a hand and to cook again in the *Enterprise*'s galley.

"Nikky, huh?" She slid a grin at me. "You guys getting serious?"

I shrugged. "I like her. It's convenient."

"So, a long-running booty call. When are you going to get back in the saddle? It's been over a year since your last real relationship."

"I like the way things are. And I don't have time for a real relationship."

"You made time for Ekaterina."

I looked out the window. Ekaterina was still a sore spot for me.

"I'm actually thinking about picking up the radio show again. The restaurant is running fine without me, at least until Zoe gets her own place. And other than that first big dinner, it looks like the Nottingham events will be pretty low lift."

Smith had finally filled Maude and a few select others at the Chicago PD in on the Nottingham operation. He hadn't given her all the details, but she knew I was doing some low-level spying for him.

"Celeste is extremely well organized. It's a little shocking, really, considering she probably wakes up in the morning blowing a 0.5."

I'd told Maude about Celeste, too. As far as I was concerned she was inside the cone of silence.

"That bad?"

"You can't imagine. It's a little unbelievable . . . the amount of alcohol she puts away would kill most people, but she shows zero effect. Not even red eyes."

"I wonder what her issue is? Why she drinks so much?"

I'd been wondering the same thing. "I don't know. She seems to have everything. She married into a filthy rich family, to a nice-looking and by all accounts attentive husband."

"Not attentive enough, by what you told me." I'd told her about Celeste's not-too-subtle hints that we hook up.

"Apparently not. But she's no trophy wife; she has serious responsibilities. It looks like she runs everything at the house. Pretty well from what I can tell."

"Well you know what they say. Money can't buy happiness."

"Yeah. But that is one seriously unhappy house. Other than Alan, everyone seems miserable."

NINE

When Maude dropped me off at Navy Pier and I boarded the *Enterprise* Nikky was already there. "Hey you," she said, giving me a quick hug. Then we got to work.

Guests would be arriving in two hours. She ran through the menu with me and I started my prep.

I liked working with Nikky. She was a great chef, and I always learned something when I was around her. It was also nice to be able to just cook once in a while, rather than have to be in charge of everything.

The boat left the dock as soon as the guests arrived, and they were seated shortly thereafter. This was a political event for one of the aldermen who was up for election, so it was much less complicated than the evening soirées both of us often did. Fewer courses, for one. And much less alcohol. I recognized a few people from the dinner I'd done at the Nottinghams', including the alderman. He represented one of the more affluent wards in the city, notably including the Lincoln Park neighborhood. Nottingham had probably underwritten the cost of this event.

Nikky's food tended toward the whimsical. She loved themes, and today's menu celebrated Chicago's sports teams, one of the few topics in the city that everyone could get behind. The meal was fairly pedestrian, by her standards, but the organizers had specified that they didn't want anything too extravagant. It was a fundraiser, and they didn't want to be accused of wasting money on profligate dining.

Guests had their choice of trayed appetizers, either North Side Stars, a red, white, and blue assortment of peppadew peppers stuffed with blue cheese; or South Side, lightly fried oysters with black caviar and crème fraîche. It didn't take the guests long to figure out the dishes reflected the color schemes of Chicago's professional teams, and already people were squaring off in good-natured arguments over their favorites.

Once seated, the servers came to the tables with platters of salad fixings, and guests were invited to have customized Slapshot Salads with their choice of cooked sweet potatoes, cherry tomatoes, roasted red peppers, kalamata and black olives, shredded carrots, black beans, chiffonaded romaine and frisée greens, and a variety of white dressings.

There were two mains: Bulls Nation, a steak with roasted tomatoes and mashed potatoes, or Sky Nation, squid ink pasta with arrabbiata sauce and burrata cheese. We wrapped things up with coffee and Da Dessert, individual parfaits with layers of persimmon gelée, fresh blueberries, and white chocolate custard.

The meal went off without a hitch, and my job was done, other than some cleanup. And maybe a quick check-in with Nikky to see if she wanted to hook up later.

We hadn't seen each other in a few weeks. It had been so long that even Celeste was starting to look like an option.

I'd stepped outside to the deck to get some fresh air when there was the irritating ring of Smith's phone.

He'd put the fear of God into me a little bit at our last meeting, about always carrying it with me. I'd never really seen him scared, but this operation had clearly gotten to him. At this point I never went anywhere without it.

"What's up?"

"Sags, where are you?"

He never called me "Sags."

"'Hi' to you, too. I'm on the *Enterprise*."

"Are you alone?"

"Just me and about a hundred other people."

"I mean right now. Can anyone hear this conversation?"

"No. What's going on?"

"I'm on speaker. SSA Stokes is with me. He's from the FBI's JTTF."

"Is that supposed to mean something to me?" I'd given up long ago trying to keep track of the FBI's acronyms.

"Miss Pfister, this is SSA Stokes, from the Joint Terrorism Task Force. Listen carefully. We've had a credible threat that there's a bomb on the boat."

"On the *Enterprise*?"

"Yes. I need you to look around."

"Look around?"

"Yes, we need you to see if you can locate the bomb."

"A bomb? Are you kidding?" I pulled the phone away from my ear and looked around. "This thing has lifeboats. We need to get off."

"You can't do that."

"Why not?"

"We've been informed that if anyone tries to leave the boat the bomb will go off."

"Why are you talking to me? Shouldn't you be calling the captain?"

"Please, keep your voice down. And try to stay calm. We did contact the captain. He's been instructed to stay away from the pier until we can determine if the threat is a real one."

I noticed for the first time that the boat was no longer moving.

"Don't say anything to anyone. Most calls like this are hoaxes, and we don't want to start a panic. But I need you to see if you can spot anything that looks like a bomb."

"Isn't there security, or some—"

"Miss Pfister. Please. If this is a real threat we don't have much time. The caller said the bomb was hidden in the kitchen. Agent Smith tells me you were there recently for a previous event, and you're working in there today. You're in the best position to see if anything is out of place, or unusual, in that area of the boat. I need you to go to the kitchen, and—"

"Galley."

"Galley, and look for anything that seems like it doesn't belong there."

"What does it look like?"

"We don't know."

"Then how the hell am I supposed to—"

"It would be at least as big as a shoebox. But small enough that it could be carried by one person and not attract attention."

"And what happens if I find something that looks like that?"

"Don't touch it. Keep the phone on, I'll be on the line while you look."

I went back inside and walked into the galley.

Everyone was busy, putting away food, washing dishes, cleaning equipment and prep stations.

I walked through the lines, opening up cabinets and peering in. Pots, pans, dishes, silverware, chafing dishes . . . everything looked the way it should.

I went through the refrigerator, just in case, and then walked into the pantry. I'd spent a fair amount of time in here, and tried to remember what it looked like the last time I was on the boat.

Nothing seemed out of place, or unusual. But I couldn't be sure.

The galley was huge. And nothing was jumping out at me as different. Short of pulling everything out of the cabinets and off the shelves, I didn't know what else I could do. And they hadn't told me how much time I had.

This was stupid. I wondered how long everyone would last if we just jumped overboard. How cold was Lake Michigan in December?

Definitely above freezing. But not by much.

Thinking about the cold reminded me of the walk-in freezer. I opened the heavy door and went in.

Large by kitchen standards, and huge by galley standards, the freezer was only about half full, primarily stocks, ice creams and sorbets, some frozen fruit, and bags of ice. Not much meat or fish; the events on this boat were high-end, and usually only fresh proteins were served.

Everything looked the way it should, stacked neatly, much of it still in the original packing boxes.

There. Sitting at the end of one of the metal shelves, second from the bottom.

An unlabeled brown cardboard box, about the size of a shoebox. Had I seen it before?

I couldn't be sure. But I didn't recognize it as part of the normal inventory.

I backed up from the shelf as far away as I could get, then opened the door and stepped out, closing it tightly. I leaned against the door and pulled out Smith's phone.

"I may have found something. In the freezer," I whispered.

"What does it look like?"

"It was a brown box."

"What else?"

"I don't know. I left it in there."

"You need to go back in and describe it to me."

I looked around the galley, my eyes drawn to the exit sign above the doors.

"Can't we just—"

"No. Please, you're wasting time. Get back in the freezer and make sure no one sees what you're doing."

I opened the door and went back in, closing it again behind me. I stood as far away from the box as I could.

"It's a brown cardboard box, no label. Nondescript. A little bigger than a shoebox."

"Are you sure that it's not something that belongs there?"

"Of course I'm not fucking sure! You told me not to touch it, remember?"

Now that I was in the proximity of what might be a bomb, my breath was coming in short gasps, my exhalations small visible clouds.

"OK. I'm sorry. Take a deep breath. It's good that it's in the freezer. Can you open the top of the box, and look in?"

"How about if I just walk out and close the door? This door's really solid, and—"

"See if you can open the box without jostling it too much."

I took a few steps toward the box, just close enough to see the top of it.

"The two flaps, at the top. They're sealed with packing tape."

"Can you cut it?"

"Are you nuts? What if I set it off? No." I shook my head, even though he couldn't see me. "I'm not touching it. You have bomb guys, get one of them in there to deal with it."

"They're on their way, but we don't have time to wait."

When I didn't respond, he added, "Someone carried it in there and set it down. Between that and the boat's movements, if it was that sensitive it would have already gone off."

There was a box cutter on the shelf near the door for opening up supplies. I picked it up and took a few tentative steps toward the cardboard box. Staying as far away as I could and still reach it, I leaned over and slid the edge of the knife as carefully as I could along the tape. My heart was pounding, and it took two tries to get it open.

I was starting to sweat, even though it was close to twenty degrees in here. "OK. The tape is cut."

"Good. Pull gently on one of the flaps and see if you can get a look in."

I used the tip of the cutter to lift one of the flaps and pull it up. Then I did the same to the other flap.

"It's just wadded up newspaper."

"Pull it aside. Carefully."

No shit, "carefully." I pulled gently on the piece of newspaper at the top.

It was one large piece and came up easily.

Whew. This didn't look too bad. I exhaled.

"There's a cell phone, some wires, a little ball of gray putty or something, and just a small glass or clear plastic tube, with two compartments, sitting on the putty. Here, I'm sending you a picture." I took a picture and texted it to him.

After a moment he muttered a low curse. "Miss Pfister, listen very carefully. Do you see the timer?"

I looked into the box again. "You mean the one on the phone? Yeah. Two forty-one. Two forty . . . it's counting down."

He took another deep breath.

"What's going on? What do you know?"

"I believe the putty is plastic explosive, and when the timer goes down it will detonate."

I took a step back. "OK. Well, it doesn't look like a lot of explosive. And all that's in there is the phone and that small tube. So I can just close the door, and—"

"We believe the tube contains Novichok precursors."

"Novichok? Precursors?"

"Novichok is a family of nerve agents. Like Sarin."

"Sarin? You mean, the, 'expose a bunch of people to tiny amounts and they die or suffer irreparable physical damage immediately,' Sarin?"

"Yes."

Holy fuck. I took another step back. "How do you know what it is?"

"The caller told us."

"And you didn't bother to tell me?" I started hyperventilating again, my small exhalation clouds forcing me to observe my own panic. "What am I supposed to do?"

"The precursors can be destroyed by incineration. But the incinerator would need to be airtight. Is there anything like that in the kitchen?"

"No . . . not that I can think of." I was starting to feel faint. "Why can't I just leave it in the freezer and close the door?" And jump overboard.

"That isn't an option. When the timer goes off the two compounds in the vial will mix, creating the Novichok agent, and then spread out in powder or liquid form. Some of it could get through the vents, some of it might freeze. If that happens it could stay viable and dangerous for a very long time."

"So what? We can dock, get everyone off, and your hazmat guys can come on the boat and take care of it."

"We can't allow the boat to dock with this on it. And there's no time to get anyone to you to deactivate it. The incident team has been dispatched, but they're at least fifteen minutes away. And there's another problem. We don't know exactly what kind of plastic explosive is in the box. There's a chance it will be powerful enough to damage the freezer door, or violate the integrity of the pressure system. If that happens, the powder or liquid mist will escape, and many people on the boat will die."

"You saw the picture. You can see . . . there's not that much stuff in here." The vial held at most a few tablespoons of liquid.

"It doesn't need much. Novichok is many times more powerful than Sarin. A drop on your skin could kill you within minutes, depending on the formulation."

I dropped the piece of newspaper that I'd been keeping in my hand on the floor and kicked it away.

"How much time is left?"

I hadn't touched anything in the box. Maybe I'd be OK.

"Miss Pfister, how much time is left."

"A minute ten seconds."

"OK. It appears to be a relatively simple set up. I think all you have to do is detach the wires from the explosive."

"'Appears?' 'You think?' What if there's a backup?"

In the movies explosive devices always had alternative activation mechanisms. If the main character did something to deactivate a bomb, inevitably another activation mechanism would kick in, usually with less time remaining.

"It doesn't look like it from the picture. Uh, before you do it, make sure the door to the freezer is closed."

"It's closed. Wait, what? You mean, in case it explodes it will just be me that gets sprayed with deadly poison?"

"Please just hurry up. But be careful."

I walked back up to the box and pulled one of the flaps as far back as it would go. The timer was down to thirty seconds.

"Should I just use my hands?"

"Yes."

"What if I get some of this explosive on me? And what if there's some of that poison on the phone or the wires? Shouldn't I use gloves?"

"There's no time. You need to hurry."

I reached into the box, and gently laid one hand on the putty and the other on the red and black wires that led from it to the phone, doing everything I could to avoid touching the clear vial containing the poison.

Here goes nothing. I held my breath, and pulled on the wires.

TEN

I turned my face away as I pulled the wires out. Once I felt them release I snuck a look back at the box.

5 . . . 4 . . . 3 . . . 2 . . . 1

I turned away again, still holding my breath.

After a few seconds I looked back. The phone counter was at zero. Everything was intact.

I exhaled and closed the flaps to the box, then stepped back.

"Miss Pfister?"

I'd forgotten the phone was still on, and jumped.

"Yeah. The counter's at zero. I think it's OK. Nothing happened."

"Good. The hazmat team will be there in a little while. You need to keep the door closed, and stay there until they come."

"It's freezing in here. How long are they going to be?" Even though it was deactivated, I didn't want to be anywhere near this box and the poison "precursors."

"They're coming by boat. It shouldn't be more than ten minutes now."

I was wondering how long it took to freeze to death when the freezer door finally opened. Three men in light-gray plastic-looking suits, gloves, boots, hoods, goggles, and respirators walked in. The only part of them I could see was their eyes.

They closed the door after they were all in the freezer. All were carrying metal cases, one of them was also holding a large trash bag.

The one with the largest case walked directly over to the box and peered inside. "The container appears intact," he said, his voice tinny and robotic.

He carefully picked up the cardboard box with both hands and set the entire thing into his case, then closed and locked it.

The other two set their cases on the floor and opened them.

Both removed small tubes. After taking out the stoppers at the top of the tubes they waved them around the space. Then they took out pieces of cloth, and wiped them in and around the box. They each pulled a vial out of their case, and used a dropper to wet the cloths.

After a few moments they gave each other the thumbs up.

"No sign of the agent," one of them said.

"Great. I'm f–freezing."

I started to walk out and one of them stepped in front of me, shaking his head.

"Miss, you have to stay here until you're decontaminated. Please give us your phone, and take off your clothes."

"Are you k–kidding? It's freezing in here. And I thought you said there was no sign of it?"

"It's standard protocol. I'm sorry."

It was clear I wasn't getting out of here until I took off my clothes. I handed him my phone and then stripped. Once my clothes were off one of the men put them in the trash bag, and then another one took out a tube of something from his case.

He opened the top, squeezed out a white lotion, and then proceeded to cover me in it. It was embarrassing and silly to be standing naked and covered in lotion by a stranger, but it seemed way less important at the moment than the fact that I was freezing.

While they were doing that I could feel the boat moving.

After I was covered in the lotion the three of them wiped it off, putting the wipes in the trash bag along with my clothes, and sealed it.

They handed me a pair of sweatpants and a sweatshirt they'd brought with them, and a blanket. I dressed and wrapped the blanket around me, and we walked out of the freezer.

The galley was empty. Everyone on the boat was outside on the deck, crowded near the railings. One of the men handed me a phone.

"Sagarine?" It was Smith.

"Ye–yeah?"

"Are you OK?"

"F–fine."

"Someone from the office will be at the dock to pick you up. We'll debrief when you get here. In the meantime, it's critical that you don't share what happened with anyone. We're telling people it was an exercise."

I was too cold to argue. "W–wonderful." All I could think about was going home and taking a hot shower.

The boat docked, and people pressed to get off. Even though they'd been told it was an exercise, the site of men in hazmat suits and hoods freaked them out.

Most of them, anyway. One of the passengers was lagging behind, taking pictures of the hazmat team, and several of me.

"Sags, are you OK? What happened? All of a sudden these guys came on board and told us to get out of the galley. Were you in the freezer?" Nikky was still on the boat, and had stepped out of the disembarkation line to get to me.

"Y–yeah. It was—"

"Miss Pfister?"

A man in a very FBI suit pushed through the crowd at the gangway and took my arm. "Come with me, please."

"I'll see you later," I said to Nikky as he pulled me past the other passengers and led me away.

The ride to the FBI office took longer than usual, traffic turning the fifteen-minute ride into forty. But even with the heat turned up full blast I was still shivering by the time we got there.

Smith met me in the lobby and we went up to the sixth floor and into a small room.

There was a table and three chairs. Another guy in a suit was sitting in one of the chairs.

"Hello, Miss Pfister. I'm SSA Stokes."

"Hi. Can I get some coffee?"

He nodded to Smith, who left the room. I guess I knew who outranked who.

"How are you doing?"

"Cold."

Smith walked back in the room and handed me a cup of coffee.

"Thanks. Listen, what am I doing here? I'd really like to go home."

"We won't keep you long. The FBI is responsible for handling terrorist threats. The presence of a potential nerve agent puts it in our purview. As I said earlier, we believe that the substances in the vial were Novichok precursors."

"You already knew that."

"We won't know for sure until we test them. We were told they were, by the anonymous caller."

"Maybe you should be talking to your anonymous caller."

"We don't know who it is."

He leaned forward. "First things first, Miss Pfister. It's extremely important that you not speak about what happened on the boat to anyone."

He stared at me until I nodded.

"For now we're telling people that the event on the boat was an exercise. No one knows that there was a live device on the boat, other than law enforcement, and you."

"And whoever put it there," I added.

He pursed his lips. "Tell me, how did you locate the device?"

"I don't know, I just started looking around."

"How did you know where to look?"

I looked between him and Smith. "You called me, remember? You were both there, on speaker. You told me your anonymous tipster said it was in the galley."

He stared at me with a look that I guessed made a lot of people uncomfortable.

I stared back. At times like this my gray eyes were useful. Most people found them disconcerting.

After a full minute of staring, Stokes said, "Do you know anything about where this device came from?"

"Of course not."

"Where were you, Miss Pfister, prior to boarding the boat?"

"This is ridiculous." I stood up to leave.

Smith put his hand on my arm. "Please, Sagarine, just answer his questions."

I dropped back down on the chair. "I was visiting my sister, who's in rehab. Face the Future Rehabilitation Center. You can check the visitor log. Do you seriously think I had something to do with this?"

He stared at me again.

"Smith, tell him. We've been working together, for God's sake."

"He knows what you do for us. This is just standard operating. We need to rule you out."

"Did you see anyone carry anything onto the boat, anything that could have hidden the device?" Stokes continued.

"No. But I spent most of the time in the galley. And what makes you so sure that someone brought it on this trip? The *Enterprise* goes out all the time. Isn't it equally, or even more, possible that it was put there before this trip? Why on earth would someone put a deadly poison bomb on a boat they were on themself?"

"Why indeed. Have you recently made any trips on the *Enterprise*, prior to this one?"

"Yeah, I did an event there last weekend."

His eyebrows went up.

"Oh, come on." I looked in exasperation at both of them. "Didn't I just deactivate the thing for you? You can't seriously think I had anything to do with this. Why would I put myself near that stuff?"

Stokes leaned back. "We don't believe you had anything to do with this. But you may know something about who did."

"I doubt it. I don't hang around with people who make DIY bombs."

"This kind of device looks simple, but it's an effective and efficient way to distribute a nerve agent. There aren't a lot of moving parts, or electronics that can fail. Just a cell phone. Novichok is extremely dangerous. Even carrying it in sealed containers has to be done very carefully. Because of that, bombs made to disperse it often use precursors. That is, two compounds that by themselves are harmless, but when mixed produce Novichok. The precursors can be created and transported easily and safely, then placed inside some kind of container where they're separated until the terrorist wants them mixed.

"In this case, there was a thin membrane separating the two

liquids. A small amount of C4 was placed around the membrane, and then connected to a detonator and the phone. A call to the phone would have set off a small explosion, which would have broken the membrane, mixing the precursors into Novichok, and then propelled it out into the surrounding area. All to say, the device could have easily been activated via phone from a safe distance. And I agree with you, we don't believe it was brought on board the *Enterprise* on this trip. Whoever planted it probably did it on the previous cruise."

"Which one was that?"

He looked at Smith, who said, "The Nottingham dinner party."

ELEVEN

"Holy shit, Sags, weren't you on this boat?"

I'd finally made it home and headed straight for the shower, and then to bed. I'd just gotten up and was sitting down to my first cup of coffee in the kitchen with Maude.

"Wait, is that you?" she said, peering closely at her laptop.

"Give me that." I turned the screen toward me.

Oh, no . . .

Prominent on the front page of the *Tribune* was a large headline: CRUISE PASSENGERS NARROWLY ESCAPE GRISLY DEATHS FROM NERVE AGENT. Next to the article was a picture of someone wrapped in a blanket.

"Yeah." I looked at the picture more closely. "Do you think it's that obvious that it's me?"

"I doubt it. But I know you pretty well."

While I was looking at the picture Smith's phone rang.

"Rosehill. Now." He hung up.

I made it to the cemetery in less than ten minutes but he was already there waiting.

"You were told not to say anything."

"I didn't."

"You were the only one who knew about this."

"Sure. Just me, you, your buddy in the FBI and whoever he told, the anonymous caller, the FBI guy who pulled me off the boat, and a bunch of hazmat guys. Oh, and whoever actually put the bomb on the boat."

"I don't think you understand how serious this is. SSA Stokes wants to arrest you for compromising the investigation."

"*I* don't understand? You weren't the one stuck in a freezer with a poison bomb."

He shook his head. "The whole city now knows how close it came to a nerve agent being released on a boat full of people.

Everyone is panicking, and it makes our job much harder. Not to mention that the Chicago police and fire departments are being flooded with calls to respond to sightings of suspicious objects. All because you opened your mouth and decided to get your picture taken." His normally even voice was raised almost to a shout.

This was ridiculous. He was frustrated, and taking it out on me. "Seriously?" I said, my voice rising to match his. "I didn't take a goddamn picture of myself. And I didn't say anything to anyone. Not even Maude. After I left yesterday I went straight home and went to bed."

I stared at him, breathing hard.

After a long moment, he said, more calmly now, "Did you see who was taking the pictures?"

"Not really. I got a glimpse of him just before your guy dragged me off the boat to be interrogated. Which, by the way, wasn't all that subtle."

"You're sure it was a man? Taking the pictures?"

"Or a woman in drag. Whoever, that's who you should be talking to."

He looked away. "We would if we knew who it was."

"Don't you have a list of the passengers?"

"Yes. But he's apparently not on it."

I knew enough about these boat trips to know that it was extremely difficult for people to get on board if they weren't invited. But figuring this out was Smith's job, not mine. I was glad it was over, at least for me.

"Well, at least it's over."

"What are you talking about?"

"Stokes said the thing was probably put in the freezer during the Nottingham party, by him or one of his guys. And this was their big thing, right? Their big attack? And it failed."

He shook his head. "This was nothing."

"Nothing? Didn't Stokes say it would have killed everyone on board? And possibly lasted long enough to float over the city?"

He sighed heavily. I noticed for the first time the black circles under his eyes, and his normally clean-shaven face was darkened with stubble. “Yes. But whatever Rykov is planning will be on a much larger scale than this. Thousands, hundreds of thousands, maybe millions of people. A few hundred people on a boat doesn’t match up with the resources he’s gathering. This was a test run. The device on the *Enterprise* was too small-scale for Rykov to be involved. And not that we needed it, but it’s more confirmation that we’re dealing with the Russians. The substances in the devices were tested. They are Novichok precursors.”

He shook his head. “Stokes wasn’t kidding. This stuff is unbelievably toxic. A drop on your skin, or you inhale just a tiny amount of powder, and it can kill you within seconds.”

Jesus. In retrospect, stripping in the freezer didn’t sound like overkill. “How does it do that?”

“It’s a nerve agent. A very bad one. Basically it prohibits your nerves from sending signals. Without those signals your muscles stop working, including the ones responsible for respiration, which means you stop breathing. An exposure to it that’s not immediately lethal can also cause death later via cardiac or lung failure, sepsis, or a host of other things.”

I wondered if Nottingham kept any of that shit in his house. I hoped not. But my desire to continue to cook for them was seriously dampened.

“How can you be sure it was the Russians? Couldn’t anyone make it?”

“We don’t think so. It’s their calling card. They always deny any involvement, publicly, but when this stuff shows up everyone knows it’s them. And they want it that way. It sends a message. Remember those two Russians, in Salisbury, England, who were poisoned with it?”

“No. I don’t follow international poisonings.” I rolled my eyes.

“In 2018. Sergei Skripal. He was a Russian military officer, and had been acting as a double agent for British intelligence. When he retired he moved to Salisbury, a small city in southern England, with his daughter, Yulia. They kept a low profile but were tracked down by Russian GRU agents. Two of them went to Salisbury and sprayed a small amount of Novichok on the door to Skripal's house. Sergei and Yulia were both found unconscious and near-dead on a park bench nearby, shortly after touching their door handle. The police officer who was first on the scene almost died after going into the house during the investigation.

"The Russian agents used a perfume bottle to carry and distribute the Novichok. When they were done they threw it into a dumpster in Amesbury, a town a few miles from Salisbury, before they left the country. A man in Amesbury found the bottle and took it home to give to his girlfriend. She sprayed it on herself, thinking it was perfume. She died a week later. Sergei and Yulia survived, but are living with a number of medical conditions, as is Charlie Rawley, the man who found the perfume bottle.

"It was a tiny, tiny amount, Sags, left on a door handle that was exposed to the elements for hours before anyone touched it. Imagine if more than that got into the air, or someone detonated a larger device in a public area—like Wrigley, or Soldier Field. Or in a train station. The immediate effect would be hundreds or thousands dead. And then it's not like it would just go away: any area in which traces of it were found would have to be completely decontaminated, which could take months, or years, depending on the venue and the conditions. Even then, it's not clear that anyone involved in the cleanup would be protected."

"What do you mean?"

"I mean that the men in the suits who came on board to take the device from you were extremely brave. When the Russians first developed Novichok in 1971 they did so with the explicit intent to avoid detection. And they successfully designed it to defeat NATO hazmat gear, so that standard NATO-issue suits wouldn't protect the wearer from the agent. The suits that we have now are better, but they're constantly making new Novichok formulations, all slightly different but equally as deadly, and it's never a hundred percent certain that the specific form of the agent won't break through the suit barriers. It also survives in water, and in the air, for long periods of time. Some of the formulations we've tested have no known half-life. Opinions are mixed as to how long it can exist in the environment, but it's a moving target, anyway. They've developed fifty different types of it, that we know of.

"As Stokes mentioned, we're fairly certain they're making the precursors here, in the US; it's too hard to import them on any scale, especially now. So they need a lab, which is where we think a lot of Rykov's money is going. It's not something that can be cooked up by a garden-variety terrorist. If someone tried he'd most likely end up killing himself."

He paused for effect, even though he didn't need to. I was completely freaked out.

"We've just found another one of Rykov's accounts, in the Caymans. The transfers into that and the other one we know about have totaled almost four million dollars in the last year. Some of that has headed back to Russia. We presume he's using the rest of it to put together the attack."

"You still think the money's coming from Nottingham?"

"We can't find a single cent of Nottingham's money going anywhere it shouldn't. But there aren't a lot of people in Rykov's circle with that kind of cash. And we know the two of them have been meeting. The bottom line is you need to continue to work at the Nottinghams until we find out what it is they're planning."

Great. "Are we done?"

He nodded, lips pressed tightly together.

"You might want to get some sleep, Smith. You look like hell."

I turned to leave and felt my other phone vibrate.

"Hello? . . . OK, sure."

"Who was that?"

"Ellis. The Nottinghams' butler, assistant, whatever. They want me to come to the house immediately."

"Are you doing another event today?"

"Not as far as I know. I'm not sure what they want."

When I got to the estate the gate was open. Zach was standing on the other side. He waited until I was through the gate and it closed before turning and walking toward the house, a slight wave of his hand to follow him the only communication.

When we got to the house he walked me straight to Celeste's office.

She was sitting behind her desk. Standing next to her was Mason.

"Please, sit down, Miss Pfister," she said.

I took the chair across from her, making an attempt to look at her and not at Mason, who was staring daggers at me.

"When we first spoke to you, I believe I was very clear that you not do anything to reflect poorly on the family."

Mason held out his phone, showing me the screen. On it was the by-now-familiar picture of me standing on the *Enterprise* near the gangway, wrapped in a towel.

"That is you, isn't it?" she asked.

"Yes."

The picture wasn't all that clear, and my face wasn't showing. How had they known it was me? I thought the only reason Maude recognized me was because she knew me.

"What were you doing on that boat?" barked Mason. Celeste turned slightly toward him, putting her hand on his arm.

"Cooking. I was sous-ing for Nikky Bullware. This events position is only part-time, you know I have other jobs."

I wasn't sure what to say, so didn't elaborate. If they wanted to boot me from the family service force for making the front page, I wouldn't be all that disappointed.

"Yes, and that's fine. But it's important that the people working for our family keep a low profile. This," she said, nodding to the phone, "is not that. What we—"

"I want to know exactly what you were doing on that boat, and how you became involved in a terrorist threat," interrupted Mason.

"I wasn't involved. I was there when it happened, like a lot of other people."

I wasn't sure how much to tell them. If all they knew was what was in the paper, they knew that there was a nerve agent on board, that it had been deactivated, and that I'd been in close enough proximity to have my clothes taken off. They wouldn't know anything about me being the one to deactivate the device, or my connection to the FBI.

But what if the bomb had been placed by Nottingham, or someone working for him? We still didn't know if anyone in his family or security team had anything to do with his secret life, although if any of them were part of his terrorist activity, my bet would be on Mason.

Maybe Mason knew about the bomb because he'd had a hand in placing it. And if so, did he know about my connection to the FBI? All of a sudden I wished I was anywhere but in this room.

OK . . . think. Whether or not this guy was working with Nottingham and Rykov, if he knew for sure I was working for the FBI he wouldn't have brought me back here. I would have been fired. At best.

"I don't know much more than what was in the paper. I was in the kitchen, cleaning up, putting things away in the freezer, and all of a sudden all hell broke loose and there were guys in suits and respirators telling us to get outside. That's it."

"You see," said Celeste, looking up at Mason. "There's nothing to worry about. I think we're done here."

Mason scowled and put the phone back in his pocket. He was obviously not done with me, but was loathe to contradict the lady of the house. He left the room. Zach followed him out.

"Thank you for coming in, Miss Pfister. I have another event for you. A few days after Martin's party."

She handed me a folder. I'd been under the impression that I'd only be doing an event every couple of weeks. These were coming fast and furious.

She must have seen the look in my eyes because she added quickly, "It's just a small one. A brunch for some of my friends at our store. I'm sure it will be an easy thing for you to do," she said, smiling. "I would normally use Percy for something as small as this, but I've just really enjoyed your work."

"No problem."

I couldn't get out of there fast enough. I went out the front door and walked down the driveway.

"Stop."

Mason was standing just after the bend in the road, out of sight of the house.

"Don't think because you're Celeste's favorite new toy that you're off the hook. I don't trust you, and I'm watching you. All of the time."

Maybe Smith was right. Why would this guy be so worked up about a picture of me on the boat if he didn't have anything to do with Nottingham's plans?

I walked past him and through the open gate, feeling his eyes on my back.

When I got home Maude and Linda were ensconced in the living room. Several laptops were open on the coffee table, stacks of folders piled around them and on the floor. Color photos of crime scenes covered one of our walls, replacing our framed pictures, which were now on the floor leaning against the one unused wall.

"Are you OK?" asked Linda. "What happened? Did you see the bomb?"

"I'm fine. And I can't talk about it."

I had no desire to be arrested. Fortunately they both knew about operational security, and didn't push it.

"Another one?" I nodded to the wall.

Linda had organized the crime scene photos into groups. There were now four columns of pictures, at the top of each a set of spray-painted numbers.

"Yeah," said Maude. "While you were facing imminent death on the *Enterprise* our bloody vandal struck again."

"'Vandalism'? Is that what you're calling these?"

She nodded, and pointed to the pictures on the far end. "The last one, at the Art Institute of Chicago. This guy really knows how to poke the bear."

The Art Institute was one of the premier cultural institutions in the city. The image she had was of the outside of it, taken in the front, from far enough back to include the two iconic bronze lions that guarded the entrance. On the ground below each of the lions was an indeterminate animal corpse, mangled and bloody.

"I'm guessing that's blood?" I asked, pointing to the lions.

They both nodded. "It's real. And those are possum carcasses," Linda added.

Blood dripped from the mouths of both lions. The picture captured some of the drops in the air, and some after they'd splashed on the sidewalk below, only slightly obscuring a white, nine-digit number.

TWELVE

It was a relief to be able to focus on prepping for Martin's party and not have to interact with the Nottinghams for a little while. I had no desire to go back to the house, even though Smith was still calling me frequently for updates.

The venue for Martin's party, the Harris Theater Rooftop Terrace, was a tented outdoor space, normally only available between April and October. More of a shade structure than an actual tent, the open sides allowed spectacular three hundred and sixty-degree views of the area, but little protection from the elements.

Still, the kind of money the Nottinghams' threw around made anything possible. Part of me thought that it was Martin's way of irritating his dad, who must have had to pay an exorbitant amount to put on Martin's yearly bash under the most expensive circumstances.

The night would be clear, which meant guests would have the benefit of panoramic views of the park, the city, and the lake. It also meant it was going to be cold. It wasn't quite the dead of winter, where seconds after going outside you'd feel the cracking of your mucous membranes as they froze. But it was cold enough that I put on my thickest coat, gloves, and turtleneck.

They would no doubt be commissioning outdoor heaters, but I'd been to enough events in Chicago in December to know that no matter what they did it would still be butt cold.

It turned out I needn't have worried. Of course whoever they'd hired to make sure it was warm was the best money could buy, and when I stepped out of the elevator onto the terrace I was hit with a blast of heat, and forced to immediately remove my coat, hat, and gloves. Now I wished I'd brought a T-shirt to work in.

Courtney, Michael, and Elliott were waiting for me. The

party started at eight, and we had three hours to get everything ready.

It wasn't to be a formal dinner. Celeste had indicated appetizer-type food to be served throughout the night, so it wouldn't be a heavy lift, meal-wise. But I needed Courtney to manage the alcohol, which would be substantial, and Michael and Elliott to help with the food. Celeste hadn't specified what "all night" meant, but we came prepared with enough supplies to last two days if necessary.

I would have liked to have Maude join us. She loved things like this, and even though she wasn't a cook, she had a knack for inserting herself in the most helpful ways possible. But she was busy with the task force. And even though Smith had told her about the Nottingham operation, he didn't want her involved. He believed that if the Nottinghams even got a whiff of law enforcement I'd not only be fired but they'd step up their overall wariness, which would affect the rest of the surveillance package he'd put together.

We installed caviar stations around the room, and Michael got to work setting up a small grill where he'd serve fresh oysters and Wagyu bites cooked to order.

I hadn't seen Martin much at the events I'd done for the family, and his food preferences weren't part of Celeste's event folder, possibly because his and Tasia's enmity appeared to extend to Alan and Celeste. So I'd done my own research. I scoured archived articles and photos for clues to what he liked.

He'd been born in Chicago, but his mom was English. I guessed that he might associate foods from his time with her with feeling happy, so I put Elliott in a station in the corner of the room where he could prepare make-to-order both Italian beef sandwiches and fish and chips. High end ones, of course. The fish was fresh halibut and turbot, the sandwiches would be made with Wagyu.

The room decorator arrived soon after we did. In a remarkably short amount of time she transformed the empty space under the tent into a Yale-themed party cove, twenty-five blue and white decorated tables, each with an empty bowl set in the center of it. Other rectangular tables were set up around the room, everything accented with blue and white streamers and lights.

At seven the band showed up. The Handsome Dans, by the sounds of their warmup some kind of post-grunge group. They set up a small stage and speakers in a corner.

Courtney had brought along four bartenders, and they put together three separate bars and placed numerous kegs around the space. No one would have to go more than ten feet to get something to drink. It seemed dangerous, making it that easy for Martin to get and stay loaded, but maybe that was the least of his addiction worries. In any case, I made sure the food was in easy reach as well in the hopes that if people got something in their stomachs early it might mitigate the effect of the alcohol.

By eight o'clock we were ready. I unlocked the doors.

At nine o'clock the only people there were me, Courtney and her bartenders, Elliott, Michael, a few of the Rooftop's staff, and the band.

At ten o'clock it was still just us. Would Martin blow off his own party? That would be a really good "fuck you" to his dad.

At ten forty-five I heard the ring of the elevator. A group of thirty-somethings in suits poured out, followed in short order by several more elevators full of well-dressed Yalies who had clearly done their pre-funk somewhere else.

They fanned out under the tent, immediately availing themselves of the open bar, kegs, and caviar.

At midnight there was a cheer. The guest of honor had arrived.

Martin walked out of the elevator, closely surrounded by five of his friends, Zach, and Tasia.

He and his buddies were wearing backpacks. Upon entering the space they moved chairs to the side of the room, then two of them pushed several of the long tables together in a line near one side of the tent.

The cheering grew louder as they emptied their backpacks onto the tables.

Mounds of pills were dumped into the glass bowl

centerpieces, accompanied by multi-colored vaping devices and wooden boxes containing perfectly wrapped joints. Martin was at the rectangular line of tables, meticulously laying out the longest and thickest line of coke I'd ever seen in my life. At both ends of the line he stacked hundred-dollar bills.

Guests surged to the line of coke to roll the bills and start snorting. Others made beelines for the tables with the drug buffet.

Yikes. This could get ugly quickly.

My original plan was to bring out the big surprise later, after the party got going. But in a couple of hours everyone might be too wrecked to notice. I gave Michael the high sign and we went into the back.

I'd asked Jake to make me another ice sculpture. This one was larger than the one he'd done of Jewelers Row, but less elaborate. It was still recognizable, though, to anyone who knew what they were looking at. We rolled it under the tent and put it in the middle on one side.

In the center of the sculpture was the John Harvard statue, sitting in Harvard Yard in front of University Hall. All iconic landmarks of Harvard University, Yale's bitter rival.

There was a moment of silence when we unveiled it, and then loud booing. Some of the guests threw their glasses at it.

Martin cocked his head, then waved his hand to settle everyone down.

He walked over to the sculpture, grinning. When he was next to it he unzipped his pants, and then urinated on it, aiming for the obvious urinal trough that Jake had carved around the Harvard landmarks.

Cheering broke out, and soon the sculpture was ringed with Martin's guests, all peeing into the trough, some aiming higher to bring down the John Harvard statue, which was already starting to deform.

Zach was smiling. I guessed his hard work would come later, after the many pounds of drugs were consumed. I grabbed a plate of perfectly seared Wagyu bites and walked over to him.

I was glad he was here. He seemed the most approachable of the security team, and presented the best opportunity to-date to gather information for Smith. He was also way less scary than Mason.

"Thanks." He took the plate and wolfed down the beef. "And nicely done," he said, nodding to the sculpture.

"So far so good."

He polished off the rest of the meat.

"Martin's dad doesn't come to these?"

I took his empty plate, and handed him a glass of sparkling water. "Neither of them would tolerate that." I assumed he meant Martin and Tasia.

"Alan?" It seemed a little sad that the only member of his family to come was Tasia.

He shook his head.

"Why not?"

He shook his head, again. He finished the water and handed the glass back to me, then turned his gaze back to the center of the room.

NDA. Got it. He was under the same restrictions I was when it came to divulging any information about the family. At least I'd given it a try.

I took Zach's empty plate back to the kitchen and grabbed what I needed to top off the caviar stations. When I returned to the tent I was gratified to see small lines starting to form in front of Michael's and Elliott's food stations.

Tasia was eating oysters, standing next to Michael's station as he served. She was talking to him in between bites. They were both smiling.

Maybe Michael would get lucky tonight. I couldn't blame her; he was a nice-looking guy, albeit a far cry from the crowd she regularly moved in. But maybe that was part of the attraction.

I'd never seen her smile. It rendered her already striking face stunning.

At two a.m. the party was still going strong, no doubt fueled by the cocaine. The bartenders had been busy all night and there was no sign that they were slowing down.

Martin had left the tent for a few moments. When he returned he had two bowls in his hand. He set them on the long table, on either end of the line of coke, entire sections of which had already disappeared.

"Those are the mushrooms," said Zach. He'd walked over to me while Martin was placing the bowls. "You have about thirty minutes to put away anything breakable that you care about."

As if on cue most of the guests started making their way toward the elevators. Apparently this part of the evening was reserved for the hardcores, some of whom were already dipping their hands into the mushroom bowls.

Over the next thirty minutes most of the guests said their goodbyes to Martin and trickled out, until all that was left were him and his best buddies. Other than Tasia, only one woman remained.

"Is she his girlfriend?" I asked Zach.

He shook his head, a little sadly, I thought. "No. She would like to."

"He's not into girls?"

"He's not into anyone."

I wasn't sure what that meant, but let it go. It wasn't too much later she gathered her things and walked to the elevator.

The music went up a notch, and two of the friends walked to the far ends of the table with the line of coke. They each planted their face in it, then snorted down the line, with no hands, until they met in the middle. While this was going on two others pushed the round tables in the middle of the room to the side, creating a wide path that ran the length of the tent.

Martin grabbed an armful of champagne bottles from the bar, then opened each one and methodically poured them onto the floor, walking back and forth along the space vacated by the repositioned tables.

He took off his shoes and stripped off his clothes. When all he had left on were his shirt, tie, boxers, and socks, he backed up to the end of the tent, and after a running start threw himself on the floor on his stomach.

He slid about thirty feet on the champagne, aided by hearty cheering. The rest of his friends removed various articles of clothing and lined up, taking turns running and throwing themselves onto the world's most expensive slip-and-slide.

I used the time to cue Elliott and Michael to shut down the open flames and deep fat fryers, and we hustled to move the equipment out of harm's way. Then we went to work making sandwiches and simple snack plates, setting them on the table next to the rapidly disappearing line of coke.

An hour later they were still running and sliding, in between drinking and snorting. In a surprise to no one, two of them slid down the floor at the same time and ended up colliding.

They were both sitting on the floor, bleeding, laughing their asses off. Zach fast-walked over with a first-aid kit. While he was tending to the two men another of Martin's friends set one of the table cloths on fire.

After sticking a butterfly on one of the slider's foreheads Zach set his first-aid kit down, picked up one of the fire extinguishers, and calmly put it out.

Over the next hour Martin's friends, alone or in pairs, proceeded to break or defile themselves or some part of the venue, during which time Zach never stopped moving, tending to minor injuries, broken glass, and small fires.

By four o'clock things finally started to slow down. All of the fires were out, and they were done with the slip and slide. One of the guests was standing in the corner, urinating onto the tent. He seemed transfixed by the stream, aiming it high, and watching it drip down, then aiming low, possibly watching to see if it would drip up. Almost everyone else was sitting down, in chairs or on the floor. Just outside the tent someone was vomiting.

"Sagarine Pfister!"

Martin was dripping champagne, in his socks and boxers, his white dress shirt down to its last button, his tie loose around his neck.

"Hey Martin."

"You," he said, pointing me in the chest, "are a great chef. I want you to do all of my parties."

"I'd love to," I said, which was true, even though it would never happen.

He looked happy, the bruised, brooding look in his eyes replaced with small crinkles from his smile. I was sure it had something to do with whatever combination of drugs he'd ingested, but it was nice to see him look happy for a little while.

The only people left now were the band, me and my crew, Tasia, Zach, and a few of Martin's friends, now in a circle with their arms around each other, singing what might have been the Yale fight song.

Tasia walked over and stood next to me. "You and your crew can leave now," she said flatly.

"I don't have to. I'm used to late nights. And besides, I need to clean up the food."

"We have someone else to do that. Zach will help you out," she said, turning away.

You're welcome.

I circulated to the rest of the team and told them we were done for the night, and to pack up.

Courtney, Elliott, and I were standing by the exit, waiting for Michael, who was saying his goodbyes to Tasia. At least she liked one of us.

"Check it out everyone!" The vomiter had come back inside, and was frantically waving for us to go outside of the tent.

As we filed out I bumped Michael on the arm. "Got a new girlfriend?"

He looked down, blushing.

I put my arm around his shoulder and we joined the others outside. The vomiter was pointing up to the skyline, toward the northwest, to the Crain Communications Building, aka, the Smurfit-Stone, its slanted roof lit up, as always, with its iconic diamond border.

Inside the diamond, prominently written in bright red lights, was FUCK YOU.

THIRTEEN

Smith had set our meeting the next day for nine in the morning. It was way too early, again, for me. But when I got up Maude and Linda were already at it in our living room.

Maude was sitting in front of her computer, leaning forward, eyes boring into the monitor. She had that look she got when she worked long hours on something that was stumping her.

"There's been another one." Linda was taping up a new set of pictures on the wall. She'd become a regular fixture in our house.

"You're putting in a lot of hours."

"I don't want to give them any excuse to put me back in the basement."

She pointed to the images she'd just put up, organized like the others underneath a nine-digit number. The pictures included one of the Chicago skyline, then a close up of the Crain building's diamond, with the FUCK YOU in the center.

"Yeah, I saw that last night from the Terrace. Pretty spectacular, in an obnoxious kind of way."

That would get the mayor going. The Crain's slanted, diamond-shaped roof was one of the most renowned elements of the city's famous skyline.

"It's definitely a step above raw meat and river dye." She nodded to the slanted roof face. "That part of the roof is made out of reflective glass panels. The words were spelled out in lights, with a substrate made out of some kind of special composition that allowed them to stick to the glass."

"How in the world could anyone do that? Even get up there?"

She shook her head. "We don't know yet. I'm looking into the backgrounds of the window washers and maintenance people. It's possible it was done using a drone."

"You think it's the same guy who did the other ones?"

She nodded, and pulled a third photo out of the stack.

It was a zoomed-in image of the center of the Crain's diamond face, taken during the day. Underneath the FUCK YOU was 098 777 453.

Maude was typing furiously.

"What are you—"

"Shhhh."

"She's adding the new number into her code software," whispered Linda.

I went into the kitchen to grab a cup of coffee and came back and sat down on the couch. Linda and I waited in respectful silence while Maude did her thing.

"Dammit."

"What?"

"It's definitely a multilayered code, with composite ciphers. And it would be very cool if it wasn't so frustrating.

"Each time we get one of these numbers it gives us more information about the code and should bring us closer to breaking it. But each time I put in the new number it uncovers another layer. Whoever put this together is sophisticated. Someone very smart is going to a lot of trouble to fuck up our city."

"There can't be that many people who know anything about multilayered, composite whatever," I said.

"That isn't the difficult part. You and millions of other people use composite codes every day. I assume you do multi-level verification on your computer?"

"Not on purpose. What is it?"

"Password protection, where you have to enter a password and then a code from your phone, or something else, like a thumbprint."

"No, I don't do anything like that." The only computer I used was at Saga, and I'd never bothered with password protection. I couldn't imagine why anyone would want to break into it.

"Well, most people do. By itself it's relatively simple. But this guy's using everything in the book. It started with a reverse telephone cipher, then a series of binary transformations, then some other stuff. He even added a layer of pig Latin."

"You're kidding." Even I knew how to do that.

She shook her head. "He, or she, has a sense of humor." A small smile played on her lips. She was frustrated, but she loved this shit.

"I don't understand how you can even get close to solving this."

"It's more the software than me, and it's nothing sexy. The algorithm just goes through millions of possibilities, and every known cipher and code structure, to make meaning out of the characters. We're going to get to a point where we need a keyword to solve it. But it doesn't look like we're there yet."

She leaned back, rubbing her eyes. "How did it go last night?"

"Good, I think. Too bad it's not Martin they need to arrest. There were several felony's worth of drugs at the party. Oh, and Michael might have a girlfriend."

"No kidding?"

"I'm not sure, but I think Tasia likes him."

"Tasia Nottingham?"

"Yeah." I thought of Alan, and the other perfectly turned-out people in the family's social circle. "I'm not that surprised. He's a real person. And she seems like a no-bullshit kind of girl."

Exactly the kind I like.

"Well, I'm not surprised either." Maude smiled. "He's a good-looking guy."

Smith had filled Maude in, that I was working for the Nottinghams, and that it was part of one of his operations. But he clearly hadn't shared with her the level of danger that was involved. If so she wouldn't be so lighthearted about Michael dating one of them.

I finished my coffee and headed out to the cemetery. Smith was waiting at our usual spot.

"You realize I've had almost no sleep for twenty-four hours?"

"What did you learn?"

"These events go late, Smith. And I don't get to sleep immediately afterward. That means I get to bed around five or six. Your nine o'clock meetings are the middle of the night for me."

He didn't look like he'd had much sleep, either. His eyes were bloodshot, and his suit was wrinkled. Extreme signs of stress for a guy who never had a hair out of place.

He was trying to prevent a catastrophe. And whether I understood it or not, Maude really cared for him. I needed to try to give him a break.

"Martin loves drugs. Tasia's still a bitch. Michael might have a girlfriend."

"That's it?"

"I don't know what you think I'm going to find out. Martin's party was a drug-fest, the only family there were Tasia and his security guy, Zach. I doubt either one of them are in on whatever you think Nottingham is up to."

"What makes you think that? Is there something specific, something you observed?"

"No. But I just don't see it. Tasia and Martin really hate their dad. And for what it's worth, they're not fond of Alan or Celeste, either."

He sighed, exasperated. "We need hard evidence. What you feel about anything doesn't count." He rubbed his forehead, looking down. "But let's suppose you're right. Maybe we can exploit the rift in the family. If Martin and Tasia are truly estranged from their father, then it would make sense they're not involved in what he's doing."

He nodded, convincing himself. "Let's go with that premise. Work on getting closer to Tasia. She might share something with you, something about her father."

"Believe me, I'd love to get closer to her. But I don't think she rolls that way."

"What do you mean?"

"I think Michael might have a better chance."

He bent his head back and looked at the sky. "I didn't mean sleep with her. I mean, try to develop a relationship."

I snorted. "That's a nonstarter. I think she hates me, too. But she seems to like Michael. Should we bring him in on this?"

As soon as the words were out of my mouth I wished I could take them back. Maude and her family had just gotten

Michael back, after he'd been missing for years. If she found out Smith had put him in a dangerous operation she'd go ballistic.

Smith must have been thinking the same thing. "No, we can't risk putting another civilian in harm's way."

No problem putting me in harm's way, apparently.

"Do you have any other events coming up?" he asked.

"A little one, tomorrow, at the store."

"See what you can get."

I shook my head. "It's one of Celeste's private parties. I don't think anyone else in the family's going to be there. I doubt they even know about it."

"Do your best. Anything else?"

"Just that I'm on Mason's radar."

"What do you mean?"

"I told you. He caught me in an area of the house I'm not supposed to be. He went nuts." I could still feel the iron grip of his hand on my arm.

"When?"

"A few days ago."

He frowned. "You should have told me about that immediately."

"I did tell you." It was a bad sign that Smith was forgetting things. "And even if I didn't, and was just telling you now, would you pull me out of there?"

I waited for a few moments. "Yeah, I thought not. And that's not all. He made Celeste drag me in for an interrogation when they saw the article about the nerve poison in the paper. They recognized me on the front page."

"How did they do that?"

"I don't know."

He ran one of his hands through his hair again, which by now was sticking straight up. "And you didn't think that merited mention?"

"I'm telling you now."

He blew out a breath. "Do you think he suspects you're working with law enforcement?"

"I don't know that, either. He definitely suspects something.

He made it clear he's watching me. But I think if he knew I was working with you I'd be out of there already. More importantly, if you had any ideas about me being able to skip around the house looking for secret papers you can forget about it. I'm not going to do anything that will make him madder. If he catches me doing something else I'm not supposed to the least that would happen is I'd get fired."

"What do you mean?"

"He practically ripped my arm off the first time he caught me coming out of Nottingham's special diamond-cutting room, even though Nottingham didn't seem to mind. What do you think he'd do if he found me going through any of their private stuff?"

Smith's shoulders dropped as he let out a heavy sigh. I didn't think he'd even considered that this whole thing might be dangerous for me. "Don't worry. You won't be there for much longer."

"Whatever. I have to go and get ready for Celeste's thing. I'll see you around."

Celeste's event was a simple affair, a short brunch in the main showroom at the Carat and Crown for twenty of her lady friends. I got there at ten, an hour before the start time, to lay out the tables and set up my mise en place for the meal.

The food would be simple: they had their choice of truffle eggs benedict or lobster omelets, fresh orange or grapefruit juice, and croissants with black truffle butter—the main attraction the Veuve Clicquot champagne that would be served by the gallon. Celeste had made sure to emphasize that we not run out.

All of the women arrived close to eleven. True to the group's description in the folder, they looked like movers and shakers, all in power suits and with expensive, professional-looking haircuts. I recognized a few politicians and CEOs from the dinner we'd had recently at the estate. Celeste was cementing her political and power relationships, another step to becoming the wife of the successor to the family estate.

They were seated and I started service. Unlike every other

function I'd done for the family, there was no one from Mason's security team lurking around. It made the event a little brighter.

I hadn't realized until now how much of a dark pall he and his team cast over the family, and for the first time I felt a trace of compassion for the wealthy. I couldn't imagine being surrounded by security teams all of the time, their presence a constant reminder of potential danger.

The lunch moved along quickly, and by noon the guests were done with their food and wrapping up conversations. These were busy, serious women. And as far as I could tell none of them had more than one glass of champagne, even though we'd gone through a case of it. Celeste's handiwork, no doubt.

As some of the women were grabbing their coats, the door in the back of the store opened. Six gem workers quietly filed out and left through the front entrance. Not one of them looked up as they went by. They were followed by Celeste's guests, most of whom had said their goodbyes.

After the last woman grabbed her coat and gave the hostess a quick hug Celeste sidled up next to me.

"Can we speak for a moment?"

"Sure."

"Your brunch was fantastic, thank you," she said breathlessly.

"I'm glad you enjoyed it."

"I wanted to give you a head's up, the family is going to Canada on Thursday. We'll be gone for three days. It's the regular trip to Yellowknife. Richard does an event for the company workers up there twice a year, to thank them."

Thank God. Since my conversation with Smith I wasn't eager to go back to the estate and be in the proximity of any of that Novichok stuff.

"The flight leaves at nine a.m. You can meet us at O'Hare."

Damn. "Oh. OK."

I must not have hidden my feelings too well, because she added, "This won't be a problem, will it? You have a passport, yes?"

"Yes. No, it won't be a problem." *Fuck.*

"Wonderful. You'll enjoy yourself, we always have the best time." Somehow she made that sound dirty.

"Is there a, uh, folder for the event?"

"Yes, I'll give it to you later. But I'll provide the important details now," she said, squeezing my upper arm conspiratorially. "There will be about four hundred guests, we're having it at the White Wolf Lodge, where the family is also staying. The dinner happens on Friday, so you'll need to gather most of what you'll need for the event ahead of time. One of our drivers will pick up whatever you purchase and take care of shipping it. The theme should be fun. And nothing too experimental when it comes to food. And definitely no buffets—we want them to feel like they're being wined and dined, not herded like cattle."

"Got it. Which flight is it?"

She laughed. "We're taking the family jet. It's—"

We were interrupted by a loud thump, a crash, and screeching tires. A woman screamed.

We both moved to the front window.

A car was streaking away from the front of the store and down Wabash. It took the turn on Madison at speed and disappeared.

The bus-stop shelter was destroyed, most of it lying in pieces on the sidewalk. A woman from the brunch was standing next to the debris.

She was looking at the ground, next to where the shelter had been.

A man was laying on his back, water from the undercarriage of the L track dripping into his open eyes.

FOURTEEN

I wasn't sure if anyone else had contacted the police yet so I called 911. Five minutes later I heard sirens. A police car pulled up in front of the building and two officers stepped out. They spoke briefly to the small crowd on the sidewalk, occasionally turning to look at the storefront.

A few minutes later one of them came into the store, the bell at the top of the door jingling with his arrival.

"Do either of you know the man who was hit?"

I noticed he'd said "hit" and not killed, although the guy was obviously dead.

"He works here. He was just leaving for the day," Celeste offered. "I don't know his name."

"He worked here today?"

"Yes, the gem workers are here a half-day on Mondays."

"I have to ask you to wait for the detective, he'll have some questions."

"Will this take long?" I noticed her coffee cup was empty.

"I don't know, ma'am. But you need to wait for the detective."

She looked behind her, eyes wide. "I need to go to my office. Our employee files are back there."

He nodded. "Please stay here, miss," he said to me, then followed Celeste to the back.

I plopped into a chair and was pulling out my phone when I heard the door jingle.

Detective John Carter.

Great. Just what I needed.

He closed the door and scanned the room. When his eyes landed on me he rolled them, then wasted no time coming directly for me.

"Why is it whenever there's a dead body around, Pfister, I find you next to it?"

"'Hi' to you too, Carter." Maude had told me that he'd gotten a promotion, and was now in the PD's Citywide Homicide section. The fact that I'd been working with the FBI for two years carried no weight with him; he had little to do with their operations, and I doubted he'd been read in on what Smith was doing. "The guy was hit by a car. I was inside when it happened."

He pointed a stubby finger at me. "Don't even think about leaving until we've had a chance to catch up."

Celeste and the officer returned to the showroom. She looked calmer and had a fresh cup of coffee in her hand, no doubt augmented with whatever alcohol she had in the back office.

Carter left me and went to stand in front of her. As they talked I saw her shake her head. After a few minutes she turned away and pulled out her phone.

Shortly thereafter Carter got a call. It was brief, and he didn't do much speaking. His shoulders sagged, and he left the store without a word.

"We can go," said Celeste. "He's going to meet us at the estate."

Huh. Another perk of the very wealthy. You got to choose where you were interviewed by the police.

"You can ride with me," she added.

I wasn't thrilled about being trapped in the back of a car with her, but fortunately she wasn't in the mood to put her hands on me. We made the trip in silence.

Alan was standing in front of the open door to the house when the limo pulled up. I followed the two of them as he escorted her in, his arm protectively around her shoulder. Once inside she made a beeline for her study.

Alan sat down on the couch, looking anxiously over his shoulder toward the hallway and Celeste's office.

Up to now I'd had little opportunity to talk to him, so I took the chair closest to the couch.

"Did you know the man who was hit?" I asked.

"What?" He glanced at me briefly before returning his gaze to the hallway.

"The man who died. Your employee."

"Oh. No."

After a moment he turned to me. "Did you see it happen?"

"No, Celeste and I were inside."

"That's good."

His eyes were empty. Not scary or psychotic empty, but in more of a "there's no one home" kind of way.

Hard to imagine this guy taking over the family business. Or, anything, for that matter.

"It was—"

"Excuse me." He got up and disappeared down the hallway.

A few moments later he and Celeste came back and took seats on the couch, his arm again around her shoulders, his brow furrowed in a look of concern that could have been painted on. The perfect image of someone who was caring for his wife.

While we'd been talking, Mason had joined us in the living room. He took his place standing a few feet behind the couch. I could feel his eyes boring into the back of my head.

The elder Nottingham was nowhere in sight. I wasn't all that surprised; he hadn't been at the store when it happened, and I guessed that in order to talk to him Carter would have to go very high on the police food chain to get permission.

We sat in silence for almost two hours, interrupted only by Celeste's trips to the office to refill her drink, when a police car pulled up in front and Carter stepped out of it. Ellis let him into the house and pointed him to the living room.

Before he could say anything, Mason stepped forward. "Will this take long? It was quite a shock for Mrs. Nottingham, and she'd like to retire for the day."

"Retire" was apparently the family euphemism for "drink her head off."

I'd seen Carter in action before, and his standard response to this question was always, "It will take as long as it takes." He worked on his own schedule, to which everyone else must bow.

It was already a huge concession for him to come all the way out here to interview me and Celeste. Witnesses usually had to go down to the station. So I was surprised when he said, "I'll try to make this quick. Thank you for making the time." He looked like he was choking on the words.

"I'd like to start with you, Mrs. Nottingham. Is there somewhere we can talk privately, maybe a study or something?"

She nodded and stood up. They walked down the hallway and I heard the door to her office open and close.

A scant five minutes later she came back into the living room. Carter couldn't have missed the strong smell of booze on her, and may have decided he wouldn't get much out of an inebriated witness.

"He wants to see you now, Sagarine," she said, sitting back down on the couch and leaning against Alan.

Carter was seated behind the desk. When I walked in he nodded to the chair across from him.

"You never answered my question. Why is it, whenever there's a dead body, you're somewhere close to it?"

"C'mon, Carter. You can't possibly think I had anything to do with this."

"If you do, you better believe I'll nail your ass. Better late than never."

"Are you ever going to let that go? That was two years ago."

He'd always suspected me of Louie Ferrar's murder, and never let me forget it. Louie had been my boss. He'd been killed in his own restaurant, now my restaurant, and the person they'd originally collared for it was found to have an alibi. Carter had no other suspects, other than me, and it remained an open case.

"There's no statute of limitations on murder. And something else I know? Murderers don't stop. You're going to slip up, and when you do I'll be all over you."

"Whatever. Can we just get on with this?"

"Did you know the deceased?"

"No."

Carter was old-school and still used a notebook and a pen to take notes. As we talked he scribbled, somehow managing to do it without taking his eyes off of me.

"You've never seen him before?"

"I didn't say that. I said I didn't know him. I saw him when

I went there for my interview. He was working in the back of the store. And I saw him walk out of the store today. That's it."

"When was this?"

"About a week ago or so."

"No, what time did he leave the store?"

"A little after noon. He left with the other gem workers, around the same time the event ended."

"What were you doing there?"

"Putting on a brunch for Celeste."

I could feel Smith's phone buzzing in my pocket. I pulled it out and swiped left.

"What do you know about the Nottinghams?"

I wasn't sure if the Chicago PD was in on Smith's operation, and even if they were, I didn't know how much I could tell him. Smith had barely told Maude any of it.

"Not a lot. I'm their event chef."

"Event chef? What the fuck is that?"

"I cook for their events," I said, rolling my eyes.

My phone buzzed again. I let it go.

"You don't want to answer that?"

"There's nothing I'd rather do than talk to you," I said, smiling sweetly.

"How long have you been working for the Nottinghams?"

"About a week."

"Have you ever seen Isaac Katz at their estate?"

"No. Is that the man who was hit?"

"Are you confused, Pfister? I'm the one asking the questions." He paused for dramatic effect. "Have you witnessed any discussions, or arguments, between Katz and anyone in the family?"

"No. Like I said, I've only seen him at the store. Twice, briefly. We've never said so much as 'Hi' to each other."

"Have you seen anything suspicious, about the family, since you've been working for them?"

"Suspicious?"

What the hell did he mean? Maybe he did know about Smith's operation. Smith had said he was going to bring the

Chicago PD in on things, but I didn't know if that included Carter. "Uh, like what?"

His eyes closed to slits. "You know something, don't you?" Carter had that cop sense, that ability to know when someone was lying or holding something back.

"I know you're wasting your time, and mine. I was inside doing the brunch all morning. I don't know the guy and I had nothing to do with him getting run over. For that matter, I doubt the family does, either. Why are you even investigating this? Wasn't it just a hit and run?"

He stared at me for a long moment before closing his notebook. "We're done. For now. And just so you know, I know you're hiding something. And I'm going to find out what."

Whatever. I left the room, and, after a brief goodbye to the family, left the house.

It was still early, but I was exhausted by the time I got home. Sparring with Carter always took it out of me. He was unfortunately very smart. And he was right about me. I did have secrets.

Maude and Linda were still in the living room. It looked like they'd been there all day.

"Hey," I said, throwing my coat on the couch.

"Hey," Maude smiled.

"What's happened?" She'd been morose when I left.

"Linda ID'd the guy who did the Crain Building. Or at least, one of them. They picked him up an hour ago."

"Oh?" I really didn't give a shit about a few pranks around the city. "Who is it?"

"Dennis Penny. He used to work for the Nottinghams."

FIFTEEN

I slept until after noon the next day. When I woke up and went upstairs, the stacks of folders, all the computers, and the pictures that had been taped to the walls were gone. Maude was nowhere in sight.

Just as I was pouring myself some coffee, I felt the buzz of Smith's phone in my pocket. I'd turned off the annoying ringtone, but even the thing's buzz was highly irritating. I sighed and pulled it out. "What? I'm busy. I'm getting ready for a trip."

"Rosehill, ten minutes." He hung up.

I left the house. When I got to our spot at the cemetery he was pacing.

"Can you make this quick?" I said, sitting down. "And why can't we ever talk on the phone?"

"Because you're not answering when I call. We think the attack is imminent, even if those idiots at Homeland won't give it the designation."

"How imminent?"

"Days. Maude's at the station. The man they found with the drone, Dennis Penny, the one they think is responsible for the Crain building defacement? He used to work for the Nottinghams."

"I know. She told me last night."

"The Nottingham terrorist threat and her vandalism case have been officially linked. It's now one joint effort, and everything is being run out of PD headquarters. That's what I wanted to talk to you about. I need you to keep your eyes open for anything at the estate that might tie into the stunts happening around the city. And see if you can find anything out about the relationship between Isaac Katz, the jeweler who was killed, Dennis Penny, and the family."

Why did he care about Katz? "I already got grilled about

that by Carter. I don't know Isaac Katz, I've never seen him interact with the family, and they've never spoken about him. They don't talk about their employees. I don't think they even know most of their names. And they've never mentioned Penny, and I've never seen him. Can I go?"

"Goddammit, Sagarine, do you think I want to be here talking to you?"

I leaned back. Getting sworn at by Smith was like a slap in the face from anyone else.

"I know it's a long shot, I know that there's only so much you can do, and I know you're not an agent. But every single piece of information we do have is telling us that whatever Nottingham's doing it's going to happen soon. My job is to make sure we're getting the most out of every thread we have going. I don't know how, or why, or even *if* the vandalism has anything to do with the attack, but until I'm sure that it doesn't, we have to follow it up."

"OK, OK."

"Do your best," he said, slightly calmer. "Keep your ears open."

"I will." It was unsettling, seeing him like this. "Do you know, did the guy they picked up, Penny, was he responsible for the meat, and the dye, and all the rest of that stuff?"

"We don't know. He's not saying anything, and he's already got a lawyer. A very high-priced one, which tells us that he's still connected to the Nottinghams. There's no way this guy would be able to afford that on his own."

This made no sense. "If Nottingham's in the middle of putting together a secret attack on the city, why would he have anything to do with high-profile vandalism stunts? It would just draw attention to him."

"I know. We're not a hundred percent sure that he does. Penny hasn't officially worked for them in years. Maybe it's a distraction. Like you said, these pranks are extremely high profile, so much so that the mayor diverted PD resources to them. In any case I need you to find out whatever you can about him and his relationship with the family."

"Fine. But you need to get Carter off my back. He thinks I

had something to do with the hit and run in front of Carat and Crown."

"Why would he think that?"

I stared at him. "Because he has it in for me. And you know why. Are we done?"

"No," he said, looking down. "The man who was killed in the hit and run, in front of the store, Isaac Katz . . . he worked for us."

"What do you mean, 'worked for you'? Was he an agent?"

"No. But he'd been giving us information about Nottingham."

"You mean he was one of your informants?"

"Not officially. But we'd asked him to report on anything he saw that could be of use."

Whoa. "You mean, like what I'm doing."

He paused, then nodded.

"*Exactly* like what I'm doing."

I stared at him, then stood up. "That's it. I'm done."

He put his hands up. "Hang on. We don't think Nottingham had anything to do with Katz's death. It was probably an accident. Just a coincidence, that he happened to be working for us."

"A coincidence? Really?"

Like every other law enforcement person in the world, Smith didn't believe in coincidences.

"But we're checking into it anyway. There are cameras in the front of the store, we're getting the footage."

"Why don't you already have it? It happened yesterday."

"This isn't television. It takes time to collect footage and go through it. And in this case the family lawyers are involved and they're forcing us to get a warrant. I'll let you know if we find anything. But don't worry, I do think it's just a coincidence."

I was still up when Maude stomped into the house at midnight, slamming the door behind her.

"What's up?"

She waited to answer me until she dropped her computer bag on the couch and went into the kitchen for a beer.

"They've linked the cases. Your Nottingham terrorist case and our vandalism."

"Yeah, Smith told me. That's good, right?"

Maude usually liked working with the FBI. It meant meatier cases, and a lot more resources than were normally available to the PD.

"No." Her mouth was set in a thin line. "I'm no longer the lead on the code numbers. They've got their own codebreakers. I've been killing myself on it, and I think I'm close. And now they're bringing in their guy and their fancy software to take it over. After I've already laid all the foundation."

That explained it. She liked figuring things out on her own, and now one of the FBI's pretty boys would swoop in for the credit.

"Well, at least it means you'll see more of Smith."

She snorted. "He's in the field, gathering intel from his informants. He shows up in the morning to share what he's learned, and then we don't see him the rest of the day. And we haven't spent a night together in weeks."

That alone would account for a fair amount of her frustration.

"Speaking of informants, you're being careful, right?" she asked.

"Sure. I'm just cooking, and keeping my eyes and ears open. No planting bugs, nothing like that."

I hadn't told her about my interactions with Mason. She had enough to worry about.

"Good."

She sat down heavily. "It gets worse. They've now put Linda in charge of investigating Frank Chimen's death. They're not sure it has anything to do with the vandalism, but now that the cases are linked they want to check every avenue. She's the last rung on the organizational ladder, so they gave her what they consider to be the least important element."

I felt my body go cold. "Please tell me you're kidding."

Maude stared at me. "Nope. And you know how she is."

I did. Linda was smart, and dogged. This was not good news for me. But there was nothing to do about it at this point.

I just needed to hope they solved both cases before she figured out what happened to Chimen, and then maybe the case would be dropped.

I didn't want to think about that, and changed the subject. "What do they have you working on?"

"I'm supposed to be bringing the FBI guy up to speed on the code. But I'm still going to work on it myself. I feel like I'm close." She opened up her computer and set it on the table. "It's unbelievably complicated. More layers than I've ever seen. The last one was something that looks like a grid letter substitution."

"Is anyone but you supposed to know what that is?"

"It uses a cipher disk. Ever play *Fallout*? The video game?"

"You know I don't play video games."

"In *Fallout 4* they include a type of cipher disk as one of the game puzzles. A simple one. This one's like that, but on steroids. It's a 512-bit, 128-character string."

She leaned in to the monitor and banged away on the keyboard, my cue to leave.

She wouldn't rest until she figured it out. I hoped it would be soon. I wasn't sure how much more gridbits and bytestrings talk I could take.

And I had an early day tomorrow. There was a lot of work to do to get ready for the Canada trip. Putting together a dinner for four hundred people in a different city was an interesting challenge, one I was looking forward to for a number of reasons.

Going to Yellowknife felt like a reprieve. For a few days there would be no early morning meetings with Smith. And it would be nice to not have to be inside Nottingham's house for a while.

SIXTEEN

I spent the next day making calls and putting together a menu that didn't involve day-of stops at Hagen's or my butcher. Fortunately it turned out that Yellowknife had solid fish and meat vendors, and as soon as they realized I was working for the Nottinghams they were more than accommodating. Not only did Nottingham's diamond mine operations account for a sizable portion of the income to the region, they knew anyone working with him had an unlimited budget.

I picked up a few vegetables and other things I thought I'd have trouble getting up there, gathered some of my specialized equipment that might not be available at the White Wolf Lodge, and called it good.

On the departure day I wanted to be at the airport early, so planned to head out at nine a.m. for the noon flight. I left Maude sitting at the kitchen table, in front of her computer.

She'd already been working long hours on the vandalism task force, and now that it was merged with an FBI terrorism operation, things had ramped up. Not to mention the constant and increasing pressure they were getting from the mayor to, as she quoted him, "Shut this shit down."

"You're still working on the code?" I asked as I was putting on my coat. "I thought you were training the fancy FBI codebreaker?"

She snorted. "He figured out I'd already gotten as far as he could, so we're working together. He's allowed me to work with him on it." She rolled her eyes.

"Still, we've been working on this nonstop and have fuck all to show for it. At least now I have access to their software. I'm using it to try my own algorithms."

She looked up. "You're off?"

"Yeah."

"Why the long face? You've got an all-expenses paid trip to

Canada, home of the free, and land of the polite. I hear it's beautiful in Yellowknife. Not to mention you get to be there for the big reveal."

"The 'big reveal'?"

"The Nottinghams go to Yellowknife twice a year to visit his mine and fête their employees. They use the trips to show off his latest over-the-top creations via Celeste Nottingham's generous neckline. She'll be sporting a brand new, ridiculously expensive diamond necklace. Nottingham's company produces two of them each year, and they reveal them on this trip. Some kind of weird, rich-people PR thing."

"Oh." I didn't care about their jewelry, although maybe if Celeste was focused on millions of dollars of diamonds around her neck she'd be less focused on me.

That was really the only downside to this trip. For the most part I'd figured out how to work my way around the estate and the events without being alone with her. In a new environment I'd be vulnerable to her stalking me.

I left Maude poring over her algorithms and took a Lyft to the airport. I had no idea where the private jets took off, but was directed to a shuttle that served the private jet terminal.

I took the shuttle and checked in at the front desk in the terminal's small building. "Are the Nottinghams here yet?"

The woman behind the counter smiled. "The flight doesn't leave until noon. They'll be here a few minutes before that."

Oh. I guess the "arrive two hours before your flight" doesn't apply if you're richer than shit. "Is it OK if I wait here?" I looked around for a chair.

"Of course. Would you be more comfortable in the VIP lounge?"

"No, thanks."

I sat down to wait. As the time dragged on I noticed one of the planes on the tarmac getting some attention. First they filled it up with fuel. When that was done they began loading it with supplies.

At eleven thirty they moved a set of movable stairs to the plane's door, and one of the men from the terminal building walked out and placed stanchions on the tarmac, between which he pulled red ribbons, effectively creating a cordon around the stairs.

Ten minutes later a shuttle bus arrived. About fifteen people, many carrying cameras, poured out and took places around the outside of the ribbon.

I didn't think the airport allowed journalists on the tarmac, but I was learning that everything was different when it came to the fabulously wealthy. I wondered again why Richard Nottingham would put any of this at risk by helping the Russians attack the country in which he'd made his fortune.

At a few minutes before noon a black limousine pulled up in front of the building. Richard Nottingham, Celeste, Alan, Tasia, and Martin stepped out. Close behind them was a black SUV carrying security staff that would presumably be joining us on the trip, and Percy. The drivers of both vehicles got out and carried a small mountain of bags to the jet, among which I recognized the four boxes of my foodstuffs and specialized equipment.

The family made their way past the cordon and up the stairs. Richard first, looking straight ahead. Close behind him were Tasia and Martin. Martin looked like he'd just gotten out of bed, or maybe had never made it there. Percy, Mason, Zach, and one of the other security staff boarded next.

Celeste and Alan were last, walking arm in arm. Alan was in his customary suit, and she was wrapped in a fur coat that must have involved the demise of many small creatures. He escorted her to the top of the stairs, and as if choreographed they both turned around and beamed perfect smiles at the crowd. After a long moment Celeste unbuttoned the top of her coat and let it fall slightly off her shoulders, a la Marilyn Monroe, revealing a low-cut dress and the largest diamond necklace I'd ever seen.

I stood there staring at the two of them with the rest of the crowd. Flashbulbs went off in earnest. This was what everyone had come for. The big reveal.

Even from where I was standing I could make out the five very large, heart-shaped diamonds that made up the center of the necklace, bordered on each side by a chain of smaller ones.

The diamonds looked similar to what I'd seen when I'd interrupted Nottingham in his room.

It made sense, given his love for the work, that he'd craft these special necklaces himself. If so, he must have had some false starts; the number of large diamonds on the necklace was half the amount that I'd seen on the table in the basement cutting room. Maybe he did them in batches, or was already starting on the next one that would get displayed in a new creation six months from now.

After a few moments Celeste pulled her coat up, threw one last beaming smile at the crowd, and the two of them disappeared inside the jet.

"Uh, Miss Pfister? Are you ready to board?" asked the woman at the desk.

"Oh, yeah, thanks."

I grabbed my roller bag and went out to the tarmac. It was strange, walking in front of a gaggle of journalists like I was on display. Even though the main show was over there were a few scattered flashes from the photographers, all likely wondering who the hell I was but taking pictures just in case I was someone.

The flight to Yellowknife was around five hours long, and after a few minutes marveling at the spacious and very soft leather seats, I spent most of it sleeping, I'd be working hard once we landed, and wanted to get my rest in now.

We landed at four o'clock, and even though Chicago was one hour ahead of Yellowknife, the sun was already starting to go down.

We were picked up by several cars at the airport. We were all staying at the White Wolf Lodge, the family's rooms on one side of the building, and Percy and I in presumably lesser accommodations on the other side.

My room was still very nice. I dropped off my suitcase and turned around and left. I wanted to see the event space immediately to talk to the staff about layout and service.

I made my way to the lobby, then down a short hallway and through the large double doors that opened to the event space.

Sixty round tables were already laid out in a grid on clean, dark wooden floors, surrounded by wooden walls and peaked, high-beamed ceilings. There was no stage, just some audio equipment set up in one corner, and several counters where staff were setting up bars. A narrow hallway led to the restrooms, and a single door to the kitchen.

They were already starting to load my things into the kitchen, and I did a quick run-through of the equipment and stock before I headed out to do some shopping.

I'd not been included in whatever the family was doing for the evening. I was fine with that, and actually a little relieved; it meant one night where I didn't have to fend off Celeste, although so far she'd never tried anything with Alan or his dad around.

The lodge was set close to the main part of town and I decided to walk. Everything was ice and snow, beautifully lit up with a hazy glow around the streetlights and open storefronts. It was well below freezing but I was prepared, bundled up as I would be in Chicago when the temperature dropped. It was colder than Chicago this time of year, but I was warm enough for the few minutes it took to get to my destination, the YK Centre Mall.

Less of a "mall" as I was used to, the YK Centre was a corner building that housed at most twenty stores. Still, I was able to pick up a few food items I needed for the dinner and spend some time in a couple of touristy shops. I bought Yellowknife T-shirts and hooded sweatshirts for Maude, Linda, and the Saga staff, and a glass mug with a caribou on it for Gigi from Old Town Glassworks. Smith got the aurora borealis snow globe keychain.

By the time I was done I was loaded down with bags. I went back to the lodge and dropped a few food items in the kitchen then went upstairs. I didn't miss the fact that one of the security team was stationed at the landing between the two sets of stairs, and there was another one I didn't recognize standing in the hallway on my floor. Locals, maybe.

Just as I was putting the key in the door Smith's phone rang.

Dammit. I set everything on the floor and pulled out the phone.

"Bad timing, again. I'm slammed."

"You were supposed to check in."

"I don't have anything yet. We just got here." No snow globe for you, buddy. "The dinner is tomorrow. I'll see what I can do." I dropped my voice to a whisper. "Listen, stop calling me. I'm working, and there's security everywhere."

I hung up, and was sticking the key card in the slot when I realized the door was already ajar. I pushed it open.

Mason and one of his team were in my room. All of the drawers in the dresser and side tables were open, the contents dumped on the floor. My roller bag was upside down on the bed, my clothes scattered around it.

"What the hell are you doing?"

Mason had been lifting up a corner of the mattress. He dropped it, and took two quick strides toward me. He stopped, way too close, and held up his hand. In it was a stainless-steel cylinder, with clamps and control buttons set below a small digital display.

He waved it in my face. "What is this?"

I snatched it out of his hand. "It's a sous vide immersion circulator."

Looking at his blank expression, I added, "It's a kitchen tool. For temping and controlling food cooked in a water bath."

He stared at it, then grabbed it back, and turned it around in his hand. "Then why isn't it in the kitchen? Why did you carry it with you, and not put it with the rest of the baggage?"

"It's fragile, and expensive. I never pack it. Be careful with it."

He threw the controller on the bed. "Who were you just talking to?"

"My roommate."

"Let me see your phone."

I pulled my own phone out of my pocket and handed it to him. He hit redial.

I watched his face as he listened. After a moment he handed it back to me.

"Sags? Sags? What's up?"

"Nothing, sorry. Butt dial. Call you later." I hung up.

Mason stared at me, then barked to his buddy.

They stomped out of the room, opening the door so hard on the way out it bounced against the wall.

I dropped onto the unmade bed.

Jesus. What was that? Did they do this to all new employees on this trip? Or was Mason focused on me because he knew I was funneling information to the FBI?

Or was this a sign that Smith was right, that Nottingham was getting close to whatever he was going to do and was stepping up security?

Now that I thought about it, if Nottingham was going to execute an attack in Chicago, what better time to do it than when he and his family were safe in Canada?

I was glad I'd listened to Smith for once. If I'd left his phone in my room instead of carrying it with me they'd have found it, and then it would have been game over.

When I was able I stood up and walked to the door. I closed it, my hand shaking on the handle, and pulled down the security bar. Then I called Smith.

SEVENTEEN

The next morning I was up before the alarm went off. I'd gotten little sleep. When I did I had nightmares of Mason finding Smith's phone and dragging me down to Nottingham's basement.

My discussion with Smith the night before had done nothing to calm my nerves.

"It's likely standard operating for them," he'd said, after I told him about Mason tossing my room. "It's his job to be paranoid. And you don't know that he doesn't do that to all of the staff on a regular basis."

I was standing in the bathroom with the water on. "You don't think he suspects I'm working with you?" I whispered. I wasn't one hundred percent sure Mason hadn't bugged my room.

To his credit, Smith didn't lie to me. "I doubt it, but we can't be sure. To be on the safe side, try to avoid going out alone. And lock your door when you're in the room."

After we hung up I headed down to the kitchen. I was grateful the event was today, and that Percy wasn't there to help with the dinner, apparently brought along only to make Nottingham's special meals. Nothing focused me more than cooking.

Most of my part of the food prep was done, and I was in the kitchen waiting to brief the hotel staff on the evening's schedule when Celeste walked through the swinging doors.

She stood close to me, whispering. "After the dinner, later on, maybe we can get together for a nightcap? You're in room four, aren't you?"

I wondered how she thought we'd be able to do anything with the security team all over the place. Or maybe this was something she did often, and they were all in on her affairs. And maybe Alan didn't care.

Thinking about his plastic face, it was hard to imagine him having any emotion about anything.

It occurred to me that if I did hook up with Celeste, it might help me with Mason. He could hardly rough up one of her lovers.

No, I thought, looking at her. I couldn't do it. She was beautiful, but not even close to my type. If nothing else, I didn't think I could spend any up-close-and-personal time smelling her unique bouquet of perfume and alcohol.

"Thank you. I'd love to, but I don't know how long I'm going to be working. And after doing something like this I'm usually pretty beat." This was a complete lie. I was always jacked up after cooking and it took a while for the adrenaline to dissipate.

I was saved from further discussion by several of the lodge's staff filing into the kitchen.

"I'm sorry, I need to get going. I hope you enjoy the meal." I forced a smile.

She gave my arm a squeeze and walked away. I noticed her looking over the hotel staff on her way out. Maybe one of them would get lucky tonight.

The staff assembled around me and I went over the menu, the service, and the bar protocols for the evening.

They would be tending the four open bars stationed around the main room. Full bars, with all of the appropriate high-end spirits and beers, plus making three specially themed cocktails that I'd designed for the occasion: Perfect Clarity, a spruce tip-infused gin martini; Aqpik Vein, with aqpik—cloudberry—liqueur and prosecco; and an Ekati Manhattan, named after the mine, made with Canadian Club Chronicles 40–45-year-old whisky and sweetened with birch syrup.

At this point in my career I rarely came across an ingredient that I'd never heard of. So when I'd done my research for this meal I'd been delighted to discover birch syrup.

It was what it sounded like: syrup made from the sap of birch trees. It was collected and made similar to the process used for maple sap, but that's where the resemblance ended. I'd asked a small family operation, Crooked Creek Birch, to overnight me a tasting sample, and after trying it decided on the spot to focus the meal around it.

Thinner, and not quite as sweet as maple syrup, the subtle flavor of the birch syrup was a complex mix of molasses and flowers that varied depending on when the sap was harvested. Early-, mid-, and late-summer harvests produced markedly different flavors.

It was also far more expensive than maple syrup. It took over a hundred gallons of birch sap to make a single gallon of the syrup, compared to the forty it took for maple syrup. Because of that it was usually used sparingly.

But I didn't need to worry about cost. I got as much of it as I could get my hands on, and inserted it into the menu in every way I could think of.

As the guests arrived they were offered glasses of champagne and treated to tray service. Waitstaff circulated with three different appetizers; two were bites of Canadian Bannock bread, half of it smoked over an open fire and served with mushrooms and whisky sauce, and the other unsmoked, accompanied by caviar and crème fraîche. Also making the rounds was my own take on "Montreal smoked meat," a national favorite that was similar to corned beef but made with less sugar. We'd put the minced meat inside wonton wrappers with lightly vinegared sauerkraut and deep fried them, then served them with three kinds of mustards for dipping.

The room filled up quickly. Everyone seemed comfortable, possibly because they all appeared to know each other, and they weren't shy about availing themselves of the tray service and the bars. Before long we were on our last trays of food, but I'd timed things right; just as we were running out the announcement came to find seats and get ready for dinner.

There was no official program. Instead, Nottingham offered brief thanks as everyone was being seated.

I'd catered a number of corporate dinners in my life. For some reason the business owners always felt the need to take advantage of their captive audience. While pretending to offer their employees a nice dinner as a gesture of thanks, they couldn't help themselves from using the event as an opportunity to push some company initiative or cultural imperative. I appreciated the fact that Nottingham didn't subject his employees to a long presentation.

He looked relaxed. Not as much as he'd been in his cutting room polishing diamonds, and he still had on his five-figure suit, but he'd left off his tie for the evening.

Celeste and Alan worked the room with him, Alan providing hearty handshakes and Celeste talking to the women. She was still sporting the bazillion-dollar diamond necklace, apparently a regular feature of these employee dinners. She leaned in frequently to let people touch it. Many of the men seemed particularly interested, possibly because of the necklace's proximity to her prominent tracts of land.

Tasia and Martin were at one of the few tables that wasn't full, about as far away from the rest of the family as possible. What must it have been like, as a child, growing up with Nottingham, the man who never smiled? Still, that by itself couldn't have engendered the obvious disdain for him by Martin and Tasia.

As usual Tasia wasn't interacting with anyone other than Martin, but she looked more relaxed, too. She was even better looking when she wasn't stressed out and frowning.

Not that it mattered. It was pretty clear she wasn't into me, and I'd stopped fantasizing about her after I saw her light up around Michael at Martin's alum event.

It was probably for the best. But I was feeling antsy; I hadn't hooked up with Nikky since I'd started this job. I'd need to call her when I got back.

Normally for a group this size I would have set the food up buffet-style. But my instructions for this event had been clear: make sure it felt like a fancy sit-down dinner. No one was to self-serve. The whole point was for the Nottinghams to serve the employees.

At the designated time we guided everyone to their seats and brought out the first course, a moose ragu mafalde pasta with smoked carrots. We followed that with arctic char, grilled and basted with late-harvest birch syrup, of the three varieties the one with the strongest molasses flavor.

After a palette cleanser of spruce tip sorbet, we brought out the meat: braised wild boar ribs with birch syrup glaze and potatoes, accompanied by baby kale and fresh pea salad from the local greenhouses.

For dessert I'd wanted to do a dessert bar, but per Celeste's desire that the guests feel catered to, I'd opted instead for dessert carts, each one offering a selection of Canadian butter tarts, panna cotta with sauce made of the lighter, floral, early-harvest birch syrup, and semifreddo made using the cloudberries—peach-colored berries that tasted like something between a raspberry and a currant—that I'd also used in the specialty cocktail.

These employees saw enough ice in their daily lives, so I didn't commission an ice sculpture. But I did have a surprise.

While the dessert carts were going around we cleared the centerpieces off the tables, and on each placed a set of wooden skewers and a single large metal tin filled with fresh snow. Waitstaff came around to each table where they drizzled a hot stream of mid-harvest birch syrup onto the snow, then took a wooden skewer and rolled it onto the syrup, creating a birch taffy lollipop.

I'd cleaned out every source of birch syrup I could find for this event, buying out entire stocks of both small, family-owned, and larger operations. But it was worth it; everyone in this region was familiar with maple syrup candy, and the chance to do it with the precious birch syrup was greeted with exclamations of pleasure and some applause.

Both Martin and Celeste had as usual put away their weight in booze. Celeste was showing no effects. Martin, on the other hand, was bleary-eyed and disheveled, and had ambled off to the bathroom after the meat course, one of the many trips he'd made during dinner to coke up.

He was on his way back from the bathroom, weaving among the tables, when he stumbled. On his way to the ground he grabbed at a tablecloth.

He pulled it down with him as he hit the floor. Glasses, many of them filled, plates, silverware, and the metal pan with snow all clattered to the floor.

Mason made a hand gesture to Zach, who quickly walked over and helped Martin to his feet, then escorted him out of the room.

Tasia stood up, and with one of her focused glares at her father, followed them out of the room.

It was a minor blip, and far less damage than I'd seen Martin do before. At least he hadn't pissed on anything. The waitstaff moved like ninjas, cleaning up the floor and restocking everyone's food and drinks. Within seconds it was like it never happened.

My part of the event was mostly over. I went back to the kitchen, and after a few directions to the staff about cleanup, I grabbed one of the snow trays, a set of skewers, and a pot of the hot birch syrup, and went upstairs.

The family's rooms were on the top floor. Zach was standing in the hallway, next to one of the rooms that I assumed was Martin's.

Zach seemed to genuinely care for Martin. But he worked for Mason, who answered to Nottingham, who was primarily interested in Martin not fucking anything up. A hard line to walk, I imagined.

"I brought this for Martin."

He nodded, and I knocked on the door.

There was no answer, so I knocked again.

After a few moments Tasia opened it.

"What?" she barked.

"I brought this for Martin."

She stood there, staring at me.

"Can I come in?"

She scowled but stepped back to let me in.

Martin was sprawled out on the king bed, his head up against the headboard, a drink in his hand.

"Hey Martin."

I set the tray and skewers on the table, and poured the syrup onto the snow. "It won't stay hot for long."

I left, closing the door softly behind me, then went back downstairs to join the rest of the staff in the cleanup.

Almost no one had left the party. They were enjoying coffee

and birch syrup candy; many of them were still taking advantage of the hosted unlimited bar. Nottingham, Alan, and Celeste were making their way around the room, talking and shaking hands.

I puttered around the kitchen and the floor, picking up plates and bringing out a few requested extras. Two hours later the last guest left and I was free to leave.

It had been a long day, but as usual I was wired. I walked into the lodge's small lounge and took a stool at the bar.

They were closing soon, and there was almost no one left.

"A pint of Nitro Porter, please," I said to the bartender.

"I'll take one of those as well. You can put them both on my tab."

I turned to see Tasia standing next to me.

"Do you mind?" she said, nodding to an empty stool.

"Go ahead." I was hoping to get a break from the family, but I could hardly say no.

She sat down, both of us wordless until our drinks arrived.

She held up her glass to me. "Nice job with dinner tonight."

"Thanks." She clinked my glass.

The beer was creamy and delicious, made by NWT, one of the local breweries. I wondered if I could get it in Chicago.

"Nice of you to bring the dessert to Martin."

I nodded, taking another sip.

"I never thanked you for his alumni event. He appreciated it, very much. Especially the opportunity to pee on Harvard."

"I'm glad."

A long moment went by. Despite Smith's request that I develop a relationship with Tasia, I wasn't up to it at the moment. I'd worked hard today and wanted a few minutes to myself. And I was suspicious at her sudden chattiness.

She broke the silence. "Why did you do that?"

"Do what?"

"Bring dessert to Martin's room."

I turned to look at her. "Because he missed it, and it was the coolest part of the meal."

"I know, but . . ." she looked down. "Most people hate him. They think he's an entitled, spoiled brat."

I finished my beer. The bartender came over and raised an eyebrow, and I nodded. It was after closing time, but he wasn't going to close the bar on a Nottingham.

I waited until my beer came before I answered her.

"You want the truth?"

She nodded.

"I think he's a good kid. I don't think he's spoiled. I think he's damaged."

The full truth was that he reminded me of my sister. Self-medicating away a hurt so deep he couldn't face life without drugs and alcohol. I wondered what his damage was.

Or maybe I was wrong, and he'd had a perfect, entitled childhood, and was just bored. Either way, I didn't think Tasia was used to people saying what they honestly thought around her.

I didn't care. If they fired me, they fired me. And it was becoming increasingly clear that Tasia and Martin had no say in any decisions related to the family.

But if she was surprised, or upset, at my response, there was no indication of it.

"I've never heard anyone say that before."

"Well, I'm an expert on the subject." I finished my beer and stood up. "Thanks for the beers."

I walked out of the lounge and went up to my room. I wouldn't have minded another beer, but I was worried about running into Celeste.

Once in the safety of my room I got out of my clothes and took a shower. Nothing felt better after a long shift than washing the food smell out of my hair. Even if it was great food, I didn't want to smell like it.

While I was toweling off my phone rang.

Jesus. Who would be calling me at this hour? No one, other than Smith, for some reason using my personal cell.

That might be the most irritating part of working for him. He didn't sleep, and he didn't seem to think other people needed to, either.

I let it ring a while before I picked it up. "What?"

"I've got some Bollinger in my room. Interested in a nightcap?" It was Tasia.

"Sure," I said, without thinking.

"Top floor, room five. Come over in ten minutes." She hung up.

I dressed and walked down the stairs to the landing, taking the other set of stairs up to the family's floor.

I walked to Tasia's door, surprised not to see any security in the hallway. She opened it just as I was about to knock.

I stepped into the room, and she put both hands on either side of my head and gently pushed the door closed. Then she leaned forward and kissed me.

EIGHTEEN

"I never got my nightcap."

We were lying flat on our backs on the bed, both of us covered in a thin sheen of sweat.

I had no idea what time it was. The sun hadn't come up yet, but at this time of year it didn't rise until ten in the morning.

After I'd gotten in the door she'd practically dragged me to the king bed, pulling my clothes off on the way. I returned the favor, and discovered she was even better looking with her clothes off.

We were finally taking a break.

And, wow.

I wasn't sure if it was because I hadn't seen Nikky in a while, or because Tasia and I had a connection, but I didn't care. She was as ferocious in bed as she was out of it.

I wondered if she did this all the time. I didn't think so; someone with her profile couldn't exactly go out for pickups whenever she wanted. But she was definitely not out of practice.

She gave a low laugh as she got up and went to the kitchen. She came back with a bottle of Bollinger Vieilles Vignes Françaises and poured two glasses.

We clinked glasses and drank.

Wow. Creamy, earthy, fruity . . . this stuff was amazing. I doubted the locals carried it, she must have brought it with her.

"That was surprising," I said after taking another sip. We'd talked very little since I'd walked in the door.

"What?"

"I thought you were a bitch. I mean, until last night."

"What makes you think I'm not?"

"Good point. I also thought you were into Michael."

"Who?"

"Michael. My coworker, at Martin's party. The oyster/Wagyu bites guy."

"Oh. Yes, he was nice. But not my type." She ran her fingers down my leg. "Clearly."

I leaned forward, looking more closely at the locket she wore around her neck. It was the only thing she hadn't taken off.

"No diamonds for you?"

"Never."

"You're not envious, that Celeste gets to wear the great necklace?"

"I hate the bloody thing. He tried to get me to wear one years ago. Trust me, Celeste is more than happy to be the clothing horse for his creations."

"What's this?" I said, touching the locket.

She put her glass down, and opened the locket. Inside was a picture of a woman. She was pretty, and looked to be in her thirties.

"It's my mother."

"That's where Martin gets his looks." The resemblance was striking. The same bruised brown eyes, soft brown hair with a slight wave.

She nodded.

"Where is she?"

She shook her head, closing the locket. "No idea. She left when we were young."

"Left you? That's hard."

"It was, especially for Martin. He cried every night for weeks after she left."

This might explain Martin's damage. A young boy suddenly losing his mother would be devastating.

"Do you know why she left? Or where she went?"

She stared out of the window. "No. I know she was unhappy. I can't blame her." She laughed bitterly. "Who wouldn't be, living with him." No doubt she was talking about her father.

"Let's change the subject." She closed the locket. "So, tell me. What are you doing here?"

"What do you mean?"

She ran her fingers from my leg up my side and down my arm. "I mean, you're talented. And you have your own restaurant, and could open up another one if you wanted to. Why do parties for the filthy rich?"

Was she fishing? Did she know something? Despite the post-sex serotonin rush, I was immediately on guard. Or would have been, if it weren't for her wandering fingers.

"This is a great job. For starters, working with an unlimited budget is a chef's dream. You have no idea what it's like to be able to use whatever I want in whatever quantity I want. That birch syrup I used tonight? It's hundreds of dollars a gallon. And I've been looking for something else to do. The restaurant practically runs itself now. What about you?"

"What about me?"

"What are you doing here? It's pretty clear you're not a huge fan of your dad. Why stick around?"

She looked over to the window, sipping. "I can't leave Martin."

"He seems like a nice kid."

"A nice, brilliant kid."

"Seriously?"

She nodded. "He's the best of us."

I didn't want to offend her, and tried not to look too surprised.

"Alan barely graduated Harvard, even with the best tutors and grades money could buy. He's my brother, and a nice guy, but he's a complete moron. I did fine at Stanford. But Martin . . ." She smiled, shaking her head. "He graduated summa cum laude, with dual degrees in economics and mathematics."

I didn't see that one coming. "So he must have started his partying afterward, then?"

"Oh, no. He's been doing that since junior high school."

"You're kidding."

"No. I meant it. He's brilliant."

"As smart as your dad?"

She nodded.

"Speaking of your dad, what happened to the security guys?

I was sure I'd run in to one of them on the way to your room."

"They're much more relaxed up here. There are no other guests in the place, and all of the employees have been vetted. Besides, other than Zach, their primary concern is my dad, Alan, and Celeste."

They hadn't seemed all that relaxed when they were tearing up my room.

"Mason doesn't seem to like Martin very much."

She scowled. It was clear she felt the same way about him as she did her father. "Mason's been with the family since before I was born. He thinks Martin threatens dad's reputation. That's part of the reason I have to stay to keep an eye on Martin. I don't trust Mason."

Something else we had in common. "I don't get it. Why don't the two of you just leave?"

She shook her head. "Dad would cut us off. I'd be fine, but Martin, he's in no shape to manage his own life."

"How did it get to this point? I mean, between you and Martin, and the rest of the family?"

She pulled her hand back and looked away.

Shit. Too much, too soon. "I'm sorry."

"No, it's OK. It's just hard to talk about."

I really wanted to know what "it" was, but I let it drop.

"I was sorry about Isaac Katz."

"Yes, that was horrible." Unlike everyone else in the family, she'd bothered to learn his name.

"Did you know him?"

"A little. He was with us for years."

"Do they know who did it?"

"I don't think so. They said it was a hit and run."

So Carter hadn't gotten anywhere on who ran into Katz. I hoped Smith had found something out from the video footage.

"There's a lot going on in the city right now."

"Isn't there always?"

"I mean, with all of the stunts."

In response to her puzzled look, I added, "You know. The

dye in the river, the 'fuck you' on the Crain building, the raw meat dump in front of Wrigley."

If she knew anything about any of that, she was the best actress in the universe. "Oh, yeah. I don't pay attention to that kind of thing. I'm surprised you have the time for that, with all you've got going. It seems like Celeste is keeping you pretty busy."

Was that a deft change of subject?

"She'd like to keep me busier."

She raised her eyebrows.

"She's been hitting on me since I interviewed."

She chuckled. "That's the norm. She jumps anything with a pulse."

Huh. Part of me was a little put out that I wasn't special. "Seriously?"

"Yes. Men, women, I've seen her give the look to the horses. It's no surprise."

"Why?"

"Alan's impotent. I doubt they've even consummated their marriage."

That explained a lot. "How do you know that?"

"Sometimes when she gets really loaded she lets things slip."

I couldn't imagine what it would take for Celeste to get really loaded. But I was having a hard time thinking about Celeste. Tasia's hand was roaming. I rolled over on top of her.

"Hang on," she said, breathless, reaching over to the nightstand for her phone. "Shit. The jet's leaving in two hours. You better get going."

I got out of the bed reluctantly and put on my clothes. "I think it's best to not mention anything to Celeste about this. I'm not sure how she'd react if she knew we'd hooked up. I don't want to lose my job."

"Don't worry. We rarely talk to each other. Mostly I just feel sorry for her."

I put on my shoes and leaned over to give her a kiss. It was a long one, and I got the strong feeling it wouldn't be the last.

The thought made me happy. Tasia was gorgeous, and smart, and she had an edge to her. I liked that edge. And I realized I hadn't thought about Ekaterina once the whole night. A first for me since she'd walked out of my life.

I left the room, closing the door softly behind me. Before I turned to walk down the hall there was a sound from the other direction.

At the end of the hallway was Celeste, standing in front of her door, staring at me.

NINETEEN

"What did you learn?"

Smith had given me a couple of days after I got back before calling me too early for an update. It was eight a.m. and I was with him in the cemetery, which was starting to feel like a home away from home.

I'd made it back in one piece from Canada, on the jet with the rest of the family. Minus Tasia, who'd misplaced her passport and had to stay over until she could get a new one. Even the fabulously wealthy needed passports, although unlike the rest of us they were able to turn a new one around in a day.

It was a relief when we'd touched down. I'd half expected something terrible to happen in the city while we were gone.

Now that it hadn't, I couldn't shake the nagging feeling that Smith had all of this wrong.

"The rift between Tasia and Martin and the rest of the family is real. Alan's a moron, and he's impotent. Their mom disappeared when they were kids and no one knows where she went. Tasia knew the dead jeweler that was killed in the hit and run, although not well. She seems to be upset by it. She doesn't pay attention to the news and isn't up to speed on the vandalism incidents. Martin is still doing drugs."

It was cold, and short puffs of mist were coming out of my mouth with every word. I wished he'd do these meetings a little later in the day.

"That's oddly specific, albeit not that helpful. Where did you pick all of that up?"

"Tasia told me."

"Tasia? I thought she didn't talk to you."

"Well, you said to try to get close to the family. I've been working on that." I tried not to laugh as I said that.

"Did you get anything else? Anything about Richard Nottingham?"

"No. Tasia doesn't like to talk about him. She hates him.

"C'mon, Smith," I said, in response to his frown. "You said I was just one piece of the surveillance you have in place."

"I had hoped after spending a couple of days with them you'd have more."

"Well, you might not have to worry about my incompetence much longer," I added quietly.

"What's that supposed to mean?"

"I mean, Celeste is running the show, and she's not too happy with me right now."

"Why not?"

I looked away.

"What did you do?"

"You sound like my fucking mother."

He stared at me. "You can lose that restaurant as easily as you gained it. What happened?"

"Celeste is mad I'm not sleeping with her."

He frowned. "So? According to you she's been unhappy about that since day one."

"Yeah, well, now she's madder." I looked away again.

He waited a few beats. "Why? What—Oh, you're kidding me. Did you sleep with Tasia?"

"She made a move on me. It wasn't like I could say no."

Of course, I could have said no.

"Celeste caught me coming out of Tasia's room."

"Do you have to have sex with every criminal's daughter?"

"Technically, Ekaterina wasn't Morzov's daughter. Besides, you told me to get close to the family."

"I didn't mean in the biblical sense."

I grinned. "What we did was hardly biblical." I got a small amount of pleasure watching him squirm. "For what it's worth, I can guarantee you Tasia's not involved in her dad's business, legal or otherwise. She really hates him. Not just that, I think she would help us. You know, if I told her what was going on."

I'd come up with that idea on the plane. If Tasia hated her dad as much as it seemed like she did, she might jump at the chance to help us put him away.

His eyes grew wide. “No. Absolutely not. Under no circumstances should you tell her anything. You can’t be sure she’s not in on it. And even if she’s not, family ties are nothing to mess around with. She might hate him, but if push comes to shove you’d be surprised how many people will decide not to sell out family members to law enforcement, no matter how much they hate each other. Besides, how do you know she’s not doing it for her father?”

“Doing what?”

“Sleeping with you.”

I snorted. “I don’t think so.”

“The security team tossed your room. So they may very well suspect something. And if so, what better way to find out than lay a honey trap.”

“What’s a ‘honey trap’?”

“When women, it’s at least almost always women, throw themselves at a man in order to gain information. Usually it involves a woman who’s way out of the man’s league.”

I bristled. “Are you saying Tasia’s way out of my league?”

He put his hands up. “No, no, I’m just saying that you can’t be sure about anything when it comes to the family. You have to keep your guard up, even with Tasia.”

I didn’t like where this conversation was going. “Fine. Forget I mentioned it. What about the dead jeweler? Did you get the camera footage?”

“Who? Oh.” Now it was his turn to look away.

“What did you find?”

“It turns out the cameras were facing the other way when it happened.”

“I suppose you think that’s a coincidence, too?”

“I don’t know if it’s a coincidence, but the hit and run was no accident. There were no tire marks at the scene, and the cameras had been turned away from their normal orientation shortly before the accident happened.”

“So that means it had to be the Nottinghams who were behind it.”

“Not necessarily. It would’ve been fairly easy for anyone to do it. But it was definitely premeditated. And I’m struggling to see how it makes sense for Nottingham to have one of his employees killed at the same time they were doing an event at his own store."

Uh oh. "He might, if he didn't know there would be an event."

"What are you talking about?"

"I'm not sure anyone other than Celeste knew about the brunch. She was the only member of the family there, and none of the security team showed up."

He nodded. "That makes more sense. In any case that's not our focus right now."

"One of your informants being murdered isn't a focus?" I didn't like the sound of that.

"We're still looking into it, of course. But Rykov just got another infusion of money. Several million dollars. We think this means they're very close to their attack."

"Can't you just arrest him?"

"We've talked about it. But there's nothing illegal about having money put into your account. If we did pick him up we wouldn't be able to hold him, and all we'd be doing is letting them know we're on to them. But I agree with you. If it were up to me we'd pick him up now. That is, if we could find him."

"What do you mean, 'if you could find him'?"

"We have no idea where he is."

"Weren't you tailing him?"

"We lost him. At least for now. That's why it's so important now that we keep tabs on Nottingham."

I groaned.

"It won't be for much longer. Maybe a few days. Between Rykov disappearing and the infusion of cash, whatever they're going to do is going to happen very soon. We believe within the next two weeks. I think there's a good chance it could happen at their annual holiday party.

"What holiday party?"

"They do a huge holiday bash every year. You haven't heard anything?"

I shook my head.

"I'm surprised. I would have thought Celeste would have already talked to you about it. It's their biggest event of the year. Everyone in the city who is anyone will be there. And if the goal is to affect the maximum number of people, there's no better venue than Union Station."

Maude was already up and at her computer when I got back.

"Nice to see you," I said. Between my trip to Canada and her long hours at the station we'd not seen each other in days.

"You too. How's the spy business?"

"Nerve wracking. But Smith says I won't have to do it for much longer. How's the codebreaking business?"

"I'm making progress. We've figured out that each set of numbers is a single letter. The code's layered, which means we have to run multiple algorithms on it to get through each layer. So far I've managed to break ten layers."

"How many are there?"

"I don't know. But I think we might be on the last one, or at least close to something meaningful."

"A meaningful five-letter word?"

"Six. There's been another incident. Someone hung a bag of hog carcasses from one of the Sears—I mean, Willis Tower spires." She laughed. "From a really long rope. An accountant came into work in the morning to find a bag of bloody meat dangling outside of his window."

"That's inventive. How would someone get that up there?"

"With a drone, although it would have had to be a big one. Which means there's at least one other person involved in this. Dennis Penny, the guy we picked up for using a drone on the Crain building, is still in custody.

She clicked her screen, bringing up an image of the entrance to the Willis Tower. A set of nine numbers was spray-painted on the sidewalk in front of the building's glass walls.

"Somebody's committed to getting your attention."

"They've got it."

"How do you know you're on the last layer of the code?"

"I can't be a hundred percent sure, but after working with a code like this for a while you start to get a feel for the personality of the person who put it together. He or she is sophisticated, and has a sense of humor. I'm half expecting the final message to be something like 'wanker,' and tell us nothing about the vandalism, much less about Smith's operation. Regardless, we have what I think are the final set of letters. YEURXU."

"Six letters? All of that for six letters?"

"Yeah."

"Great, I guess. Now what?"

"I think it's a simple Vigenère shift cipher."

In response to my blank look, she said. "Each of the letters, YEURXU, corresponds to a different letter, according to the cipher pattern, that once transformed gives us the coded word or phrase. The Vigenère cipher pattern is determined by a keyword. Once we know the keyword, we're able to transform YEURXU into the word or phrase we want to identify.

"Here's an example. Suppose the keyword was 'SAGS'. We'd write SAGS underneath YEURXU. Since SAGS is only four letters, we'd write SAGSSA underneath YEURXU. So, underneath the Y would be S. The letter A in this cipher corresponds to 0, and given S is the 19th letter in the alphabet, it corresponds to 18. So we shift the Y back by 18 places, bringing us to the letter G. Continuing on, with SAGS as the keyword, YEURXU translates to GEOZFU."

"What does that mean?"

"Nothing, because SAGS isn't the keyword."

My head was starting to hurt, but it still didn't seem like it would be all that hard for Maude to figure out, given her computer skills. "So you just need a six letter keyword? Can't you get the computer to run through millions of them a second or something?"

"The keyword can be any length, and there are over a million words in the English language. And it doesn't have to be a real word, it could just be a random list of letters. Even so, you're right, the computer can run through the possibilities in a few minutes. It already has, in fact. The problem is that the computer identified what it calls 'plausible candidates' for the coded word, and there are tens of thousands of them. I need to comb through them, to identify what I think is the actual coded word.

"I have software to help weed out nonsense, but it will still take a while. And, this all assumes that both the keyword and the coded word are in English. If we consider all of the world's alphabets, including Unicode, we're talking thousands of years of additional computer time to even come up with the plausible candidates.

"The bottom line is, until we have the keyword we're not going to be able to solve it. At least not soon."

"I've never seen you give up before."

"I'm not giving up. It's just going to take time."

"Why are you doing this here? Instead of at the station, with the FBI guy?"

"The powers that be have now decided that the codes don't have anything to do directly with the terrorist threat, so it's taking a back seat to digging into any connections with the Nottinghams. They've got me doing pattern analysis on Rykov's previous operations in Europe, and monitoring social media. But I can feel it, that this code is important. I'm going to keep working on it."

She leaned back and stretched. Her eyes were red and puffy, and her hair hadn't been combed. It stuck straight up in spikey blonde peaks in a look that she often crafted on purpose.

"How's Jeb doing?" she asked. Sometimes I forgot Smith had a first name. "Don't you see him every day?"

She shook her head. "He's running the informants. I don't see him at work and we haven't had a date in weeks."

"He's OK. He looks tired. Like you."

She looked down. "I've been read in on the operation, and I think this could be really bad. This Rykov guy, as far as we know it's his first time in the US, but he has a long list of suspected terrorist actions in Europe and Africa, most of which resulted in significant casualties. He usually doesn't get involved unless it's something that involves a high body count. And the Russians, well, we know they've been actively working on destabilization, psychological warfare, here for years. But this is on a whole different level. Can you imagine, if they execute a terrorist attack on a large scale in Chicago? The FBI think it's going to be something with Novichok." She shuddered. "Do you know what that stuff does? I can't think of anything worse."

TWENTY

"Will I ever get to see your room?" Tasia and I had just knocked off an afternoon quickie in my backyard bungalow. "Supposedly, staff are allowed up there, if they're invited . . ."

I'd been staying in the cottage since we'd returned from Canada. It was comfortable, and it was easy for us to see each other. The only drawback was that I was getting almost no sleep. Tasia was a voracious lover, and we were hooking up every chance we could. I had no doubt Ellis was sharing my whereabouts with Celeste, and likely Mason, but being in the presence of Tasia apparently gave me the seal of approval to stay in the cottage even when I wasn't cooking.

"Do you think that's a good idea? My room's down the hall from Celeste and Alan's."

I'd mostly been kidding. I had little desire to spend more time inside the main house, and less any closer to Celeste.

She'd been cold and distant to me once we'd returned from Canada. I didn't mind, at all, and appreciated not getting hit on every time I was around her.

But I didn't want to be fired, either. At least not yet. And I didn't think rubbing it in her face would be helpful.

"Why isn't this your place, like Martin's? Why live in the house?"

"I'd love to. Dad wanted to keep me in the house. As punishment, I think. We could always go to your place," she added. "Where is your place?"

"Andersonville. I share it with Maude."

"Who's she?"

"My best friend. We've been roommates for almost three years."

"Do you ever . . ."

"No. She's dating—"

I realized I'd almost said "an FBI agent."

Damn. I'd have to be more careful.

It was hard not to tell Tasia what was going on. Despite what Smith said, I trusted her completely.

And she trusted me. Among other things, she'd given me the family code to the front gate, which made it easier to come and go.

The better I got to know her, the more I believed she not only had nothing to do with her dad's terrorist shit, but she'd do anything to help us take him down.

Regardless, I had to trust Smith's judgment.

"She's dating someone. A guy."

"Ah."

"What's your story?" We'd never spoken about exes, or anything like that. I knew very little about her.

"You mean, dating?"

"Yeah, if you don't mind my asking."

"No, I don't mind." She took a sip of Bollinger. She'd filled up the refrigerator in the cottage with as much of it as it would hold. "I was engaged, once."

"To a guy?"

"Yeah," she said, grinning. "Blakeford Wainwright. His family was as rich as it sounds. My dad set it up. Like it was the sixteenth century or something. I think he thought merging the families would help his business."

"I can't see you going along with that."

"Of course not. But he told me if I didn't do it he'd cut me off."

"That must have been strong incentive to marry the guy."

She shook her head. "I've never cared about his money. But then he said he'd throw me out of the house if I didn't go through with it. I couldn't do that to Martin."

"I get it. I feel the same about Gigi."

"Your sister?"

I'd told her I had a sister, but little else.

"She's in rehab. She's been living on the street for years, doing drugs, getting pimped out by her dealer. I'd do anything to help her."

With Maude working late at the station all of the time it was nice to be able to talk to someone about Gigi. I didn't think I was violating any of Smith's secrecy rules by telling Tasia about her.

"How's the rehab going?"

"Good, I think. She's been before. Several times. I keep hoping this will be the one."

Tasia looked away. "At some point Martin's going to have to stop. I wonder how he would do in rehab . . ."

Neither of us spoke for a long moment. Tasia finished her glass and refilled it.

"So," I said, trying to get the mood back, "how come you're not married to this guy? The one your dad set you up with?"

"I told my dad that if he made me marry him I'd leave the country and he'd never see me again."

"And he believed you?"

"No." She laughed. "And he wouldn't have cared if I did. But he knew I was bluffing, that I'd never leave Martin."

"So what happened?"

"Dad invited the Wainwrights over to the house for a weekend to get to know us. The first night they were there I snuck into Blakeford's room and woke him up with a knife at his neck. I promised him that if he didn't call it off I'd kill him in his sleep on our wedding night."

I spurted champagne out of my nose laughing. I could totally see her doing this.

"The next morning he told his parents he wouldn't marry me. They left that day. Dad hasn't tried anything like that since. Anyway, he's got Alan to carry on the family name."

"Not Martin?"

"He would have loved Martin to do it. He knows how smart he is. But I guess he felt he'd waited long enough for Martin to 'straighten up,' as he calls it. Dad's not getting any younger, and even if Martin did decide to clean up his act, he's shown no interest in the business. Not to mention he hates my dad as much as I do. More."

I wondered again what Nottingham had done to engender

that much hatred. But she'd been reluctant to talk about it, and I didn't want to cut the conversation short.

"Is Alan up to it?" Since she'd told me Alan was a moron I'd seen him prove it on multiple occasions.

"No. But Celeste is. Say what you want about her drinking and libidinous inclinations, she's smart. Alan might become the head of the business, but she'll be the brain. I was glad when he married her. It took the pressure off of me to be involved in all of that."

"No desire to run things?"

She shook her head. "None. I fucking hate diamonds. And when dad's gone I'm taking Martin and leaving."

"To where?"

"I don't know . . . somewhere away from this place. Do you have a couple of extra rooms?" She glanced at me sideways.

"Somehow I think if you were at my place you wouldn't be staying in one of the guest rooms."

"I hope not." She took the glass out of my hand and set it on the nightstand, then crawled on top of me.

There was a discrete knock at the door of the cottage. I pulled on sweatpants and a T-shirt and opened it.

It was Ellis. "Mrs. Nottingham would like to see you," he said. If he noticed Tasia in my bed there was no sign of it.

"OK. I'll be right there."

I closed the door. "Gotta go. The lady of the house is calling."

She frowned.

"I don't want to get fired. She's already mad at me."

Tasia left while I was taking a shower. I dressed and went to Celeste's office.

She was behind the desk, sipping tea. Probably the Long Island kind.

She'd been cool to me since she'd caught me coming out of Tasia's room in Canada. There'd been no more sexual innuendos, or invading my personal space. But I didn't doubt for a moment that she knew that Tasia and I were hooking up. Tasia told me that Ellis was Celeste's eyes and ears in the house, and told her everything.

She gestured for me to sit across from her, then tossed a thick folder on the desk in front of me.

"The annual Nottingham holiday party is being held at Union Station, in five days. This is the family's biggest event of the year."

I swallowed hard. Smith had said this was coming up, and that it would be a prime opportunity for whatever Rykov and Nottingham were planning.

"Bigger than the *Enterprise* dinner?"

She scoffed. "Much bigger. There will be seven hundred guests. It is our most important event of the year. Everyone you've seen at previous events will be there, plus additional very important people, and selected press."

"What kind of theme are you looking for?"

"Everything you need to know is in the folder." She looked down at another set of papers. My signal to leave.

On the way back to the cottage I stopped in the kitchen.

"Hey Percy."

"Hi." He smiled.

Once he'd realized I wasn't there to take his job, our relationship had done a complete one-eighty. I'd given him a hand a few times when he was putting the informal family dinners together, and occasionally given him some suggestions to elevate his meals. I'd also shared some of my molecular gastronomy tricks. He'd bought his own centrifuge, and had been experimenting.

Like Mason, Percy had been with the family for years. He was a decent chef, nothing amazing, but he was diligent, and they didn't need a rock star to make a couple of family dinners each week and put together Nottingham's daily lunch tray.

He was at the counter now, working on the lunch. It was the same thing every day: small piles of the cheese cubes, a few meat ribs, flatbread, all washed down with a glass of milk.

He opened the refrigerator to take out one of the unmarked glass bottles that appeared every week. He pulled off the foil top.

"Yikes. What is that?" I said, breathing through my mouth

to avoid the sour, funky smell. I hadn't actually been around before when he opened it.

"It's Kumis. Fermented mare's milk."

"Seriously?"

Percy had said he made all of Nottingham's meals. And I already knew a little about his ascetic tastes from the dinner on the *Enterprise*; he'd not touched any alcohol, and ate sparingly. But fermented milk? I wasn't afraid of exotic food, but this stuff smelled like a cross between cheese and sewage.

He nodded. "He drinks it every day."

This could explain why Nottingham always looked so miserable. "Why?"

He laughed. "No idea. But he's religious about it."

There were pretty strict regulations in the US for anything to do with food from a horse, and also importing milk products. "Where do you get it?"

"We have a supplier, a horse dairy farm. One of three in the country. They deliver it fresh twice a week. Along with the ribs."

Fermented milk and horse ribs. Jesus. Any lingering doubts I had about Nottingham's childhood roots were immediately snuffed out.

I went back to the cottage, taking large breaths through my nose to get the smell of Kumis out of it. I packed up my stuff and headed home. On the way I called Smith to let him know the Union Station event was confirmed.

When I got home I dropped off my bag, then borrowed Maude's car and went to visit Gigi. I hadn't been able to see her since I'd gotten back from Canada, and now that I had the big event coming this would be my last chance for a little while.

I enjoyed visiting her at the clinic. Our interactions were so different now. She wasn't drugged up, or laser focused on where she'd get her next fix. And while she wasn't all that chatty, there were glimpses, every now and then, of the sister I remembered, before the abuse and the drugs.

I was looking forward to having her live at our house when she completed rehab. But that wouldn't be for a while. The counselor had said that her recovery was more likely to stick if she stayed in rehab at least three months, with regular therapy.

I was fine with that. I wanted her to be in the best shape possible to stay clean.

If she was up for working when she got out I could find something for her to do at the restaurant. Or even help with the events, if Richard Nottingham turned out to not be a terrorist, and I kept my job with the family. For this reason alone I hoped Smith was wrong about the whole thing.

A girl could dream.

I pulled into the parking lot and walked into the lobby to the front desk.

"Hi. I'm here to see Gigi Pfister."

The woman frowned. "She's not here."

"Where is she?"

"She checked out, two days ago."

"What?"

"She left the facility, two days ago."

"Why did you let her leave?"

Her frown deepened. "Gigi is not a minor, and this is not a prison," she said, officious. "She did leave against medical advice. She signed the form."

"Where did she go?"

"I have no idea. We don't track people who leave."

I took a deep breath. "OK . . . how did she leave? Did she call a car?"

"No. She was picked up by a man."

"Can I please speak to Hannah?"

I was treated to another frown but the woman picked up the phone and made a call. A few minutes later Hannah came to the lobby.

"I'm really sorry, Sagarine. I tried to encourage Gigi to stay. But she was adamant."

"Did you see who picked her up?"

"Yes. It wasn't the one that tried to do it before."

Frank Chimen had attempted to get Gigi out of rehab when she'd first showed up. They hadn't let him into the facility, and she never knew that he'd come for her. But they'd told me.

“Did you get his name? What did this one look like?”

“No name. Thirties, white, skinny. Scruffy beard.”

Great. That described half of the dealers in the city.

“OK. Thanks.”

“Uh, if you do find her, we can’t take her back. At least not right away. All of the spots are filled, and when people leave against our recommendation their place is given to someone else. I’m sorry.”

Dammit. “I know. Thanks.”

TWENTY-ONE

As soon as I got back in the car I called Smith.

"I can't do the Nottinghams' events any more. Gigi's left rehab. I have to go look for her."

"Settle down. Where are you?"

"I'm just getting on I-90."

"OK. Meet me at Rosehill at our usual spot. I can be there in twenty minutes."

Smith was already there by the time I pulled up.

"So what's going on?"

"Gigi's left rehab. Against their recommendation. I think a dealer came for her, and she's back on the street. I need to go look for her. I can't deal with the Nottinghams right now. And I can't spend time prepping for Union Station. I'm going to tell Celeste to bring in someone else."

He put his hands on my shoulders. I shrugged them off, and he put them up, placating.

"You can't leave, not now. This event is almost certainly where the main attack is coming."

"You don't know that for sure."

"I'm as sure as I can be. There isn't a better venue for a nerve agent attack. It's an enormous event space that sits just above the largest transportation hub in the city. Hundreds of thousands of people go through there every day. There's also no more important guest list; it's a who's who of everyone who's anyone in the city, including everyone who makes the city run. We're setting up an entire operation to intervene before they're able to release the nerve agent. We'll have agents outside the station and as close as we can get to the actual festivities. Every first responder in the city will be on alert. You can't quit, not now. There's too much at stake. Gigi's left rehab before, hasn't she?"

"Yes," I said, angry. "So what?"

"So, she can go back again. But this, if this happens? If they release Novichok at Union Station? There'll be no coming back from that."

He was right, but I didn't care. I'd decided long ago that there was nothing more important than my sister. "I can't do it. I have to look for her. I'm calling Nikky."

He shook his head. "You can't. They already think she's unavailable. If you drop out now and bring her in it will look suspicious. If they think we're onto them they may change the location, or the time, and we lose our chance to intervene. So you wouldn't just be stepping out of the operation, you'd be ruining it."

"I don't understand why I need to be there, if you're already sure that's where and when it's going to happen."

"The Nottingham holiday bash is always tightly controlled. No one gets in without an invitation. We can't get anyone inside at the actual event. I need you there, watching."

"Watching for what? And do you really think Nottingham's going to poison a room full of people while he's there?"

"No. That's why you have to be there. To see if and when Nottingham leaves the building. When he does it's as clear a sign as we're going to get that the attack is imminent."

"So I'm supposed to stick around and get poisoned?"

"No. If you see him leave, you contact us. We can be there within a minute."

I didn't care what he said. I had to look for my sister.

I shook my head.

He sighed. "Where do you think she is?"

"I don't know. Probably somewhere looking for a fix. Her primary hangouts were the homeless camp under Wacker downtown, and the tent city further south under the Dan Ryan Expressway near Taylor. I don't know who her dealer is now. Her last one is dead."

He looked at me. "Frank Chimen? The guy they found floating in the river?"

I looked away, expecting a lecture.

He surprised me. "We'll talk about that later. Look, if I put someone on the street to look for her, will you do this?"

"Who?"

"I know one of the undercover agents, he goes out when we conduct operations that involve drugs and the gangs. I can ask him to look for her."

"So I'm supposed to trust some UC of yours that I've never met, who has his own stuff to do, to find my sister? Does he at least work for you?"

"No, but I'm his superior. And he's not involved in any operations at the moment."

"Would he honestly look for her?"

"I'll make sure of it."

I stepped toward him, pointing at his chest. "I mean it, Smith. If you fuck me around on this I'll walk away in a heartbeat." Part of my inducement to work with Smith in the first place had been to keep Gigi out of prison. And he'd kept his end of the bargain, making sure that the times she got picked up by law enforcement, for soliciting, or drugs, she had a get-out-of-jail-free card.

"No, I know. Mike Rivers is good. Give me a list of her past hangouts and I'll have him check them out. If she's not there he'll talk to his contacts on the street. We'll find her."

His guy might have better luck than me, anyway. "OK."

"Good, thank you," he said, exhaling and stepping back.

"As long as I've got you here, let me brief you on what's going to happen Saturday. First of all, we're going to be on the lookout for Rykov. He won't be able to get inside without one of our surveillance teams spotting him, and if we see him anywhere near the building we'll grab him before he goes in. But if he does manage to get inside you'll need to let us know. And then keep an eye on him."

"How am I supposed to do that, and watch Nottingham at the same time? I'm in charge of the whole event, you know. I'll have actual work to do."

"Don't they let you bring whoever you want to this thing?"

"Yeah. It's all hands on deck."

"Then bring more people than you need. Just make sure you're available to keep an eye on him."

"I can bring anyone?"

He nodded.

"Even Maude?" He'd said before not to involve her, that they might object to having her around since she worked for the PD.

"At this point they're not going to do anything to draw suspicion, and they're not going to wreck their big event by keeping you out of it. If they are aware she works for the PD they'll know she helps you out with this kind of thing from time to time. I was going to suggest using her, anyway. She'll be able to help you look out for Rykov. Your other main job will be to keep an eye on Nottingham. If you see him leave, you let us know immediately."

"OK. But I mean it. I want to know the second your guy finds Gigi."

I left him and drove home to pack a large bag, and then went back to the Nottinghams. I'd be staying at the cottage until we did the Union Station bash. There was too much work to do to deal with going back and forth to my place every night.

I puttered around the kitchen and the pantry, making an inventory of what they had and what I needed to buy. It took a while, as I had some new ideas for the menu, different than what I'd originally envisioned before talking to Smith.

By the time I retired to the cottage it was well after midnight. I took a shower and dropped into bed, a little relieved Tasia hadn't come by. I needed to sleep.

I was just nodding off when I heard a car pull up in front of the main house.

The car doors opened and closed, and I waited to hear the sound of the front door. Instead there were muted voices. One of them sounded like a woman.

They moved from the front of the house to the backyard.

I went to the window and peered around the edge of the blinds.

A slim sliver of light grazed the yard as the door to the basement opened. I couldn't get a look at who was going in. Several sets of footsteps shuffled on the pavement pad before the door closed.

Now that I thought about it, I'd heard people going in and out of that door in the middle of the night before. But on those nights I'd been with Tasia, and had better things to do than check out who was coming and going.

Late night meetings through the back entrance. Was it Rykov?

I made myself stay awake, listening. Ninety minutes later the basement door opened and closed again. A few moments later the car in the driveway started up and drove away.

TWENTY-TWO

Smith had said to bring whoever I wanted to help with the event, so I could focus less on the meal and more on keeping tabs on Nottingham with one eye out for Rykov. But it was one thing to ask for help, it was another to recruit people who didn't know they might be exposing themselves to a deadly nerve agent.

Asking Michael was a nonstarter. His family had just gotten him back. And normally I would've brought in Declan, Elliott, Michael, and even Zoe. The four of them could do the whole thing on their own.

But I couldn't put them in harm's way, either. So instead I'd adjusted the menu, constructing dishes that while clearly high end, wouldn't involve a lot of attention just before or during service, and that could either be passed on trays or hold up as part of a buffet. Things like the caviar stations, that this crowd had come to expect, anyway, and Lobster Newburg, a dish that I could make ahead of time and didn't suffer, and perhaps benefited, from some time in a chafing dish.

It also never hurt to go nuts with shellfish, so for the tray service I added lobster bisque shots and mini crab cakes with remoulade. These were in addition to bite-sized Pâté en Croûte, and charcuterie boards that included Wagyu and other extremely precious meats like Jamón Ibérico, Culatello di Zibello, and bresaola, and rare and expensive cheeses, including Pule, made from the milk of Balkan donkeys from Serbia, which retailed at almost $600 per pound.

I still couldn't do it alone. So I'd reluctantly asked Maude. She at least worked for the police and would know what she was getting into. Even though I'd suggested it to Smith, I didn't feel great about it.

"Are you sure you want to do this?" I asked her, for the fifteenth time.

We'd just arrived at Union Station and were standing on Canal Street, in front of one of the large pillars that lined the face of the building.

"Very sure. I'm kind of looking forward to it. I don't get to rub elbows with the fat cats very often. And I trust Jeb. If he says he'll stop the whole thing before anything happens, he will."

I looked up and down the street. Smith had said the area would be crawling with surveillance.

"I don't see any of them. Do you think they're here? He said they'd be blanketing the place."

"The van at the corner, the homeless guy, the green and white taxi, for starters," she said, without looking around.

"Did he tell you that?" She was miked up, and Smith's voice would be in her ear the entire evening.

"No. It's just obvious if you know what you're looking for."

The party was being held in Union Station's Great Hall, one of the city's most renowned architectural achievements. Spacious and majestic by virtue of the domed ceiling alone, the room was festooned with ornate plasterwork, marble floors, and columns, all enveloped by soft ambient lighting that was enhanced by the skylights overhead.

We walked through the Hall to the kitchen service area.

"That guy there, and there." Maude nodded her head slightly to a security guard and a janitor. "And there's probably a bunch of them downstairs on the concourses."

Normally Union Station, like most big event venues in the city, required that people renting their space use their preferred caterers. But, as always, the rules were different when the Nottinghams were involved.

Their driver had brought over all of the food and equipment I needed, and we spent the next several hours setting up.

Like all of Nottingham's parties, most people arrived on time, and at six o'clock sharp a flood of VIPs walked into the hall. I was able to identify a number of them who'd been to Nottingham's dinner party, and several from Nikky's event.

It was a replay of the first dinner I'd done on the *Enterprise*, with several times as many guests. Alan, Celeste, Tasia, and

Martin made their entrances shortly after six thirty. Richard Nottingham was one of the last to show up, flanked as always by his security team.

He, Alan, and Celeste worked the room, shaking hands, every now and then Nottingham would engage in brief one-on-one conversations with a very important person.

Tasia and Martin took up their positions on one side of the room, next to one of the bars, as far away from their dad and the mass of people as was possible. I didn't think it was a coincidence that they were near the hallway with the bathrooms. Martin wouldn't want to venture very far to refill his nostrils.

Tasia looked great, tonight wearing black leather pants and a black satin shirt. I caught her eye a few times and she smiled.

It meant a lot, that smile, especially since she didn't do it very often. I was looking forward to seeing her later. Provided we weren't all sick or dead from Novichok.

The extended tray service we were employing for most of the food was augmented by caviar stations and a rotating set of buffet options. Not just because most of it could be prepared ahead of time, but so I could circulate as needed in the main room to keep an eye on Nottingham.

Maude and I had worked it out so that one of us would be in the main room at all times. When one of our trays emptied, the other would step out. It was a little tricky and required focus, which I didn't mind. It kept my mind off Gigi.

We also had the benefit of the extra servers I'd trained to keep the champagne flowing, handle the two full bars, and clear plates.

I felt bad for them. They had no idea what they might be exposed to tonight.

Maude and I got into a rhythm and the time passed quickly. Two hours into the party, Nottingham hadn't left the room once, not even to go to the bathroom. And there had been no sign of Rykov. Maybe this wasn't going to be the night.

I hoped so. Between watching Nottingham, keeping an eye out for Rykov, serving a meal for seven hundred guests, and Gigi's disappearance, my nerves were stretched tight. I was relieved when things started to wind down. The ending time was ostensibly ten o'clock, and it was getting close to that.

By now my part of the evening was done. We'd cleaned up the buffet and I was walking around with the last tray, primarily as an excuse to stay on the floor. Most people were filing out, although a few looked like they were here for the long haul, making good use of the open bar. Nottingham as always was still working the room, focused on one of the few groups of remaining guests.

Another group was standing near the back, just outside the hallway to the bathrooms. They'd been drinking pretty heavily all night, which was unusual for one of Nottingham's parties, as they tended to be more about business than celebration. But it didn't look like these guys were in any hurry to stop.

I used the opportunity to take the tray over to Tasia and Martin.

"Hey Martin."

"Hey Sags." He didn't look as wasted as usual, and I'd noticed he'd made relatively few trips to the bathroom to coke up.

"See anything you like?" I held the tray down to Tasia.

"Definitely," she said, looking me up and down. "You'll be at the house tonight?"

"Oh yeah."

"Great.

"See you soon."

She stood up. "Be back in a sec. Ready to go?" she said to Martin. "I think we've fulfilled our familial duty."

He nodded, and we both watched her walk down the hallway to the bathroom.

I started to head back to the kitchen when I heard, "Here's one. A Catholic priest, a schoolteacher, and—"

The drinkers were telling jokes. Bad ones. I kept going until I heard the sound of a glass breaking behind me.

Martin had pushed his way in between two of the men and was standing in the middle of the group, empty-handed, broken glass on the floor next to him.

"You think that's funny? What the fuck is wrong with you?"

I'd never seen him raise his voice, much less yell at anyone. Now that I thought about it, I'd never even seen him angry. Sullen, bored, brooding, occasionally grumpy, vacant, drunk, high . . . But never angry.

He grabbed one of the drinks from the man next to him and threw it in his face, then tossed the glass on the floor at his feet.

The men were backing up, still laughing.

Zach was there in a flash, pushing his way between them, grabbing onto Martin's arm to pull him away.

Martin stood his ground. "You want to know what's really funny? Drop dead, funny?" The room had quieted at the sound of the broken glass, and out of the corner of my eye I saw Mason fast-walking over.

He shouldered past the men and shoved Zach out of the way. He grabbed Martin's arm roughly and pulled him out of the circle. Martin struggled to keep up as Mason dragged him across the floor and through a door out of the main room. Zach tried to follow them but was turned away by one of the other security goons who'd stepped over to block the door.

As always, their treatment of Martin was ruthless and efficient, and barely noticeable to the partygoers, who wasted no time returning to their upscale revelry.

Tasia returned from the bathroom. "Where's Martin?"

"Mason took him away."

"Why? What happened?" she said, looking around.

"I don't know. One minute he was sitting here, the next he was breaking glass and throwing a drink in the face of that guy." I pointed to the circle of men, still drinking and laughing. "He was telling a joke, and Martin went nuts. I thought he was going to kill him."

She paled. "Where did they take him?"

"I don't know. They went that way." I pointed to the back of the room. She wasted no time in heading over to it, stopping on the way to speak to Zach who was still trying to get through the door.

"It's a bust." Maude had come out of the kitchen and was standing next to me. "Rykov's been spotted across town. Smith says we can wrap up . . . *Hello*. Earth to Sags." She snapped her fingers in front of my face.

"Sorry. They just took Martin away." I turned toward her. "We're done?"

"Yep. No attack tonight, apparently."

"How do they know Nottingham's not leaving anything here, like they did on the *Enterprise*?"

"They're going to bring in dogs, do a sweep, leave some agents around the station. The first responders are staying on alert. But our job's done."

"Good. I was running out of reasons to be out here."

Nottingham, Alan, and Celeste were still talking to the few remaining people. Neither Martin nor Mason had come back, and there was no sign of Tasia.

Maude and I returned to the kitchen to pack up our stuff, then left through one of the back doors.

We didn't call for a car right away. It was a cold and clear December night, perfect for strolling.

"Wanna get a drink?" Maude asked.

"Don't you have task force codebreaking to work on?" She'd already taken almost the entire day off.

"I'm stuck, and giving my brain a rest. Sometimes it helps to step away, give my subconscious a chance to figure it out."

"Sure. But let's do it somewhere else." Tasia had taken off, and I didn't want to run into anyone else from the family while I was relaxing.

We took a Lyft back to Andersonville and walked over to the Hopleaf.

Sporting sixty-two different beers on tap and in bottles, the Hopleaf had been an Andersonville institution since 1992. Multilevel, with brick and wood interior and a solid seasonal food menu, it had been our go-to since we moved into the neighborhood.

We got our beers and took a seat on the upper level.

"Thanks for helping tonight. I know you're not a fan of undercover work."

"It was OK, I actually had a good time. I wish we'd been able to catch Nottingham doing something, though."

It had been a stressful day, and we were both fine sitting in silence.

"How are things going with Smith?" I asked after a few minutes. "Are you guys still not getting any time together?"

"We're not, and it's pissing me off. I think he's seeing more of you than me."

"I'm sorry about that." The understatement of the year.

"How about you and Tasia? Something tells me this is more than just a convenient booty call."

I looked down into my beer, smiling. "I think it might be. I like her."

"Strong sentiment, coming from you. And I don't blame you. She's rich, and hot."

"Not just hot. She's smart, and kind of . . . fierce, you know?"

"I do. You like women with an edge. And you could do worse. Actually, you have done worse. Speaking of murderous felons, ever hear from Ekaterina?"

"No. Not since she tried to kill me." I didn't want to think about her. "Tasia and I have more in common than you would think. She's very protective of her brother."

"From what I've heard, she needs to be. He's a mess."

"Their mom disappeared when they were little, and it hit Martin the hardest. She takes care of him."

Thinking about Tasia and Martin made me think about Gigi. Maude knew it, and said, "Have you heard from her?"

I shook my head. "Smith's got one of his guys looking for her."

"I know. Mike Rivers. He's one of the best." She reached over and held my hand. "He'll find her. And you know they say it takes several trips to rehab before it sticks. She stayed longer this time than ever, didn't she?"

"She did. Two weeks. I thought with Frank Chimen dead it would be harder for her, you know, to get pulled back to the street."

"I don't think we should talk about Frank Chimen. I am with the police, you know."

"I know." I looked at my phone, a little surprised that Tasia hadn't called.

"I'm going to head out," I said, finishing my beer. "Tasia's usually pretty upset when they have to haul Martin out of one of the parties. And tonight was worse than most."

"What do you mean? He didn't seem that out of control, and least not compared to what you said he's done before."

"He wasn't. That's what made it worse. And it was strange . . ."

"What?"

"I don't know. It just seemed like they pulled the trigger pretty quickly. It wasn't like he was pissing on one of the guests."

"That's a low bar . . . not peeing on anything."

"No, I mean, he seemed to be less wasted than usual. But it was weird. I've never seen him so angry."

I stood up and we exchanged a tight hug, then went outside. I watched her walk down the street while I called a car to take me to the estate.

TWENTY-THREE

The main house was quiet. I had no desire to go in, and didn't need to, so I walked around the side to the cottage. After I took a shower I laid down on the bed to wait for Tasia. I was wide awake, as usual after an event.

By three a.m. she still hadn't showed, or answered any of my messages.

I went outside and stood on the stairs in front of the cottage. Light was coming in through the French doors at the back of the main house. She might be inside.

I crunched down the gravel path to the doors, nodding to the security guy posted at the basement stairs. They knew who I was by now, and going into the kitchen at night wasn't an issue.

I stepped into the silent house and walked into the kitchen, then out to the living room. Statue Guy, the guard perpetually stationed at the front window, didn't bother turning around. I continued down the hall to Celeste's office.

Occasionally I'd seen Martin in there, availing himself of Celeste's billion-dollar vodka. He could buy his own, but I think he liked to annoy her by stealing her good booze.

The door was unlocked, and I peeked in.

The room was dark and empty.

I knew the security team schedule by now. There was always one of them walking in close circles in the backyard, next to the stairs to the basement. The only time there wasn't someone there was for the few minutes between shift breaks.

Statue Guy never moved from the front window. I wasn't sure if he ever slept. Or maybe it was several guys. Other than Mason, all of them looked alike.

Two were stationed outside in the front of the house at either side.

Zach stayed close to Martin, and Mason floated the house, usually within close proximity to Nottingham.

I'd heard Nottingham's car pull up earlier. By now he was either in bed or in his diamond cutting room, which meant Mason would either be upstairs or in the basement.

When Smith had first talked to me about this operation I hadn't been all that worried. The FBI didn't always get things right, and I'd had a hard time believing that Nottingham would throw his whole life away to do a dirty job for Putin.

But over the last few days my anxiety had grown. Tonight, at Union Station, surrounded by hundreds of party guests and thousands of others, it was starting to feel real, and I was getting scared.

Scared for the city, and for my friends and family. The FBI wouldn't have allotted all of those resources on something they thought was a long shot. Smith strongly believed that there was going to be an attack. More importantly, Maude did, too. And I trusted her judgment.

Smith wanted me to look for documents, anything that could shed light on the upcoming attack, or link Nottingham and Rykov. Either thing would provide enough cause for them to pick them up and possibly prevent something terrible from happening.

I'd never get a better chance.

I pushed the door open and walked in, closing it softly behind me. I stood still and waited for my eyes to adjust to the dark.

I turned on my phone light and stepped behind the desk. The top drawer was filled with Celeste's folders of upcoming events. I flipped through them.

This woman was really organized. She'd make a good wife to the eventual patriarch, as long as her liver didn't give out in the meantime.

The second drawer held more folders, empty ones. On top of the stack was a passport.

It was Tasia's. Celeste must have taken it in Canada, forcing Tasia into a delayed departure. Her revenge for sleeping with me.

I thought I heard a sound in the hallway and quickly closed

the drawers and turned off my phone light. I felt my way around the desk and to the door, and then opened it slowly, peering into the hallway.

No one was there. I stepped out and pulled the door closed. I walked back out to the living room, and then to the French doors, exhaling heavily when I made it outside.

Whew. I didn't know what I'd been thinking. That was beyond stupid, going into her office.

Now I was a little spooked, and really wanted to find Tasia. I crunched down the other gravel path to Martin's cottage and knocked on the door.

There was no answer. I peeked through a small slit in the blinds.

It didn't look like anyone was there, but I couldn't see the bed.

I knocked again, then tried the handle.

It was unlocked. No surprise that he didn't care enough to lock up his place. And with security crawling around it wasn't like it would be easy for someone to make it to the backyard and break in. I looked behind me.

The security guard was facing the other way. I opened the door quickly and stepped in.

The bed was made, and there were no dirty dishes on the counter. Courtesy no doubt of regular maid service.

Laying in between the two pillows on the bed were several stuffed animals. Very old, by the looks of them. A strange thing for a man his age to have.

On the side table next to the bed were framed pictures of their mother and one of Tasia. A woman's scarf was balled up next to them. Next to it was a journal.

I took a quick look behind me, then picked up the journal and opened it.

Neat, clear handwriting covered the pages, each entry dated.

I flipped through. Near the back were sets of drawings. All labeled.

The Chicago River, Wrigley Field, the Crain Building, the Monadnock Building, the Willis Tower, the Art Institute, the Bean in Millennium Park.

All of the places where the pranks had taken place, plus another one.

I looked at the dates.

The drawings had been done weeks ago.

Martin was behind the vandalism. Or, at the very least, he was working with whoever was responsible for them.

I put the journal back down on the table. I needed to call Smith and let him know. He'd want to talk to Martin.

I wasn't eager to get Martin picked up by law enforcement. He'd never been anything but nice to me. And I couldn't believe he had anything to do with hurting anyone. He was too hurt himself.

Then there was Tasia. If I ratted on her brother she'd dump me in a heartbeat. I'd do the same thing to her, if she got Gigi in trouble with the police. Not that she needed any help getting into trouble.

But, still, the FBI had originally linked the vandalism with the terrorist attack. And even if they were wrong, I didn't have a choice. I had to tell Smith.

I opened the door to the outside, pulling Smith's phone from my pocket. As I turned to go down the stoop, I heard, "Miss Pfister. Come with me, please."

Statue Guy led me through the French doors, his hand in an iron grip on my upper arm.

We went down the hallway to the far side of the house, an area that had been off limits to me. The hallway ended at a large door. We stopped in front of it and he knocked.

"Come."

He opened the door and pushed me through.

It was an office. The polar opposite of Celeste's, this one contained no plush rug, no couch, no pillows, no windows, no books, no flowers, no bar. Nothing on the walls, other than a small clock. Just a couple of filing cabinets against the wall and several computer monitors on the desk.

Mason sat behind the spartan metal desk, staring at me while his colleague pulled me roughly down into a straight-backed chair across from him.

"What were you doing in Mr. Nottingham's cottage?"

So it was Mr. Nottingham now.

"I was looking for Tasia."

"Why?"

I wasn't sure how to answer that. I assumed at this point that he knew that Tasia and I had been sleeping together. And it didn't seem politic to say that I was worried, after watching him bum-rush Martin out of the family's holiday event.

He stared at me.

I didn't know what to say. I was tired, and it was hard to come up with something. So I said nothing.

It seemed like minutes went by, the only sound in the room my own breathing.

The silence was broken up by a knock at the door. Mason ignored it.

"We can sit here all night. You're not leaving until you tell me the truth."

The knock turned to banging. Mason frowned, and nodded to Statue Guy.

He opened the door and Tasia pushed past him into the room.

"What's going on?"

"Security. It's none of your concern."

"You're damn right it's my concern." She stepped forward and put her hand on my arm. "She's coming with me."

"No she's not. We caught her going through Martin's things."

If Tasia was surprised, or dismayed, by learning I'd been in Martin's cottage, she didn't show it. "She had permission from me."

Mason stood up. The two of them glared at each other.

Eventually he sat back down, and waved his hand dismissively at the door.

She pulled me up and we walked out into the hallway.

"What—"

"Shhhh."

I followed her to the front of the house and then outside. One of the drivers was waiting. She got in the back of his car, waving at me to join her.

"Where—"

"SHHHH."

I joined her in the back and he pulled out of the driveway and went through the gate. We drove in silence for a half an hour, south and toward the lake. He dropped us off at the corner of Irving Park and Ashland, then drove off.

As soon as he was gone, I said, "I'm sorry, I went to Martin's cottage to look for you, and the door was un—"

"Martin's gone."

"What do you mean, he's gone?"

"I mean I haven't seen him since Union Station."

"Where does he usually go, when Mason drags him out?"

"It depends. Usually he just gets taken home. But he hasn't been there. And he's not answering my calls."

"Has he disappeared before?"

She nodded. "Yes. But never without letting me know. And he always answers my calls. Always."

"Why not tell the security team? Isn't that what they do?"

"I think they're the ones that took him."

TWENTY-FOUR

"Maybe he's out at a party?"

We'd stepped into an all-night diner near where we'd been dropped off, and were sitting next to each other in a small booth in the back.

"No," she said, shaking her head. "No matter where he goes, or how messed up he is, if he's awake he answers my call. I've been calling him for hours and haven't heard a thing. I'm really worried."

She looked it. And I doubted she'd had any more sleep than I'd had in the last two days.

"What makes you think the security team has him? I mean, Mason took him out of the party, but that happens all the time. And I thought Zach was his friend."

"He is. He doesn't know where Martin is. He's worried, too."

I liked Zach, but still felt compelled to ask. "Do you believe him?"

"Yes." She looked down. "He's always been protective of Martin."

"OK. Well, why don't you go to the police?"

She snorted. "Given the amount of money my father can throw around it would be unfathomable that at least a few of them aren't on his payroll. And I have no idea which ones."

"You think your father is behind this?"

"I think his security team is, and Mason doesn't do anything without his direction and approval."

"Why would he want them to take Martin away?"

"I don't know. He was on his best behavior last night. It doesn't make any sense."

She put her arms around my neck and I hugged her.

"They wouldn't hurt him, would they?" I asked.

"No. I mean, I don't think so."

I wasn't so sure. "I'm sorry, I'm not sure what I can do."

She leaned back. "Can't you get your law enforcement friends to look into it?"

My stomach dropped. "What are you talking about?"

"C'mon, Sags, I'm not a dummy. I know you're working with someone in law enforcement."

I couldn't think of anything to say. I just shook my head.

"There's no other reason why you'd want to work for this family when you have so many other options. You've been spying on us."

"I told you, I was looking for something else to do. And I like being able to cook without a budget."

"Sure. OK. What about the fact that you have two phones, one of which you never answer when I'm around? You either have a secret girlfriend, or you're working with someone in law enforcement. I'm pretty sure I'm keeping you busy enough that you don't need another girlfriend. So who is it? The police?"

"No." My head was spinning.

"The FBI?"

I blanched.

"FBI, then."

God, I was terrible at keeping secrets. At least other people's. I wasn't cut out for this.

"Look, I don't know what you're doing for them, and I don't care. I don't even care if they're after Martin."

"Why would anyone be after Martin?"

"I don't know. He does a lot of drugs, he probably looks like the weak link in the family, and there are people who love to take down the rich."

"Is that what you think I'm doing?" I leaned back, incredulous.

She put her hands up. "I said, I don't know. And I don't care. I just want to find my brother. Please." She leaned forward, and put her arms around me again.

I didn't know if Tasia was aware that Martin was behind the vandalism. And now that the FBI had linked the vandalism to the terrorist threat, it meant that Martin could be involved in that, too. I couldn't see it, but I'd been wrong before.

I needed time to think.

"OK. I'll see what I can do."

When I got home Maude and Linda were in the kitchen.

"Hey guys. How's it going?"

"Great," said Linda, smiling. "We're making progress on the Frank Chimen murder."

For the third time in twenty-four hours I could feel myself breaking out in a cold sweat. I hoped she didn't notice.

"Murder? I thought it was a drug overdose?"

"It was. But it wasn't self-administered. The ME found a puncture wound on the side of his thigh. Not somewhere they usually inject. And it turns out the amount was way in excess of what it would take to kill someone. There's no doubt, he was murdered. We're getting a hold of video footage from the surrounding businesses and calling for anyone who might have been around at that time to see if they saw anything. It's only a matter of time until we find out what happened."

I snuck a look at Maude, who was studiously avoiding my gaze.

This was Linda's first case as a lead detective, and she'd do anything to close it. So far I'd been protected in my extracurricular activities by Smith, but only when I'd promised to stop. I wasn't sure he would keep it up.

"Well, good luck."

I always thought when people said they "smelled fear" it was poetic license. But now I knew it wasn't.

Fear smelled like sour sweat. I couldn't wait to get it off me.

I left the kitchen and went downstairs to take a long shower. When I was done I called Smith.

"Martin's behind the vandalism."

"What? Oh."

"I thought you'd be more excited to know that."

"We don't think the pranks and the terrorist threat are linked anymore. At least, I don't. I never did."

Thanks for telling me. "And, uh, he's missing."

"Why are you telling me this?"

"I was hoping you could help find him."

"Talk to the police. Missing persons isn't my job."

He was being a dick. And it would be getting worse very quickly.

"Tasia knows I'm working with you."

I could hear his sharp intake of breath.

He managed to get out "Rosehill. Twenty minutes," before hanging up.

I walked to the cemetery, listening to the crackling of my wet hair as it froze in the cold air.

Smith didn't wait until I was next to him to start yelling at me, apparently no longer caring that anyone heard us.

"I was extremely clear, that under no circumstances were you to tell her anything about this operation."

"I didn't tell her, she guessed. And she doesn't care."

He was pacing, stopping every few steps to point a finger in my face. "I could arrest you for this."

I pointed back. "That's not fair. I didn't tell her. And you knew when you put me up to this that I'm not an agent. I'm not trained, and I don't know what I'm doing. It's a miracle everyone doesn't know."

He continued to pace, shaking his head.

"C'mon, Smith. She's not going to say anything to anyone. She's worried about her brother. And I am, too."

He stepped in front of me, his voice dropping down to normal volume. "I told you, missing persons is not my job. She needs to talk to the police."

"She can't. She thinks her dad owns them."

"There's nothing I can do."

"Fine. But I'm done with this. Find someone else to spy on the Nottinghams."

I turned to walk away.

He pulled on my shoulder, spinning me around. "No, you're not."

I shook off his hand. "Keep your hands off me. And yes, I am. I got caught, looking around for the things you wanted me to look around for," I said, pointing at him again. "I was literally dragged into Mason's office. If it weren't for Tasia I might still be there. Or wherever they took Martin. Or worse. You said this wouldn't be dangerous. Well, it got dangerous. I'm out."

"You can't be out."

"Wanna bet?"

"Can you just keep it together, for two more days?" His voice had shifted from angry to pleading.

"How do you know it's just two more days? You thought it would be over yesterday."

He sat down on the bench and patted the place next to him. After a few moments I joined him.

"Remember the pipeline explosions in the Baltic Sea, three years ago?"

"Vaguely."

"There were a series of underwater explosions that effectively destroyed two gas pipelines. There's no definitive proof who was responsible, as a number of entities, including several countries, and anyone producing liquified natural gas, benefited from it. After it happened we went back and looked over Rykov's accounts. Eighteen months before the explosion he got an infusion of money, a little over two million dollars. He got another one six months later. Then two days before the pipeline blew, four million dollars moved in and out of his account. While people point out that the explosion might have hurt Russia, and Russia says Ukraine was responsible, Russian hard-liners definitely benefited, as it had the effect of creating increased tensions between Europe and the US over energy policy."

"That's all less than marginally interesting, and so what?"

"This morning five million dollars was deposited into Rykov's account. We believe this is the last one. And if so, it means the attack is happening within forty-eight hours."

"I don't get it. What's all of this money for? I mean, how expensive can it be to set off a bomb? Don't random psychos put them together in their basements, from instructions they read off of the internet?"

"Something on the scale we think they're planning requires

more money. A lot more. Why do you think there aren't more large-scale terrorist attacks? Think about it." He paused, giving me time to think about it. "Given what's already transpired, we're pretty sure they're going to do it with Novichok. If so, we told you before, they'd need to find or build a lab to make it."

"Don't they do that in Russia?"

"They do, but they'd have to transport it here, and it's difficult to move around, especially in the quantity they would need. There's the danger of it being found during transport, and also that it might leak. Even the release of a tiny amount would be noticed. So they're likely making it here, which means he had to pay to set up a lab."

"I thought Stokes said they were using precursors?"

"They did with the test device, and probably will with the main one, or ones, as well. But import and exports of those chemicals are tightly controlled, too. For something like this I don't think they'd risk trying to smuggle them into the country. They'd make them here. So they'd need a lab to make the precursors, and it would need to be equipped to allow testing of a small amount of the final product. That means specialized equipment. Then once the device, or devices, were made, Rykov would need to hire people to help place them. People are expensive; most of us aren't eager to cause widespread death and destruction. But some can be convinced if the amount of money they're offered is enough to change their lives. Life-changing money means enough to quit jobs and move away. Millions of dollars, basically, to retire comfortably and get somewhere they would never be found. This is the biggest expense, money for people.

"So, no, we're not one hundred percent sure it's happening in the next two days, but pretty damn close to it. His pattern is to bring in and pay his accomplices shortly before the attack, to minimize the chances of being found out."

"If that's the case, why were you so sure it was going to happen at Union Station?"

"It's not an exact science."

No shit. I rolled my eyes. "I think you need to consider that you might be wrong about all of this. Nottingham's not a great guy, but you haven't told me anything that proves he's planning a terrorist attack. You haven't linked him or anyone else in the family to the thing on the *Enterprise*. All you've done is found out that Rykov is getting money from someone. And you have nothing whatsoever that points to Nottingham as the guy providing it. And another thing. You said he'd broken all ties to Russia, and that he's gone to great lengths to appear English. But he's not hiding his gastronomic proclivities."

The tea he loved and that we'd served him on the *Enterprise* was Kalmyk tea. And the tray of food that Percy prepared, horse ribs and cheese cubes, was a staple of some Siberian ethnic groups. Not to mention the Kumis. So while Nottingham physically modeled a white ethnic Russian, it was likely that whoever ran the orphanage he grew up in was not.

He stared at me blankly. "We found the lab." For some reason he'd not wanted to give me that piece of information at the beginning.

I swallowed hard. "Where? How?"

"A warehouse in North Lawndale. We found the precursors and test samples. It's Novichok. Fortunately it's one of the formulations that we're familiar with. The size of the lab, the containers, the samples . . . the amount they're making? It's a hundred times what was left on the *Enterprise*."

"How did you find it?"

"A couple of kids broke in." He paused. "One of them is in the hospital. The other one . . ." he looked down.

"As far as Nottingham's food goes, it's not like he's spending time in Russian restaurants. Almost all of what you're describing happens at his estate. He's been an inactive sleeper agent for decades, and he's nearing the end of his life; it's not out of the realm of possibility that he's been lax about that one piece of security."

He put his hands on my shoulders and looked me in the eye. "Regardless, I just don't have any more time or energy to spend convincing you. So I'll say this one more time: I am one hundred percent certain there's going to be a terrorist attack in the city, very soon, that Rykov is organizing it, and that Nottingham is helping him. And that it will involve Novichok."

I didn't want to believe him. But I did.

The lab made it real. Dead children made it monstrous.

"What's going on with Gigi?" I asked, stalling for time, even though I could feel myself giving in.

"Agent Rivers is on the streets as we speak, looking for her."

He leaned back. "I know going back to the Nottinghams is a big ask. I wouldn't do it if I didn't think it was critically important."

"Mason is watching me. I can't do anything without them seeing me. And I'm worried about what they'll do if Tasia isn't around. They disappeared Martin, and he's Nottingham's son. What do you think they'll do to me if they catch me snooping around? And I told you before, I doubt there's anything laying around, anyway, that would be of any use."

"You don't have to look around for anything. We're past that. At this point I just need you to let me know Nottingham's movements in and out of the house. And especially if he takes another trip out of the city."

Smith was persuasive, no doubt why they had him running the informants.

"Two more days. That's it," I said.

The specter of a terrorist attack didn't bother me quite as much as the idea that Nottingham might get away with it. I wanted him to pay. For whatever he was trying to do to the city, and whatever he'd done to Martin.

And possibly for something else. After getting a look at the inside of Martin's cottage, another idea was taking root. An appalling one.

"Fine. But you need to find Gigi."

He didn't bother trying to hide a sigh of relief. "We will. Don't worry."

We both stood up. "I mean it, Smith. If you're stringing me along about her—"

"I'm not. We're doing everything we can to find her."

I nodded. "I'll go back tomorrow. Right now I need to get some sleep."

I went home, and after as cursory a discussion as I could get away with, left Maude and Linda for the downstairs and fell into bed.

After staring at the ceiling for what seemed like hours I gave up trying to sleep.

I put my clothes on and walked to the L stop on Argyle. Then I waited for the train.

TWENTY-FIVE

The L's Red and Blue lines run all night, making Chicago one of three cities in the world with twenty-four-hour train service.

The clientele at three in the morning is what you'd expect, primarily sleeping drunks and homeless people trying to stay warm. I didn't take the L late at night very often. Just once, recently, the morning before I met with Smith at the diner. When all of this had started.

I'd never met Frank Chimen. Over the last several years he'd become the most important person in Gigi's life.

"I need to get back, Frank will be mad." Or, "I need to see Frank."

Her code for "I need a fix."

She'd had a variety of dealers and pimps over the years. Chimen was the worst of them. I couldn't remember the last time I saw her when she didn't have bruises on her face. Sometimes older yellow ones, other times fresh purple and red. More often than not a mix of the two.

Maybe that was why he kept her around.

Chimen made his living off of desperate, addicted girls, of which there was no shortage. Gigi was older than the rest of them. I knew this because occasionally I'd give her a lift and would see them when I dropped her off. Girls that looked ten years or more younger than her, teenagers who should be in high school.

The younger girls were in higher demand. But Gigi . . . she'd almost aged out. So he used her for his punching bag. He wouldn't want to damage the faces of the younger girls, who were better earners.

The experts said I was enabling her by letting her crash at my place and giving her money. But the way I saw it, one night of good sleep and food where she didn't have to sleep on the street and pimp herself out or get beaten up by her pimp was one night for her to think about what it might be like to get out of this version of her life.

The last time she'd stayed with me I thought it was odd, in July, that she wore long sleeves. She'd crashed on our couch, and as I pulled the blanket up over her I saw a set of cigarette burns on her arms. That's when I decided that Frank had to go.

I knew her hangouts, where she went to get a fix. Where Frank Chimen spent his time. I got off at the Clark/Lake L stop and walked to the homeless encampment underneath Wacker.

"Is Frank around?" I asked the people huddled around small fires, or leaning against makeshift shelters, doing my best to sound in desperate need of a fix.

It wasn't hard, I'd seen Gigi enough times in this state to know exactly what she sounded like. And how she looked. I shuffled on unsteady feet, and made my hands shake.

No one had seen him. I walked the length of the encampment.

"Is Frank around?" I asked anyone within earshot.

"Over there," said a man, his face peering out of a sleeping bag. He pointed to one of the stone pillars that held up upper Wacker.

A man was leaning over a young woman who was sitting on the ground, her back against the pillar.

He slapped her in the face. "Where's the rest of it?"

She was crying. He spit on her and stood up.

I shuffled over to him. "Are you Frank?"

"Who wants to know?"

"I need a fix."

"You got money?"

I pulled a wad of crumpled ones out of the pocket of the hoodie I was wearing.

He snorted. "That's not nearly enough, babe."

He looked me up and down before he leaned over and pulled the hoodie down off my head, then reached over and unzipped it, pulling it partially off my shoulders.

He looked me up and down again.

"Maybe you can pay with something else."

He put his hand on the top of my head and started to push.

"Not here," I said. "Why don't we go somewhere more private?"

He smiled. "Sure, why not." Then walked away.

He didn't look back. He knew I would follow him.

He walked out from lower Wacker toward the river. He stepped over the low barrier and went toward the playground next to the water.

The Riverwalk was closed every day between eleven p.m. and six a.m., when they turned off the lights and closed the flimsy gates. Infrequent security patrols walked the sidewalk.

Chimen stepped over another small barrier and walked down a shallow ramp to a small dock.

"Private enough for you?"

He leaned next to the low railing, his hands moving to his zipper.

I hadn't planned exactly where I was going to do it, just that it needed to be somewhere where there weren't a lot of people around.

This was a perfect spot. His body would be washed downstream, turning up miles from the city, if it turned up at all. They might not even discover he was dead.

I dropped to my knees, at the same time slipping the syringe out of my pocket. Before he'd finished unzipping his pants I jabbed it into his thigh and pushed the plunger in as far as it would go.

"Hey!" Almost immediately he started to gasp.

It took a minute or so before he slumped back against the railing. I stood, leaning in close to hold him up. Anyone going by would think we were making out.

I don't know if he was still breathing when I levered him over the side of the low railing. I heard his body splash into the water, then pulled my hood up to cover my face and walked back up the ramp to the Riverwalk.

I climbed over the barrier and went to Wabash, then walked south, joining the ambling trickle of people on the sidewalks.

Once I was several blocks away from the river I turned toward the L station. I walked up to the platform and waited for the train to take me home.

This morning I managed to check out three of Gigi's spots before I gave up. No one had seen her, at least no one who was able and willing to talk to me.

I took the L back home and fell into bed.

This time I fell asleep immediately, and was out like a light when my ringing phone woke me up at ten.

It was Ellis. "Mrs. Nottingham would like to see you."

TWENTY-SIX

Ellis greeted me at the front door and escorted me back to Celeste's office.

She was going through her desk drawers and stuffing files into her valise.

"The family is taking a trip," she said, not looking up.

"Oh. Where are we going?"

She ignored me, continuing to go through the desk.

"Uh, what time should I be at the airport?"

"You won't be coming. Your services here are no longer required. You may clean your things out of the cottage."

She turned to pick a few tchotchkes off of the windowsill behind her.

"Oh, OK," I said to her back. "Thanks for letting me cook for you."

She turned around and looked at me. A little sadly, I thought. Then she went back to packing.

That was it. I stood there awkwardly for a moment, then followed Ellis out the door.

She hadn't needed to call me in to tell me they were letting me go. She could just have easily done it over the phone. Or had Ellis do it. I wondered why.

As we walked through the living room and to the cottage it occurred to me that if Smith was right, and the attack took place soon, Nottingham would make sure his family was safely out of the area when it happened.

Not only that, but even if the FBI was able to stop the attack, Nottingham would be gone. I didn't know where they were going for their family trip, but I guessed it was somewhere without an extradition arrangement with the US. Like Russia.

The thought of him getting away made me furious.

Ellis stood just inside the door while I packed, no doubt

making sure I didn't abscond with any of the furnishings or bottles of Bollinger.

"Am I allowed to use the bathroom without an escort?" I asked, only half joking.

He nodded. I went into the bathroom and closed the door, then quietly opened up my small travel bag. After a few moments I flushed, then walked back out.

"I think I left a couple of things in the kitchen." He nodded again and followed me out and back into the house.

The kitchen was empty. I wondered if Percy had been invited on the family trip.

I opened the refrigerator. On the top shelf were two bottles of Nottingham's Kumis.

"I thought I had a few things in here," I said loudly, rummaging around. "I guess I was wrong."

As I was standing in front of the refrigerator Percy walked into the kitchen. I closed the door quickly.

"Hey, Percy. Getting ready for the trip?"

He shuffled to one of the cupboards and rooted around in it, pulling out a thermos and some containers and setting them on the counter.

"They've relieved me of my services. I'm making Mr. Nottingham a lunch to take with him."

"Wow. How long have you worked for them?"

"Twenty-five years."

Damn. "I'm sorry. What are you going to do now?"

He shook his head, his eyes vacant. "I don't know."

I'd watched him since I'd started with the family. He wasn't exceptionally talented, but he was a solid chef and a hard worker. Two valuable traits in a kitchen. "Listen, when you're ready, come by Saga. There might be an opening."

Turnover in the industry was high, and we were always looking for people.

"OK," he mumbled, already focused on making Nottingham's last nasty lunch. To go.

I left the kitchen and joined Ellis back in the cottage.

"Do you mind?" I said. "I'm going to change."

"I'll see you in the foyer when you're ready." He turned and left.

As soon as he went back into the main house I pulled out Smith's phone.

"They're leaving."

"Who?"

"The family. Celeste was packing, and told me my services were no longer required."

"OK." He took a deep breath. "Do you know where they're going?"

"No, but she looked like she was in a hurry."

"Is Nottingham there?"

"I don't know. I haven't seen him this morning. But his car is still in front."

"Good. Let me know when you see him leave."

"That's not going to happen. I'm grabbing my things and then they're escorting me off the grounds."

We hung up and I pulled out my other phone and opened the rideshare app. I scheduled a pickup in ten minutes and grabbed my bag.

"Who were you talking to?"

I jumped. Mason was standing in the doorway.

"Rideshare," I said, showing him my phone.

"No, who were you talking to on your other phone?" he said, glancing up into the corner of the ceiling.

Small black dots in the corners. Cameras so small I hadn't noticed them.

I should have known. This was how they'd discovered me in Martin's cottage; no doubt there were cameras in his place, too.

Mason hadn't reacted when I'd rooted around in Celeste's office. The cameras must be reserved for the cottages. It wasn't much of a surprise; the very wealthy eschewed being spied upon. No way would Richard or Celeste tolerate being surveilled by their own security team.

"I'll take that," he said, putting out his hand for my phone.

I handed it to him.

"The other one."

When I didn't move, he stepped forward and reached roughly into my pocket. He pulled out Smith's burner phone.

He opened it and spent a few moments scrolling through the call history.

There was just one number. He knew what that meant.

He dropped the phone on the floor and stepped on it, grinding it into small pieces.

Then he slipped my phone into his pocket.

He grabbed my arm and pulled me outside, and then toward the small stairwell that led to the basement.

TWENTY-SEVEN

Mason yanked me down the basement stairs and opened the door to the house. He pushed me inside and slammed it behind him.

In front of us were a set of stairs. It looked like they went up to the off-limits wing of the house.

To the right was the long hallway that led to the kitchen.

He pulled me down the hallway and into Nottingham's diamond cutting room. He pushed me to the floor next to the table and pulled out a set of zip ties.

My heart was hammering so hard I thought it would break out of my chest as he put one of them around my wrists, and then looped it around one of the table legs. He pulled it tight.

Then he left, shutting off the light and closing the door behind him.

I wasn't sure how long he was going to leave me here, or what they were going to do to me. But I didn't want to stick around to find out.

The table was bolted to the floor. I pulled on the zip tie, giving up quickly as the plastic dug into my flesh.

It was pitch black, but I knew from my previous visit down here that Nottingham kept his tools on top of the table. Some of them were sharp, almost any one of which would easily cut through a zip tie.

None of which I could reach.

I banged up against the table. Maybe I could knock something off of it.

It didn't budge.

I slammed into it as hard as I could. The only thing I managed to do was smack my forehead against the edge. Warm blood trickled down the side of my face.

I sat there, breathing hard. After a moment I flipped myself so I was laying on my back with my arms over my head. I swung my legs up and toward the table.

My toes bounced lightly just above the surface.

I readjusted, bending my elbows and bringing my arms and body closer to the table, then tried again.

Progress. I was now barely able to touch one toe on top of the table. I tried to move it around, to push something off.

Cramp. And dammit. I brought my feet back down and curled into a fetal position, trying to breathe through the sharp pain in my side.

I rested for a few moments, then tried again. If I were only an inch or so taller, or a little bit more flexible, or if I'd ever done even one sit-up in my life, this would be easy.

I moved so my elbows were sharply bent and my neck was angled to the point that my chin was pushing into my chest and my head was vertical, up against the table leg. Then I swung my legs up and over as hard as I could.

The toes on both feet hit the table hard, sending tools and stones skittering off of it. I swept both legs around to clear anything else off that I could reach.

One of my feet hit the lamp. I turned my head and closed my eyes as it crashed to the floor next to me.

I'd managed to sweep at least some of the tools off the table. Now I had to find them. I'd heard most of them hit the floor on the far side, out of reach. But not all of them. I brought my legs back down and spread them, then brought them together to gather whatever had landed near me.

When my legs were together I could feel something hard against the inside of my knees. One of the tools. I moved my bound hands up the table leg so I could sit up, then pushed the tool closer to my feet and between them. I grabbed it between my feet and brought them up, then dropped the tool within reach of my hands.

It was one of the metal nails that Nottingham used to hold the diamond against the polishing wheel.

I sat up straight, facing the table. I put the nail in between my knees and moved my bound hands back down the table leg to press the plastic into the nail.

The nail slipped over on its side. I set it up again, holding my legs together tighter now, and brought my hands down toward it.

This time I poked the nail in my wrist. Not too deep, I didn't think. And at least this time the nail stayed straight up.

I tried again, and succeeded in poking the nail into my other wrist. I shortened my strokes, and after a few more tries felt the tip of the nail meet the plastic. I poked at the zip tie a few more times, then pulled my wrists apart.

There was no give, the plastic dug into my skin.

I continued to move my hands up and down, poking the tip of the nail into the plastic. Every few strokes I completely missed the zip tie and pushed the nail into my skin. Soon my wrist was bleeding freely.

When was my last tetanus shot?

After a few minutes I stopped to pull on the tie, and to give my legs a rest from holding the nail between them.

No progress. I kept going, poking the zip tie and my wrists regularly with the nail, until after several tries I finally felt the plastic start to give.

I redoubled my efforts, moving my hands faster, only stopping every now and then to pull on the tie as hard as I could, ignoring the open wounds I'd made on both wrists.

It took what felt like an hour before I was able to break the tie. I pulled my hands apart and wiped wet blood on my pants.

I stood up on wobbly legs and felt my way to the wall and turned on the light. Then I tried the door.

It was locked. Mason must have known I wouldn't be able to get out.

I didn't have to think too hard about why he'd bothered to zip tie my hands, even with the door locked. He probably enjoyed thinking about me frantically trying to get myself out of the tie, only to be stymied by the door.

There was a keypad for the door in the hallway, which meant there must be one on the inside, too. Nottingham wouldn't have a room in which he could be locked in with no way out.

I looked around at the walls. Other than the photographs of diamonds, there was nothing.

In the room were the table and chair, Nottingham's tools, and diamonds in various stages of refinement, most of which were on the floor. Other than that, all that was there was the sawing table and Bunsen burner, and a file cabinet against the back wall. I walked over and pulled on the drawer.

Not locked. I supposed Nottingham didn't expect anyone else to be in his special diamond room.

Inside were a few files, and a ledger. Filled with numbers.

Was this what Smith had hoped I would find? I couldn't make any sense of the tables of numbers, but he would.

I was flipping through the pages when I heard the keypad in the hallway.

The door opened and Nottingham walked in. Mason was behind him.

Dammit. I should have tried to grab something to use as a weapon. Now all I could do was stare at them.

They both looked at the scattered debris on the floor around the table.

"You can go, Mason."

"Are you sure, sir?"

Nottingham didn't say anything, and after a moment Mason walked out, leaving the door slightly ajar.

Nottingham nodded to the chair. He wasn't armed as far as I could see, but even if I managed to get by him, which might be possible, given his age, Mason was lurking just outside. There was no way I'd be able to get past him.

I set the ledger, now smeared with some of my blood, on the file cabinet, then walked slowly to the table and sat down.

"Find anything interesting?"

"I don't know. Did I?" I said, nodding to the ledger.

"We've been watching you since you started working here. Did you really think we wouldn't know what you were up to?"

He said that in an "I know I'm the smartest guy in the room" voice. Which right now was accurate. I felt like an idiot.

"I don't know what you're talking about."

"You were told when you interviewed that you would undergo a thorough background check. I know everything about you."

"Everything."

"You live in Andersonville, in a large house on Ashland. You are the head chef and owner of Saga, a restaurant in Portage Park."

"Big deal. Everyone knows that."

"Your roommate is Maude Kaminski, who works for the Chicago Police Department. She is dating FBI SSA Jebediah Smith, for whom you do undercover work."

"I'd hardly call it—"

"Shut. Up."

His ice-blue eyes glittered. He wasn't smiling, but if I didn't know better I'd think he was enjoying himself.

"In your spare time it appears you are involved with, or at least in proximity to, people who die in suspicious circumstances. They all happen to be people who threaten you, or your substance-abusing sister, who funds her habit with prostitution."

"You shut up about my sister, you mo—"

"The FBI arranged things so our previous event chef had to leave, and force us to bring someone in quickly. And there you were."

"If you know all of this, why did you give me the job?"

"Keep your enemies close, as they say. Besides, there's nothing that you've been able to tell your FBI friend, is there?"

"If you were so sure of that, you wouldn't be here."

He shook his head. "We're leaving shortly, and by the time the FBI figures out what's going on it will be too late. It's mostly just curiosity."

I didn't believe that for a second. Richard Nottingham would never do anything out of idle curiosity.

But then he smiled. For only the second time since I'd met him.

A small one. A victory grin. He turned around to leave.

I really hated this guy.

"You had that jeweler killed, didn't you?" I said to his back. "Isaac Katz."

"He was also working for the FBI. I told you, we do thorough background checks on all employees. Those checks don't stop after someone's been hired. I know all about the FBI's surveillance efforts," he said, his hand on the doorknob.

"I did find out one thing."

"What's that?" he murmured, pulling open the door.

"I know why you're doing it. Why you've decided that working with a country you haven't seen in decades to carry out a terrorist attack is worth giving up everything you have."

He let go of the handle and turned around. "Oh, yes?"

"You're being blackmailed."

His expression didn't change. But there was the barest flicker in his eyes.

"That was a real thinker. Why would the famous, wealthy and powerful Richard Nottingham bother with anything that Russia wanted? Why would a man like that throw away his seat of power, and attack the country that helped him achieve it?"

I paused for effect.

"They threatened to tell the world your dirty little secret, didn't they? A secret that would destroy the most important thing in the world to you. Your reputation. And even with all of the money in the world, it wouldn't matter a single bit if everyone knew about you. A life in Russia would still be better than the whole world knowing what you are. Well, your secret's out. Wherever you go, whatever you do, everyone is going to know."

The truth was that the only person who knew it, other than his family, was me. But he didn't need to know that.

"Once I'm there it won't matter what people think. It will be chalked up to Western disinformation."

We stared at each other. But he wasn't leaving.

"Martin figured it out, didn't he?" I said, breaking the silence. "He knew what you were up to."

He sighed. "Martin is very smart. I had such high hopes for him."

"Did you kill him?"

He snorted. "Of course not. He's my son."

"Your son who you abused."

"I didn't abuse anyone. I loved him."

I noted his use of the past tense. "I'm not sure 'love' is the right word."

I'd finally figured it out, between what I'd found in Martin's cottage, and what happened at Union Station. When the group of drunks were telling jokes. One of them about a priest and an altar boy. The joke that infuriated Martin and made him totally lose it.

It all made sense now. Alan's impotence. Martin's substance abuse problem.

And the late-night car arrivals. I thought I'd been hearing women's voices, those nights when the cars came.

But they weren't women's voices. They were children's. Young boys. Brought to Nottingham several times a week.

When I figured it out I'd jettisoned any charitable thoughts I'd had about Richard Nottingham. His lost childhood in Russia, his life choices stripped away by the KGB who took him away from what he loved to do most.

He was a child abuser, and he'd been getting away with it for decades. As far as I was concerned, of all of the world's dirtbags, he was the lowest of the low.

I didn't think hell existed, but if it did, there was a special place there reserved for men like him.

"Let me guess. You stopped 'loving' both of your sons around puberty, right? You're a sick, perverted, child molester. That's why your kids hate you so much."

I expected the usual justifications, of which I was well acquainted.

They were happy; They appreciated my attention; They asked for it; I never made them do anything they didn't want to do; Children have a right to experience sex; etc., etc. . .

But he just shrugged. He didn't care enough about what I thought to waste his breath on rationalizing his behavior. The supreme narcissist.

"That's why their mother left, isn't it? She couldn't stand to be around you."

He shrugged again, which I took as tacit agreement.

"You know they're going to catch you."

He shook his head. "No," he said, looking at his watch. "They won't. We'll be gone within the hour."

That meant whatever he had planned was happening soon. And he'd said, "we'll" be gone.

Celeste was going with him, which meant Alan was, too. And certainly Mason.

"Is Tasia going with you?"

I'd been briefly mortified when I learned about the cameras in my cottage, that they might have seen Tasia and I in bed together. Now that was the least of my worries.

He frowned. "She's made her choices." He looked me up and down. "Extremely bad ones."

He turned to leave.

"Wait, isn't this where you tell me what you're going to do? Where it's going to happen? Gloat about how you're so much smarter than everyone else?"

He walked through the door and closed it behind him. I heard it lock.

I waited for Mason to come back in the room, to take me to wherever they took people.

After another half hour I was still waiting.

So Nottingham wasn't going to have me killed.

That was a relief. Someone would find me here, eventually. And at least my wrists had stopped bleeding.

But I needed to tell Smith what I knew. Nottingham was leaving within the hour.

It wouldn't do any good to yell. Even if there was anyone left in the house I doubted they'd hear me. The living areas were far away from this room.

I grabbed the largest nail I could find off the floor and used it to bang on the door.

Three bangs, then stop. I listened for any sounds in the hallway.

I banged again. Three times, then stop.

I kept it up for another half hour, but no one came. And it occurred to me that if they did, they might not be able to figure out the keypad.

Whatever was going to happen might go down while I was

in here. Maybe it would be like one of those zombie apocalypse movies, and when I finally made it out everyone would be sick, or dead. Maybe that's why Nottingham didn't bother killing me.

I slumped back down in the chair. A few of the diamonds were still on the table, although not the big, heart-shaped ones Nottingham had been working on when I'd stopped by to watch. Those had gone into Celeste's necklace.

An hour went by. I stared numbly at the pictures on the walls.

Diamonds, in various stages of refinement. Possibly cut by Nottingham himself.

When I'd first popped my head in to watch Nottingham cutting his diamonds I'd seen him reach under the table. At the time I'd thought he'd been thinking about calling security.

I leaned down and peered underneath the table.

There it was. A small black button, sitting just inside the edge.

I pressed the button, and waited.

Nothing happened.

It could be one of those silent alarms. Even if I couldn't hear it, it might be ringing loudly upstairs.

I pressed it again, and again.

I pressed it every ten seconds or so, for what felt like hours.

I kept it up until I heard footsteps in the hallway.

"In here! In here!" As soon as the words were out of my mouth I realized that it might be Mason, or one of his buddies, responding to the silent alarm.

I couldn't imagine that ending well. I stopped yelling.

But it was too late. There was the beep of the keypad, and the door clicked open.

TWENTY-EIGHT

Zach poked his head into the room.

"Am I glad to see you," I said, standing up and walking to the door.

"How long have you been down here?" His eyes grew wide when he looked at my face and arms. Dark blood had made thick circles around my wrists that was smeared to my elbows. "Are you OK?"

"I'm fine. It's been a few hours, I think. What are you doing here? Isn't everyone gone?"

"I wasn't invited on this trip with the family. I'm looking for Martin. Have you seen him?"

"No." I walked into the hallway. "Do you have a phone?"

He pulled out his cell phone and handed it to me. I called Smith.

He answered on the first ring. "Hello? Who is this? How did you get this—"

"It's me. Listen, I've been trapped in Nottingham's basement. He's leaving the country with his family. He may already be gone. Whatever he's doing is going to happen soon. Where are you?"

"In front of his house."

I gave Zach his phone back and ran up the stairs, through the kitchen, and into the foyer.

The front door was wide open. Uniformed police were streaming in and out of the house. The driveway was crowded with cars, most of them marked police vehicles.

Smith was standing next to his black SUV, talking on his phone. As I walked over to him he ended the call and opened his door.

"Are you OK?"

"I'm fine. I saw Nottingham, about an hour ago. He—"

"You can tell me on the way. We know where the attack is going to happen."

I jumped in his car and Smith pulled out.

"How did you know I was here?"

"It was the last place your phone pinged before it went offline." Of course, he always had trackers on his damn phones. "What did you learn?"

"Nottingham was getting ready to leave the country. I think Celeste, Alan, and Mason were joining him. Maybe a few others."

"Do you know where they were going?"

"He didn't say. But I think Martin might know. Have you seen him, or Tasia?"

"No."

"Let me use your phone."

He handed it to me and I called Maude. She picked up on the second ring.

"Have you found her?"

"It's me."

"Thank God. Where have you been? Jeb told me he was looking for you, he had me worried."

"I'm fine. Listen, I think I know what the keyword is to your code."

"Hang on." I heard rustling around, then keyboard clicking. "OK, go ahead."

"Try 'pedophile.'"

"Seriously?"

"Yeah."

More clicking.

"That's it! . . . Huh," she said, after a moment. "It says, 'Jardin.' Maybe you're wrong. That's not a word. At least, not in English."

"Jardin?"

"Yeah."

"Hang on . . . I think there should be seven letters. We're missing one."

"What do you mean?"

"Martin's behind the vandalism. I read his journal, he had one more prank planned, in Millennium Park. He must have gotten picked up by his dad's security before he could do it. Let's see. Jardins, Jardiniere, Jardine . . ."

"That's where we're going," murmured Smith.

"What are you talking about? Where?"

"The Jardine Water Treatment Plant. We received a warning call. Like the one we got when that device was planted on the *Enterprise*. The caller told us there was another nerve agent device at the treatment plant. It's been evacuated. Hazmat is there now."

I hung up the phone and looked at him.

"When did you get the call? The warning?"

"About two hours ago."

This didn't feel right. Nottingham was on his way out of the country. The only reason he'd be leaving is if the big attack was happening today. A little nerve agent in the water treatment plant that might kill some workers wasn't on the scale of what Smith said they were planning.

Nottingham hadn't argued when I'd told him that Martin had figured out what he was doing. Maybe it was Martin who'd made the warning calls.

"We have to find Martin."

"I told you, missing persons isn't my job."

"I think he knows what his dad's been planning. You heard me tell Maude, Martin's behind the vandalism. It was all to put attention on the code that told us where the attack was going to take place."

"We don't need him now. We know where it's taking place. Besides, you can't be sure he's not working with his dad. They might be in on it together. And if Martin did know where it was going to happen, and was supposedly so angry at his dad, why didn't he just tell us? Instead of messing about with bloody pranks and codes?"

Arghhh . . . "Smith, I talked to Nottingham. Martin's not leaving the country with them. You have to believe me, he hates his father. Nottingham's a pedophile, he abused both of his sons for years, and he's been having young boys brought to him every week. There's no way Martin's working with him."

Smith's lips curled in disgust, but he said, "That doesn't change the fact that if he does know what his dad was planning he should have told us. I'll tell you one thing, when this is over, and we do find Martin, he'll be arrested. Knowing where a terrorist attack is going to happen and not sharing that information is a felony."

I shook my head. It would be just like the FBI to make Martin a scapegoat for his father.

The Jardine Water Treatment Plant was built next to Navy Pier. We were on Ohio Street, ten minutes from the plant. Smith stopped at a red light.

"You don't seem like you're in much of a hurry. For that matter, you don't seem all that worried. Am I missing something?"

"The water treatment plant is a completely different animal than a cruise ship. These facilities are some of the most heavily guarded, secure pieces of infrastructure in the country. Access in and out of the plant is tightly controlled, and most of the operation is automated. There aren't a lot of employees, less than fifty total, and those employees are heavily vetted. It's unlikely that anyone was able to sneak a device inside the plant. But even if someone did manage to get something inside, Stokes and his team are already there, and everyone's been evacuated. We were ready, with a massive and immediate response," he said, a little smugly. "Hazmat is crawling all over the place. If there's something there, they'll find it."

"That doesn't make any sense. Why would Rykov need all of that money to kill a few workers?"

He shrugged. "Even the mention of a potential threat to the city's water supply would be enough to scare a lot of people. People have rioted for less. Our job is going to be to shut this down as soon as possible, and make sure everyone knows their water is safe."

I couldn't imagine Nottingham would go to all of this trouble just to shake public confidence.

"What about all of the money Rykov got? Why would he need that if he hadn't actually planted a device?"

"Maybe he did plant one. Maybe they didn't expect anyone to call it in," he said, dismissing the thought, although I noticed his hands fidgeted on the steering wheel, and I felt the car speed up.

"We've also had confirmation that Nottingham's helicopter took off a few hours ago. He's gone. Once we find the device I think it will finally be over."

"What about Rykov?"

"We don't know where he is. Chances are he's on the same flight out as Nottingham."

TWENTY-NINE

We drove the rest of the way in silence. Smith pulled into the driveway that led to the plant's security gate. He showed his badge and we were allowed through.

The Jardine Water Treatment Plant was the largest capacity water filtration plant in the world. Along with the Sawyer Water Purification Plant, located about ten miles south, the two plants pulled water from Lake Michigan to provide over a billion gallons of fresh water each day to most of the city's households and over a hundred of its suburbs.

We drove past a small crowd near the security gate and some uniformed police, then parked in the three-sectioned lot close to the plant entrance. The lot was nearly full, mostly with black SUVs, a few marked police cars, and a fleet of vans.

"Stay in the car," he said, getting out.

"Don't worry." I had no intention of going anywhere near a possible nerve agent.

He crossed the parking lot to a blue tent that had been erected on the far side, currently crowded with police and blue-jacketed FBI agents.

SSA Stokes was standing next to a table, on which were some electronics and several laptops.

The rest of the scene was controlled chaos. Hazmat workers in suits, hoods, and respirators roamed the area, many congregating near the vans. Police tape barred the entrance to the plant, next to which stood a uniformed officer wearing a gas mask.

At this point no one was walking into the plant, but a lot of the suited hazmat workers were coming out. Most of them took off their hoods as soon as they got past the police tape. I took this to mean that they thought the threat was over.

They looked like the same ones that had escorted me off of the *Enterprise*. Light gray plastic-looking suits, with hoods, gloves, masks, black boots, and oxygen tanks on their backs, many carrying silver metal cases.

I vaguely recalled from a school field trip years ago that most of the plant's operations were underground, the area below us occupied by a network of thick steel pipes. To get to them one would have to get through the front gate, into the plant entrance, and then past a variety of secure doors to even get close to the flowing water.

This whole thing still didn't make any sense. What would be the point of trying to attack a water treatment plant? As Smith said, it was the hardest of targets. Not only that, because of what happened on the *Enterprise* he said law enforcement had been ready for it. It sure looked like they were. The entire place was crawling with law enforcement of various affiliations.

Smith had said he thought the attack on the *Enterprise* was a test run. If so, what had Rykov been testing? The device had never been activated, so they hadn't been trying out the nerve agent. All it had done was get law enforcement ready for what Smith had described as a "massive, immediate response." Looking over the scene I thought that was accurate; every hazmat qualified person in the city must be here.

While I'd been staring at the plant Smith returned to the car.

"It's over. I need to clear up a few things with Stokes and then I'll get someone to escort you out. I'll only be a few minutes."

I nodded distractedly.

He walked back to the blue tent and I turned my gaze to the plant.

The flow of suited workers coming out had slowed to a trickle, most of them making their way to the parking lot and their vans.

Then it hit me.

The test run on the *Enterprise*. The guy on the boat deck taking pictures, and then the leak to the media.

The call today to warn law enforcement that there would be an attack here.

I jumped out of the car and ran to the command tent. I got within ten feet of it when a uniform stepped in front of me.

"Please, step back, miss."

"Listen, I just need to—"

"I said step back." He grabbed my arm.

"Smith!" He turned away from Stokes and looked at me, then walked over.

"I told you to stay in the car." He nodded to the uniform, who released my arm.

"Did you say they're done, Smith?"

"Yes. The site's clean."

"Then who's that guy?"

One of the hazmat workers had walked out of the plant, but instead of going back to the vans he was headed in the opposite direction. He had a metal case in his hand, a little larger than what the rest of them were carrying.

And he still had his hood on.

THIRTY

"Most of them can't wait to get their hoods off. And where do you think he's going?"

Smith went back to the tent and spoke to Stokes. He pointed at the suited man, who was now nearing the security gate at the entrance.

Stokes picked up his walkie-talkie. Within seconds two of the uniforms at the gate stepped in front of the man. He brushed past them, and they grabbed his arms.

He dropped his case then broke free and ran for the poled barrier. But he struggled to run in the high rubber boots and was quickly tackled to the ground by the officers. They put handcuffs on him and brought him to the command tent, picking up the metal case on the way.

Stokes pulled the man's badge off of the front of his suit. "Steve Bishop?" he said.

When the man didn't respond, he nodded to one of the uniforms. "Take off his hood."

The officer fiddled with the hood, pulling off tape and undoing various fasteners before he was able to pull it off.

It was Mason Cooper.

Stokes took the metal case from the officer and placed it on the ground. He undid the two latches on either side of the handle and carefully opened it.

Inside, resting on molded gray foam, was a clear tube filled with liquid in two separate chambers. The tube was several times larger than the one I'd found on the *Enterprise*, but similar in that there was a gray, clay-like substance molded around the center where some kind of membrane separated the chambers.

Two other small balls of the clay was stuck to the inside of the case, near the handle.

Wires connected both sets of clay to a cell phone.

Stokes didn't waste any time. "Set up a jammer," he called over his shoulder. He turned back to Mason. "Who are you?"

"That's Mason Cooper," said Smith. "He works for Richard Nottingham."

"Where were you going with this? Are there others?"

Mason stared straight ahead, his mouth set in a firm line.

After it was clear Mason wasn't going to say anything, Stokes said, "Get me Bill Marshall."

One of the agents left the tent, returning shortly with one of the hazmat guys, still in his suit.

"Do you know who this is? Is he one of your team?" Stokes handed him the badge Mason had been wearing.

Marshall looked at the badge. "Yes, Steve Bishop. He's supposed to be going over the aeration section of the plant."

Stokes leaned down over the case. He slowly pulled the wires from the cell phone out of the clay, then closed and locked the case and handed it carefully to Marshall.

"Put this into containment, and see that it gets to the lab so they can ID it as soon as possible. How many men do you have on the site?"

"Over fifty. I've got my own guys, plus some bomb-squad guys from the PD, and FBI teams. There's even some National Guard here. Basically anyone who's ever worn a hazmat suit. I'll have to look at the list again to get an exact count."

"Count them, now. Match everyone on your list with their badges. We need to know if there are other people here who aren't supposed to be." He turned and walked back to the center table.

Marshall nodded. "I can do that with everyone who's still here."

Stokes whipped his head around. "What do you mean, 'everyone who's still here'?"

"A few of the men left already. Perez, Stavoli, and Timms, PD guys."

Stokes cursed. "See if you can get a hold of them and get them back here."

By the look on his face, I didn't think Marshall thought that was likely. "What were their jobs on this operation? The men that left?" Stokes asked.

"Those three were inspecting the aeration and sedimentation sections of the plant."

Stokes blanched and turned to the uniform. "The plant employees are by the front entrance. Find the head operator and bring him here." He turned back to Marshall. "You need to sweep the plant again. We have to assume there are more devices inside."

Now everything made sense. Smith had been right, the device on the *Enterprise* had been a test run. But not the kind of test he was thinking.

"They weren't testing the device," I blurted out. Everyone turned to look at me.

"On the *Enterprise*. They were testing the response. That's why they planted that bomb in the freezer, and why you got an anonymous call telling you it was there. They never intended for it to go off—they wanted to see how you reacted when you found it. Remember that guy on the boat, who took the pictures that ended up on the front page of the newspaper? After the *Enterprise*, Nottingham and Rykov knew exactly what the hazmat gear looked like, as well as the badges, and their testing cases. They copied them. Then by leaking it to the media they made sure everyone would be on high alert. It wasn't an accident they planted it on a boat filled with politicians, who they knew would put pressure on you to step up your focus."

Smith nodded. "So that when the call came in that there was a nerve agent device at the plant, we would be ready—"

"With your 'massive and immediate response' guaranteeing a flood of hazmat people and law enforcement would be on the site. So many that in the confusion it would be easy to sneak in a few impersonators."

"At least the employees are out of the plant," offered the second in command.

Stokes turned to him. "These are remotely detonated," he said, pointing to the case. "When it's set off, the membrane between the two chambers will break, allowing the liquids to mix. We haven't tested it yet, but I'm guessing it's Novichok. The second explosion will open the case." He pointed to the gray putty that was concentrated near the two latches on either side of the handle. "When that happens, the material will spray out from the case. Then—"

He stopped when the uniform he'd sent to the front entrance returned. Next to him was one of the employees.

"Are you the head operator?" asked Stokes.

"For this shift, yeah."

"Are there areas of the plant where the water is exposed? Where it's open to the air, not running through pipes?"

He nodded. "The sedimentation and aeration sections."

Stokes and Smith locked eyes.

"Can you do an emergency shut down of the plant? Stop the flow?"

He nodded. "We do it occasionally for maintenance."

"Good. I need you to shut it down, now."

"Oh, no, we can't do that. It has to be shut down in a specific series of steps, otherwise we run the risk of untreated water getting out into the system. And the sedimentation tanks will fill up. If that happens, the whole operation has to go offline while we clean it."

"But it's possible, to shut off the system, immediately?"

"Yes, but—"

"Go with Bill Marshall. He'll escort you into the plant. You need to shut it down, now."

"I'm not sure I can do that without authorization from the city."

Stokes stepped forward, closing the gap between them to a few inches. "You have authorization from me. If you don't do it right now I'm going to have you taken into custody and charged with participation in a terrorist attack."

The man paled, and nodded. He and Marshall left for the vans.

"What are you worried about? Won't whatever's in the tubes dissolve in the water and get flushed out? And isn't there chlorine?" I knew I should keep my mouth shut, but I couldn't imagine something that small significantly contaminating millions of gallons of water.

Stokes shook his head. "Adding chlorine to Novichok will hydrolyze it into toxic metabolites, like hydrofluoric acid and cyanide. And depending on the formulation, the LD50 of Novichok in water is anywhere from days to months."

In response to puzzled looks, he added, "Chlorine won't make things better. And it could take months for the original concentration of the nerve agent to drop in half. If it gets into the water at the plant, and then is allowed to flow into the distribution system, we're looking at the complete ruination of the city's water supply."

The uniform scoffed. Stokes looked at him darkly.

"This stuff is ten times stronger than Sarin or VX. A drop of it on someone's skin, or ingested, could kill them. Less than that would make most people very sick." He pointed to the case on the ground. "The amount in that one case is enough to contaminate every drop of water in the system, and it may be that there are at least three more left in the plant. That's enough Novichok to contaminate the entire plant along with every fountain, every sink, every toilet bowl, every hose, and every fire hydrant in the city, along with the four thousand miles of distribution pipes underneath it. Anywhere the Novichok touched would need to be sanitized or replaced, to make sure there was no residual agent remaining. That's why we need to make sure it doesn't get out of the plant. Even if the plant has to be scrapped, we can't let any of the agent out into the city. That is, if it hasn't already happened." He turned to the uniform. "Under no circumstances let anyone leave the area—no one—until we sweep the plant again for more devices, and everyone's been thoroughly searched and vetted."

The uniform left. I looked over at the hazmat vans. A large group of the workers had put their hoods back on and were heading back into the plant.

After a few minutes Stokes' walkie-talkie crackled and he picked it up. He went ashen.

"They can't shut off the flow, at least not quickly. The controls have been sabotaged. And we know why Mason Cooper wasn't able to place his device. His designated area to leave his device was shut down for maintenance this week. He couldn't get in."

"What about the sedimentation and aeration sections?" asked Smith.

"They're searching now to see if any of the cases were left behind."

He turned again to the uniform. "Do an ID check of every employee and all of the staff. Anyone whose ID doesn't match their face, take away their phones." He looked up at the sky, then shook his head. "Never mind, take everyone's phones."

"Time for you to go back to the car," said Smith to me. "You'll need to wait there until we clear this up. I mean it—don't get out of it until I give you the all-clear."

I was fine with that, and didn't waste any time getting back to the car. But I wished I had my phone. I'd call Maude and tell her to pick up as much bottled water as she could, and separate our water heater from the pipes.

An entire city, over five million people, without water? And on top of that, once everyone found out their water supply might contain a deadly nerve agent there would be panic.

Forget about conserving water. We'd need to get out of town.

Hazmat workers were still filing back through the front doors of the plant. They'd be looking for the metal cases, hopefully intact, in the areas that the three missing workers had been stationed, and in any other part of the plant where the water was not in tanks, or running through pipes. Where it was exposed.

One of the suited men peeled away from the group before he was inside the plant. He walked to a car in the parking lot and got in.

Maybe he was heading out to try to track down the missing workers.

But he pulled out and drove in the other direction, away from the security gate, on the road next to the lake that wound around the plant. East Ohio Street.

There was no exit on the other side. That road ended at a

fence that separated the secure plant grounds from a public park.

As the car drove past I saw the driver had taken off his hood.

It was Rykov.

THIRTY-ONE

I leaned on the horn. I kept it up until Smith looked over. He waved at me to knock it off. I kept honking. Finally he walked over.

"I just saw Rykov."

"Where?"

"In a car. He's heading around the plant to the other side." I pointed north. "He had a hazmat suit on."

"Are you sure?"

"I think so. It went by fast, but you gave me his picture, remember?" Rykov's Stalin mustache was unmistakable.

Smith hesitated, and then got in and started the engine.

While he did he pulled out his phone. "We think we saw Rykov heading around the plant to the north." He paused to listen. "OK."

He put the phone back in his pocket. "Stokes is sending some uniforms after us. And he says to be careful. If Rykov's here, he has the detonator."

Smith gunned it, and we sped down Ohio Street to the corner. He took the turn at speed. We could make out Rykov turning up ahead to the far side of the plant. I could hear sirens behind us.

By the time we made it around to the other side Rykov was parked at the far end, just before the fence that separated the plant from the park.

Smith pushed the accelerator to the floor, then slammed on the brakes when he neared Rykov's car.

Rykov jumped out of his car and ran toward the water. He was carrying one of the large metal cases in one hand and his phone in the other.

"Where's he going?"

"It looks like he's looking for a signal so he can detonate the case."

"I thought the area was jammed?"

"The jammer is good to about a hundred meters. We're at the edge of the range."

Rykov had crossed the road and was still moving toward the water, stopping every few feet to look at his phone. Maybe he'd run out of land before he got the signal.

"Why would he want to detonate the case now?" Rykov was still wearing his hazmat suit, but was without his hood or gloves.

"I don't know. Stay here."

The two marked police cars drove up as Smith stepped out of the car, pulling his gun out as he did.

"Rykov, put down the case and the phone, then step away." Smith was taking slow steps toward Rykov, his gun pointed toward him.

Rykov had his back to the water and was taking his own small steps toward it, alternating looking at his phone and behind him for the edge of the parking lot. A small strip of grass separated it from the large rocks that dropped sharply down to the water just a few feet from where he was standing. He'd run out of room soon.

"Rykov, stop. Right now. Or I'll shoot you where you stand."

He stopped at the edge of the pavement. Then he looked up at Smith and smiled. His finger tapped his phone.

The metal case blew up in his hand. Pieces of it flew in all directions, some of them directly into Rykov's body.

His hand was gone, but he was still standing, covered in the liquid that had come out of the case.

Smith ran back to the car, furiously waving off the uniforms that were starting to approach Rykov's body.

"Don't go near him. This scene is contaminated. Get in your cars and drive back to the end of this road. Stay in your cars until you get checked out by the hazmat team."

He pulled out his phone. "Rykov's detonated one of the cases. We need a decontamination team here now."

I leaned over to open his door and he shoved it hard with his hip, shaking his head.

"Stay in the car. Keep the windows rolled up," he yelled.

"Did any of it hit you?" I yelled back.

"I don't know." He walked away from the car and away from Rykov, looking over his own body and clothes.

A minute later one of the hazmat vans came around the corner. They parked fifty yards from Smith. Three fully suited and hooded men got out and approached him.

"Over there." He pointed to the still body of Rykov laying on the ground. He was on his side, his face laying in a small pool of drool and vomit, his eyes open.

Two of them walked to Rykov. The other one stayed next to Smith.

Smith stripped off his jacket, pants, shoes, shirt, boxers, and socks. He stood there, shivering while the hazmat worker put everything in a plastic bag and sealed it.

He escorted Smith to the van, next to which a portable shower had been set up. Smith stayed under the stream of water for several minutes while he was scrubbed with a long brush. While they were doing this an ambulance arrived. Masked EMTs threw a blanket around his shoulders and escorted him to the back of it. It drove off, siren blaring.

I waited in the car for what seemed like hours while they processed the scene, wiping the pavement and the grass around Rykov in increasingly larger circles.

A black SUV came around the corner and parked next to the hazmat van. Stokes stepped out and walked to the car.

He knocked on the window, making a "small space" sign with his fingers. I started the car and rolled the window down a crack. He slipped a phone in the space and made the signal to roll the window back up. Then he walked back to his SUV.

The phone rang.

"How are you feeling, Ms. Pfister?"

"Fine, I think. How's Smith?"

"They're taking him to the hospital."

I noticed he hadn't answered my question. "How long do I have to stay here?"

"Until they're sure that the car hasn't been contaminated. Can you tell me what happened?"

"There's not much to tell. Rykov detonated his own case while it was in his hand. Did any other cases go off?"

"No, not as far as we know."

As we were talking one of the men who'd been processing the scene knocked on the window and gave the thumbs up.

I cracked the window again.

"You can get out," said Stokes.

"Are you sure?" I looked around. "There's nothing floating around in the air?"

"It was in liquid form, designed to contaminate water. Nothing was aerosolized. If it had been, SSA Smith would not have survived. But avoid that area," he said, pointing to a boundary that one of the suited men was spray-painting on the ground.

I stepped out and joined Stokes at his SUV. He waved to one of the other men. "This agent will escort you out of the plant, and to your home if that is where you wish to go."

"Where are they taking Smith?"

"Northwestern Memorial."

"Is he going to be OK?"

He shook his head. "We don't know yet. If any of the nerve agent touched his skin he's going to be a very sick man."

THIRTY-TWO

The first thing I wanted to do when I got home was take a shower. I ran downstairs and flung off my clothes. I got in and reached for the tap before I realized I wasn't completely comfortable using the water, despite what Stokes had said.

I stepped back out without turning on the water. I wiped myself off with a towel, then put on clean clothes and called a Lyft to take me to the hospital.

Maude was already there, along with other members of the PD and a few FBI agents, all crowded in the hallway just outside of Smith's room.

He was in quarantine. We could see him through the glass being tended to by several nurses in full protective gear. He was sitting up, waving to Maude through the glass.

"How's he doing?" I asked, after Maude and I exchanged a long hug.

"He's a little dizzy and he's got a headache. And his nose is running."

"That doesn't sound too bad."

"Those are indications of mild Novichok poisoning. It means some of it is in his system. And full-blown symptoms can take some time to manifest." She took a large breath and blew it out. "But so far, so good. He hasn't been nauseous or had any trouble breathing." She looked me up and down. "How are you?"

"Fine. I was in the car when the case detonated."

Smith was talking to the nurse and smiling. "He looks happy, under the circumstances," I said.

"He is. They found the three other cases, still intact."

"That's a relief." The understatement of the century. "Any news on Nottingham?"

She frowned. "He flew out of town on one of his private

jets. They were heading for Canada. I'm guessing he's off to Russia by now."

"And Mason?"

"He's at the station. They've been grilling him nonstop since they brought him back."

"What about the other three guys, the ones that left cases in the plant?"

"No sign of them. They found the bodies of the men they replaced," she added quietly.

She looked back into the room. Smith waved at her again.

"How did you figure out the code word?" she asked, waving at Smith.

"A combination of things. Martin was behind the pranks, and he was trying to point us to his dad."

"Why didn't he just tell us?"

"I don't know. He's a strange guy. And maybe he'd planned to, if we hadn't figured it out in time. But he's been missing since the holiday party."

Maude nodded, still looking at Smith.

"How long are they keeping him in there?"

"He's showing mild symptoms of low-dose exposure. But they want to keep him for observation for a few days, just in case. They might let him out sooner, as long as he's with someone at all times. Needless to say, I'm taking the next few days off."

They let Smith out of the hospital that night, on the condition that he be accompanied by Maude, and would go back at the first sign of any shortness of breath, excessive sweating, or nausea. They gave her a syringe of atropine and told her when and how to use it, just in case.

I went home and fell asleep with my clothes on.

The next morning I was at the kitchen table when the two of them walked in.

True to form, when Smith had been discharged he went straight to the station to get in on Mason's interrogation. He and Maude had been up all night, but they were too wired to go to bed. They joined me at the table.

Smith looked fine. I wasn't thrilled, though, that I couldn't look at him now without imagining his pale white ass.

"Mason is talking a blue streak," he said excitedly.

"I'm surprised he's talking at all."

"I think he decided that talking was better than a needle in his arm. And as soon as we showed him pictures of Nottingham leaving the country, he opened up. He'd been under the impression that he was part of the escape plan. I don't think it ever occurred to him that Nottingham would leave him behind."

"Even so, why would he do something like this? Try to bring down the whole city? Was he a Russian sleeper agent, too?"

"No. And we still don't know why, other than he's been with Nottingham for decades. It might just be blind loyalty."

"Do you think it's over?" I still hadn't taken a shower. And I'd been a little nervous making coffee.

He nodded. "I think so. They're doing another sweep of the plant. But they've tested at every stage and all around the facility, it doesn't look like any part of the plant or the water was exposed to Novichok. And you were right. Mason confirmed that the device you found on the *Enterprise* was planted so they could see the response of the hazmat teams. Their plan was to put the devices in the plant during the hazmat sweep, then slip away and detonate them before the operators were allowed back in. No one would have heard them go off, and it would have taken a little while to find the debris. By that time the contaminated water would have already flowed out of the plant and into the distribution system."

"Was it really as bad as Stokes said? That they would have had to shut down the entire distribution of water?"

"Almost certainly. There is another plant that serves the city, Sawyer, but it's only for the suburbs and parts of the south side. And with the contamination in the pipes they wouldn't have been able to reroute it."

Maude shook her head. "It seems unbelievable that a small amount of that stuff could do that much damage. There's so much water going through that plant every day, wouldn't it have just gotten diluted?"

He shook his head. "The amount that we found on the *Enterprise*? If you mixed that in with a million gallons of water it would still be strong enough to kill some people, and make others very ill. The amount that was in those three cases was a hundred times what was in the *Enterprise* device, more than enough to make the water deadly. The toxicity of this stuff is measured in parts per billion. And it wouldn't have been a one-time thing. Novichok sticks around. Small drops, left in a sink, or a faucet, or fountain, would be enough to kill anyone who came in contact with it. No," he said, shaking his head. "We dodged a bullet. If we hadn't found Mason," he looked at me, "if you hadn't noticed him leaving the plant, we never would have known."

"Why didn't Mason plant his case?"

"Where he was supposed to plant his case was shut down, they didn't know that area would be under maintenance. But they'd built in a contingency plan. They were instructed to leave the facility if they weren't able to plant their cases, and then once off site to deactivate them." He shook his head. "And they built in redundancy: two or three, maybe even one of the cases would have been enough to destroy faith in the water supply. Mason was trying to get off site undetected. They knew if we knew they'd planted the cases before they detonated that Stokes would do what he did: jam the site to stop cell phones from working, and try to shut off the water flow. Rykov was intending to put his case near the entrance to the plant, in the bushes. Detonating that one first would have slowed any attempt to get back to the plant and delayed them finding the debris from the cases. The Novichok from the other devices would have had ample time to get through the system."

"Then why did he take it to the far side of the plant and kill himself with it?"

"With the jamming he knew he wouldn't be able to set off any of the cases in or near the plant. But there was still value in releasing an extremely toxic nerve agent close to a water-treatment plant. Public safety goes hand in hand with confidence. Detonating a bomb that close to the water supply would panic people, even if it didn't actually affect the water. And he was never going to be taken alive. Fortunately Stokes evacuated the public park early on and there were no journalists hanging around, or people taking cell-phone shots from the other side of the fence."

"So no one knows what happened?"

"People know there was a terrorist threat at the plant, and it's going to leak that there was a contaminant release nearby. They've shut off access to the park next to the plant, and there's a tent set up around the detonation area that still needs to be decontaminated. Fortunately it doesn't look like it got into the lake, and they dug all of it out of the soil before it could get into the water table. They're still going to decontaminate the entire area with enzymatic cleaners, just in case. Then they'll monitor it for a while. The city is doing what it can to make sure the public isn't worried about the water supply. Among other things, they're filming the mayor taking a tour of the place later today to demonstrate confidence."

"Who were the other guys who planted the cases?"

"Three other members of Nottingham's security team."

"Have you found them?"

"No. We've got an APB out on them, but I'm not optimistic. All of them had significant amounts of money deposited into their accounts the day before the attack. My guess is they're already out of the country."

I'd been afraid at the start. Then relieved when Smith had said it was over.

Now I was angry. The idea that those guys would get away scot-free to live comfortable lives was disgusting.

"Any sign of Martin?"

Smith nodded. "Mason told us where they were keeping him. He was in a building in North Lawndale, not far from where we found the lab. He's at the hospital now, under guard. He was a little banged up. He'll be fine, but he's got some things to answer for."

"What do you mean?"

"I mean, he obviously knew about the threat to the Jardine plant long before it happened. The fact that he didn't tell anyone and instead orchestrated a long drawn-out set of macabre pranks to give us clues that we might or might not have solved makes him complicit."

There was more behind it than that, but I let it go.

"Is—"

"Tasia's with him. She's fine," added Maude.

I hadn't had a chance to pick up a new phone. And even if I had, I'd been unwilling to talk to Tasia until I knew anything useful about Martin.

"Has your guy found Gigi?"

"No. We're still looking for her."

I stared at him.

"I've added another one of our UCs to help. If she's out there, we'll find her." He looked at his watch. "I need to go home and pick up some things, then go back to the station."

He looked at Maude expectantly.

"I think you're fine," she said. "I'm going to get some sleep."

He leaned over and kissed her, then waved goodbye to me.

"No more babysitting?" I asked after he'd left.

"No, they pronounced him Novichok free."

"That's great."

She nodded, looking down into her coffee. "Listen, Sags, uh, I think you should know. Linda's still working the Frank Chimen case."

"Yeah, I knew that."

"She's found some things. Some footage. I'm not supposed to give you any details, but they're bringing you in tomorrow for a formal interview. I told them I'd tell you about it. You have to be at the station at eleven." She paused. "Is there, uh, anything you need to be worried about?"

It seemed like a funny question, after narrowly escaping the city losing its water supply.

"Not in the grand scheme of things."

She gave me one of her "you need to tell me the truth" stares.

"It will be fine. Really." She didn't look convinced. "I need to head out, too. I have to check in at the restaurant and run some errands."

"Do you want company?"

"No, thanks. You should get some sleep. But can I borrow your car?"

"Sure."

I took her car and drove to Saga. It felt like years since I'd been there.

The door in the back was open. Zoe was taking deliveries for the day's service.

"Hey. How's everything going?"

"Great. Packed house tonight," she said, looking down to sign the invoice from the delivery guy.

"You have everything you need?"

"Sure do. Everything's under control."

"Great. Call me if you need anything," I said awkwardly.

I liked that I could totally rely on her, but I had mixed feelings about no one needing me at my own restaurant.

On the one hand, it freed me up to do other things. Maybe I could open up a new restaurant, or bring back my cooking radio show.

On the other hand, I loved cooking. And I sure as hell didn't want to make working for Smith a full-time job.

Part of me was a little sorry it was over with the Nottinghams. Cooking for them had been a blast, outside of the occasional scary security guy tossing my room, and locking me in the basement.

At least I had something to remember them by. I reached into my pocket.

Still there.

I left the car parked at the restaurant and walked a mile down to Belmont, then to Pawn Chicago. The chime above the door jingled as I walked in.

THIRTY-THREE

Thoughts of Gigi's disappearance and the impending interview made it hard to get to sleep. The sun was just coming up when I finally nodded off, which meant I was sound asleep when Maude knocked on my door.

"Sags, Jeb's on the line. He wants you to meet him at the cemetery."

"Tell him I'm sleeping. And when I get up I'm going to the hospital to see Tasia and Martin."

"I did. He's insistent. He says if you don't meet him he's coming here."

Damn. "Fine. Can you tell him I'll be there in twenty?"

I dragged myself out of bed, took a shower, and got dressed. Then I walked over to Rosehill.

As soon as I was within earshot, I said, "Is this really necessary? I thought we were done with all of this."

He patted the bench next to him and waited until I sat down.

"Maude told me you're going to the hospital to see Martin and Tasia today. I wanted to share some information with you before you do that. First of all, thank you."

Huh. I couldn't remember him ever thanking me for anything.

"I know I put you in a hard position, and what I asked you to do ended up being far more dangerous than what I'd envisioned."

"It's not like I had much of a choice."

"Still, you went above and beyond. I hope you feel it was worth it. If we hadn't stopped this attack it would've been one of the most devastating assaults the country's ever experienced. And not just because it would have shut down and bankrupted the city; there's no telling what people would have done if we'd run out of water. Thousands of people would have died. At least. You had a lot to do with stopping this, and I want you to know that."

I wasn't sure what to say. "Any news of Nottingham?"

"He took his private jet to Pearson in Toronto. From there we know he boarded another flight to Istanbul. We expect from there he'll go to Russia."

"Good riddance."

His brow furrowed. "I thought you'd be more upset. That he got away."

"You can't win 'em all."

He stared at me a moment longer before saying, "Mason is still in interrogation, talking up a storm."

"I'm still surprised he's talking to you."

He nodded. "He's angry. He was shocked that they left without him."

"I'm surprised, too. He'd been with Nottingham for decades."

"He had, and he knew about Nottingham's past. And maybe that was the plan, originally, for him to join them. But Nottingham may have felt some urgency, especially after confirming you'd been feeding information to us the whole time."

That still didn't answer the question. "Why would Mason do that?"

"As far as we can tell it was out of loyalty."

"How can you be sure?"

"We're not, but he also knew about Nottingham's . . . proclivities."

"'Proclivities.' That's a funny word for molesting children."

"The point is, if he knew about that and was fine with it, it's not that big of a leap to go from procuring young children for the guy to agreeing to participate in a terrorist attack. He was completely devastated when we told him Nottingham was out of the country. He didn't believe us until we pulled up footage of the family flying out on the jet, and then images of them on the tarmac in Canada."

It was hard to imagine Mason being devastated about anything. And even harder to give a shit.

"OK." I stood up. "Thanks for the info. Is that all? I need to get to the hospital before I go to the station for the interview."

He frowned again. "What interview?"

"About Frank Chimen's death."

He stared at me. "Is there anything you need to worry about?"

"That's the same thing Maude asked me."

"Well?"

"No." I hope not.

I turned to go.

"There's, uh . . . something else," he said to my back.

There always is.

"What?"

"I told you, Mason's been spilling his guts. About everything. How and when the Russians activated Nottingham, his relationship with Rykov. Along with a lot of things about the family."

He waited for me to turn fully back around before sharing the last piece of information he'd gotten from Mason.

Damn. "Do Tasia and Martin know?"

"No. Not yet. I was heading to the hospital to tell them."

"I'll do it."

He blew out a small breath. "I was hoping you'd say that. It will be better coming from you."

"Are we done?"

"No. I need you to get whatever you can out of Martin."

"What do you mean?"

"I mean, we need to understand why he didn't tell us as soon as he knew about what his dad was planning."

I shook my head. "I'm not going to interrogate him while he's in the hospital. That's your job. Besides, maybe he didn't know exactly what his dad was planning. Maybe he just suspected. And even so, he did try to warn us."

"An obtuse code as part of acts of vandalism doesn't qualify as 'warning us.' The bottom line is Martin obviously knew something about the attack and he should have told us immediately. This isn't just for me. It's for Martin."

"What do you mean?"

"I mean, the more we can learn about his circumstances, and his motivation, the better it will go for him."

I had a hard time believing that Smith cared about what happened to Martin. "Why do you care about him all of a sudden?"

"I've been thinking about the abuse," he said quietly.

For a man like Smith, Nottingham's behavior toward his own sons would be unfathomable.

"OK. I'll see what I can do. But I'm not going to interrogate him. What in particular should I be asking about?"

"Any evidence he was working against his father, and not with, or for, him. It would go a long way toward at least partial exoneration."

"I can guarantee you, Martin was not working with his father."

"I know, but the more evidence we have, the better it will be for him."

"OK. Have your guys found any sign of—"

"No, but they're still looking for her. They've been to Wacker, Uptown, Avondale, and the tent city under the Dan Ryan. They'll be on it until we find her. It's the least we can do."

I looked away. I hoped Gigi was still alive. At least I knew she wasn't with Frank Chimen. But there was no shortage of dirtbag, drug-dealing pimps on the street, any one of whom would be happy to give her drugs in exchange for working for him. Or just to be available to beat up.

"It may be whoever she's with doesn't want anyone to know. Maybe they think she's a good earner."

"Jesus, Smith."

"I'm sorry. I didn't mean—"

"I know exactly what you meant." What hurt the most was that he was right.

"We're not going to stop looking until we find her. I promise."

Smith didn't make promises he didn't intend to keep. But some things weren't meant to be. Neither one of us said what we were thinking.

Gigi was very possibly already dead. Junkies who went through withdrawal, got clean, and then went back to using often overdosed. They'd take the same amount they'd taken before when their bodies had built up a tolerance, and what they needed in the past to get high was now enough to kill them.

If so, she'd be in the morgue. A Jane Doe, waiting with a toe tag for a family member to identify her.

Or worse, laying on the street somewhere.

I cursed again our uncle who'd caused all of this to happen. Part of me wished he were alive so I could kill him again.

I left Smith and took the bus to the hospital, and went up to Martin's room. A uniformed officer stood in the hallway next to his door.

Martin was in bed, pale but awake. Tasia was on a chair next to him, holding his hand. His other one was handcuffed to the bed.

"Hey Martin. How're you feeling?"

"All right," he mumbled.

I walked around the side of the bed and put my hand on her shoulder. "Can I talk to you? Alone?"

She looked at Martin. He was staring out the window. "It's fine, go."

We walked into the hallway. I tried to give her a hug, but she leaned back.

"How are you doing?" I asked.

"Fine." Her voice was clipped, and she was using a tone I hadn't heard since before we started sleeping together. "Where have you been? I thought you'd be here sooner."

"I was a little busy."

I told her about the incident at the water treatment plant. At least, the things I could tell her. They were trying to keep the gory details out of the public domain.

"Oh. In that case, forget everything I was thinking about you when you didn't answer my calls or come by earlier." She stepped forward and put her arms around me.

"How's Martin doing?"

"Not bad, all things considered. He spent three days in a room by himself, with no food or water, so he's dehydrated and exhausted. He was forced to go through alcohol withdrawal, so it wasn't entirely a bad thing. When he gets out of the hospital they're taking him to the police station. I'm not sure why."

I hugged her close. "Mason's in custody, and he's talking," I said into her ear.

She leaned back, eyes flashing. "I hope that doesn't mean he's getting any kind of deal. He's the one who stuck Martin in that room."

"No chance. His choice was the needle or life in prison. And once he found out your dad left him behind he was happy to tell them everything."

She nodded. "Good. I hope he rots there. And what do you mean, left behind?"

"He's out of the country, he left with Alan and Celeste. They went to Canada and they think they're going to Russia."

"Russia?"

Oh, shit. I realized that she had no idea about her dad's background. "You better sit down for this."

We pulled two chairs in the hallway together. I held her hand while I told her about her father's Russian roots and his status as a sleeper agent, dormant for decades until now. His part in funding and providing men to Rykov for the attack on the water treatment plant that would have killed thousands and shut down the city.

She looked shaken. "This is unbelievable. I knew he was a bastard but I had no idea he was capable of this."

"They think he was being blackmailed. That the Russians would get the word out about his child abuse."

We'd never talked about it, but she didn't seem to think it odd that I knew.

"He was always very concerned about his fucking reputation," she said bitterly. "So they think he got away?"

"For now."

Her shoulders slumped. "I'd always hoped, somehow, that he'd have to pay for what he did to my brothers . . ."

"You never know. Things have a way of coming around. Speaking of that, were you aware of what Martin was doing, while all of this was going on?"

"What are you talking about?"

"The high-profile vandalism that's been happening around the city for the last few weeks. The dye in the river, the 'Fuck You' on the Crain building. Martin did that."

She laughed, relieved. "That sounds like him. And that explains why they handcuffed him to the bed."

I shook my head. "It's more than that. All of the pranks had numbers associated with them. They were a code. An exceptionally complex, difficult one. The police cracked it, but it took a long time."

"That doesn't surprise me, either. I told you, he's really, really smart. And he gets bored. I'm sure it was fun for him, putting that together, and seeing how long it took for everyone to figure it out."

She wasn't getting it. "The code spelled out 'Jardine.' The water treatment plant. Where the attack took place."

I looked at her, until I saw the recognition in her eyes that she knew where I was going with this.

"No," she shook her head. "No way. Martin would never, ever, in a million years, have anything to do with harming anyone. And he'd never work with our father. You know that, Sags."

"I do. But it sounds like he knew what your dad was up to . . ."

"I told you, Martin's beyond smart. It wouldn't surprise me if he knew everything about our father. But there's no way in hell he would do anything to help him. He hates him, even more than I do."

"OK, but . . ."

"But what?" her voice was starting to rise.

"They were barely able to keep Rykov from poisoning the water supply. If Martin did know what his dad was up to he should have told someone."

She looked away from me, then started to stand up.

I pulled her gently back down into the chair. "Tasia, it was a really, really close thing. Your dad and Rykov almost succeeded in shutting down the whole city. Do you understand what I'm saying?"

She looked down, then said quietly, "You're saying that Martin's in a lot of trouble."

I nodded. "Yes. So if there's anything you can tell me, or that he can share, that shows he wasn't working with your father, and most importantly, something, anything, that explains why he didn't tell everyone sooner what was going on, he needs to tell the police. Rykov is dead, and your dad is out of the country. All but one of the men who were involved are either dead or have disappeared. They're going to want a scapegoat."

"They have Mason, don't they?"

"Yes, but for something this big it's not going to satisfy them. Mason was technically an employee. They're going to want to prosecute someone in the family. Talk to Martin. Get him to open up about his motivations. Find out what he knew, and when. There's at least one person in law enforcement who thinks Martin shouldn't bear the brunt of all of this."

"OK." She stood up weakly.

She looked awful, the full weight of what I was telling her sinking in. I hated what I had to tell her next.

I stood up, facing her. "There's something else. Mason told them a lot about your family, and about your mother."

"My mother?"

"She didn't leave you."

I took a deep breath. "She's buried, in the backyard of the house."

"What? What are you talking about?" her hand tightened around mine.

"Your dad had her killed, when she found out he was abusing Martin."

She looked at me in stunned silence.

"They found her body behind the oak tree."

"So she didn't leave us," she said quietly, leaning back against the wall. "He killed her. Now it makes sense. He'd done it to Alan, first. But then Alan aged out. He and my mom started arguing, all the time, when Martin was five. He must have gone after him then. And my mother knew it. She would have tried to stop him. Or at least tell someone. And he killed her for it."

I waited a moment before asking, "Is there anything I can do?"

"No, thanks. I need to tell Martin. And then talk to him about what he knew about what our dad was doing."

She put both of her hands around mine. "Thank you for telling me. Will you be around tonight?"

I wasn't sure where I'd be. It would depend on how my interview with the police went.

"I hope so."

THIRTY-FOUR

I waited in the lobby of the police station for ten minutes before a uniform came to get me.

He escorted me upstairs to an interview room.

It wasn't my first time in one of these small, gray rooms. He pointed to the uncomfortable metal chair positioned on one side of the table, then left.

I waited. This was part of how they approached interviews. Make the suspect wait to soften her up.

A half hour went by before Linda walked in, carrying a notebook and a laptop. I started to smile at her. It died on my face when I saw who was behind her.

Detective John Carter.

"Hi, Sa—Ms. Pfister," said Linda. "This is Det—"

"I know who it is."

They both sat down, Carter taking the chair directly across the table. He stared at me, unblinking.

"Detective Carter asked to sit in on this interview that we're conducting related to the death of Frank Chimen. Before we start, I need to read you your rights."

She did the Miranda thing, then set the laptop on the table and opened her notebook.

"We're here to talk with you about your whereabouts on the morning that Frank Chimen was found in the Chicago River. Tests have indicated that he died from an opioid overdose, administered before he ended up in the water. Can—"

"A lot of people aren't aware," interrupted Carter, "that the downtown area is extensively monitored with CCTV cameras. It's part of the city's public safety system. There are literally thousands of them installed around the Loop and elsewhere," he said, gleefully, emphasizing the word "thousands."

"Guess what we found when we looked through them?"

Linda looked at him sideways. It was her interview, but he was the senior officer.

I really hated this guy. "You, up against a wall, getting it from behind by one of the Latin Kings?"

His face reddened. "This murder has your—"

"Can you tell us where you were that morning?" interrupted Linda.

"I went downtown."

Carter perked up. "How is it you know exactly what morning we're talking about?" he said, smirking. "We didn't tell you the date."

I rolled my eyes. "I saw his body while they were pulling it out of the river. You don't tend to forget the day you see something like that."

"Sure, you—"

"What time was that?" interrupted Linda.

"Around seven."

"Is that unusual for you to be there that early in the morning? You live in Andersonville, and your restaurant is in Portage Park."

"Yes. I was there for a meeting."

"A meeting with who?"

Dammit. "I can't tell you."

Smith had warned me not to share the details of our arrangement with anyone, that in exchange for helping the FBI on occasion he would protect Gigi from arrest and jail, and keep my own transgressions hidden from the police.

In particular, he'd warned me to not speak of my role in this operation. Even though most of the PD were aware of the attack on the plant, only a handful of them knew about my involvement, and Smith wanted to keep it that way to preserve me as a confidential informant for future operations.

Part of me was sorely tempted to tell Linda and Carter about it so I'd be off the hook for any of Smith's future operations.

But I didn't want to go to jail. And now that Gigi was back on the streets I needed to preserve her protection.

"There's a surprise," Carter scoffed.

Linda opened the laptop and hit a few keys, then she turned it toward me.

"This is from that morning. Is this you, on the Dearborn bridge?"

There I was, walking across, just as the sun was coming up.

"Yes."

"Going to this meeting you can't tell us about," said Carter sarcastically.

Linda took a deep breath and turned her laptop back toward her. "We've determined Frank Chimen's time of death was between one and four a.m." She hit a few more keys, then turned it toward me again.

"This was taken at two forty-five a.m. that same morning. Is that you?" she said, in a voice that sounded like she hoped it wasn't.

The picture was a grainy green and white image of two people standing on the Riverwalk near a boat launch, upstream of the State Street Bridge.

One of them was clearly Frank Chimen. The other person was wearing a hooded jacket, his or her face not visible from this angle.

"Is that you, Sags?" she asked gently.

"No. Why would you think that's me?"

"Because we know you're a murderous—"

"Our analytics team determined that the approximate height and weight of the person talking to Frank Chimen is a match for you. And you, uh, you have a connection to the deceased."

"What connection is that?" I said, even though I knew what it was.

"Frank Chimen was your sister's pimp and drug dealer."

"For the record, that's motive," said Carter. Gloating.

"She has lots of dealers."

"Yes, and isn't it interesting that so many of them have been found dead in the last two years? And what a coincidence that Frank Chimen died from a massive opioid overdose, something we know you can get your hands on easily from your drug addict, whore of a sister."

"Drug dealing is a dangerous business. Maybe he was an addict himself." I pointed at Carter. "And you keep my sister out of this."

Carter and I stared at each other until Linda cleared her throat.

"We've determined that it wasn't an accidental overdose. The amount of opiate in his blood was several hundred times more than the lethal dose. And there was a puncture wound, from a syringe, in his thigh. Not a place that addicts normally choose to inject." She'd told me that before, but not officially.

"Ms. Pfister, just to be clear, are you saying that is not you standing next to Frank Chimen in this image?"

"Yes, I'm saying that. And before you ask, I did not kill Frank Chimen."

"Where were you around three a.m. on that morning?"

"Where most people are. At home, in bed. Asleep."

"Can anyone verify that?"

"I was alone."

Carter scoffed.

"But I have a roommate. She can verify I was there."

"OK," said Linda. "We'll just—"

"I understand you recently moved to a multi-level house in Andersonville. Easy to come and go there, with so many floors," said Carter. Of course he knew where I lived.

Linda looked disturbingly unsure.

"Look, you have me on video on the bridge at seven that morning. If it was me that killed him, why in hell would I go back to the river that same morning?"

"That's easy," said Carter. "To see your handiwork. Lots of criminals return to the scene of their crimes. You can't help yourselves."

"That's idiotic. Let's suppose that is me," I said, pointing to the image. "And that I somehow injected Frank Chimen with fentanyl. How—"

"How do you know it was fentanyl? We didn't tell you." Carter sat back in his seat, his arms crossed.

"Everyone knows Frank Chimen is a fentanyl dealer. And that's the majority of what's on the street right now. And it's the most common cause of overdoses." I turned back to Linda. "Let's suppose it was me, that somehow I injected him with a lethal dose of fentanyl from a loaded syringe that I happened to be carrying around in my pocket. And then let's suppose I figured out some way to get him in the water, at, what time did you say that was?"

"A little before three a.m."

"How in hell would I have known that his body would get caught up, right under the State Street Bridge? Isn't it more reasonable to presume that I would have put his body in the water so it would float downstream and carry away the evidence?" I'd sure as hell thought so at the time.

Carter's face was beet red. He knew I was right; there was no way whoever dumped the body in the river at three a.m. would've been able to predict that it would get stuck under a bridge.

I leaned back in my chair. "So, are we done?"

Linda looked at Carter. He didn't say anything, although if looks could kill I'd be as dead as Frank Chimen.

"We're done," said Linda. "Thanks for coming in."

Carter pointed his stubby finger at me. I hated that finger. "This isn't over."

Linda followed me out of the room. When we were out of earshot of Carter, she said, "I'm sorry, Sags. I was just following up. As soon as he knew you were on the interview list he insisted on being a part of it."

"I know. It's OK. Thanks Linda."

"But . . ." she paused. "They have other angles, and are still doing work on the footage. Cleaning it up. And these are just the first images. There will be more. In addition to the cameras put up as part of the city's safety efforts there are private ones. We're getting the footage from those, too. It's only a matter of time before we're able to ID the other person in the picture I showed you. Are you sure there's nothing you can tell us that will rule you out?"

"I told you everything I know. Why is everyone so hot, anyway, on finding out what happened to a drug-dealing pimp?"

"Everyone's not. It was my part of the terrorist case. The vandalism incidents were linked to the threat, and Chimen was linked to the vandalism. Even though the terrorist threat is resolved this is still my case. And it's my first one. I don't have to tell you what that means."

I knew Linda, and I did know what it meant. She wouldn't rest until she solved it.

THIRTY-FIVE

As soon as I got home I called Smith to meet me at the cemetery.

"I just had my interview about Frank Chimen's death. It happened the same day as our meeting at the diner. They know I came into the city that morning, and they know that's unusual for me. I couldn't tell them why, and because of that they think I had something to with Chimen." Partially true, at least.

"You're right. You can't tell them. And why should it matter? Are you afraid they'll find something?" he chuckled. He was so much more relaxed now that the Nottingham operation was over.

I didn't bother answering, which told him all he needed to know.

His smile turned to a scowl. "Dammit, Sagarine. We've talked about this. I told you, you have to stop." He shook his head. "I'm not covering for you this time."

"You didn't seem to mind when Brajen Krol turned up dead."

Last year Brajen Krol had emerged as the head of a new gang in the city, the one that had been trying to break in on the thriving fentanyl trade. Michael had been part of his gang when Maude found him.

Michael left the gang, and Brajen Krol had vowed to kill him for it. Maude had been terrified Krol would go through with it.

"He was going to kill Michael for leaving the gang. Maude let me know she'd be OK if I helped her out with the situation. And I did. If they link me to Frank Chimen's death, what happened to Brajen Krol is going to come up, too. And when it does, she's going to get dragged into it."

His eyes were wide. He clearly hadn't a clue about what happened to Brajen Krol.

"Number one, I don't believe you. Maude wouldn't do that. And number two, even if she did, I know you'd never drag her name into an investigation." He knew I had my faults, but I'd never betray Maude.

"You're right, I wouldn't. But that doesn't mean they wouldn't find out. You know as well as I do that anything can turn up in the course of an investigation. And you know that Carter's got it in for me. He'll turn over every stone to put as much on me as possible. And if her name did come up, associated with Brajen Krol's death, the least that would happen to her is that she'd lose her career."

His upbeat expression disappeared.

"I'm not asking you to cover for me. I just need them to know I was with you that morning, which is the truth. And that I had nothing to do with Chimen's death."

I waited.

"For what it's worth, Chimen was Gigi's dealer, he pimped her out, and he was beating her up. Regularly."

"I don't care. I don't believe Maude would do that. If you had anything to do with Chimen's death, I can't help you."

"Even after all I did for you on this thing with Nottingham?"

"There's a line I can't cross."

"Any more, you mean."

He scowled.

"Fine." Time to bring out the big guns. "What if I could tell you how Nottingham funneled the money to Rykov? I understand you're still in the dark about that."

Maude had told me that how the money had made its way to Rykov was the last piece of the operation that they hadn't been able to unravel. Smith and his team had turned over every financial leaf to figure it out, but it remained a mystery. Mason hadn't been clued in on the financial side of things.

It was more than just idle curiosity. These days the majority of major criminals were prosecuted for laundering money, sometimes instead of the more heinous crimes they'd committed, largely because the top men usually had lackeys to do their dirty work for them.

The big guys kept their hands clean, and it was hard to get

their minions to turn on them. More than one lower-level criminal had been killed for snitching. The reach of the bosses extended into prisons, and it wasn't feasible to put everyone into witness protection.

Al Capone's famous arrest for tax evasion was the archetype for bringing down top bosses on tangential crimes, and by necessity the FBI had gotten very good at following money trails.

They were stumped at how Nottingham had done it, and concerned that there was a financial pathway that they didn't know about. So finding out how he'd been able to send millions to Rykov was not a trivial matter.

Smith's face gave away his struggle between his desire to solve the financial mystery and his belief that I shouldn't continue to get away with murder.

"I don't believe you."

I shrugged. "If after I tell you, you still don't believe me, you don't have to do anything. But if you do, I need you to talk to Linda, do whatever you have to do, to get her to stop looking at me for Frank Chimen's death."

The muscle in his jaw clenched and unclenched. "Fine. But only if it turns out to be right."

"You'll take care of this? You promise?"

He mumbled assent.

"Is that a yes?"

"Yes, dammit."

I trusted him. Smith was nothing if not honorable.

"The money that Nottingham sent to Rykov came from selling diamonds."

He rolled his eyes in disgust. "No, he didn't. Obviously we looked into that. Diamonds are tightly regulated. Each one is marked with an identification number, and it has to carry a provenance with it. Any large diamond purchases or sales are flagged. We also looked into Carat and Crown's inventory. Nothing is missing, nothing's been stolen. And if I know anything about Richard Nottingham it's that he's always cared too much about his reputation in the industry to mess around with black market diamonds."

I reached into my pocket and pulled out a handful of stones.

"Are those diamonds? Where did you get those?"

"From Nottingham's diamond cutting room. I was locked in there, remember?"

"So you stole them?"

"You're missing the point here, Smith."

I got up off of the bench and dropped one of the stones on the concrete sidewalk. I stomped on it with my boot, then picked it up and handed it to him.

"Look at it."

He turned it over in his hand, then shrugged. "So?"

"See that chip?" I said, pointing.

He peered at it closely.

"Diamonds don't chip . . ."

"That's right. They don't. This isn't a diamond. It's a cubic zirconia. These are all cubic zirconia."

"How did you find that out?"

"I took them to a pawn shop."

"Seriously? You stole Nottingham's diamonds, and then tried to sell them?"

"C'mon, Smith. After what I went through I didn't think taking a few diamonds off of a terrorist pedophile who'd already left the country was that big of a deal."

The fact was that I needed some cash to put Gigi back in rehab, if and when we found her. I'd pulled out all the stops to get my parents to pay for her last stint. After years of failed rehab they weren't eager to "throw good money after bad" as my dad put it. But they'd never agree to do it again.

Of all the facilities she'd been in, she'd lasted the longest at Face the Future, which wasn't cheap. She'd made real progress there; I had hope that maybe the next time would be the one that stuck.

"I don't understand. How does cubic zirconia in Nottingham's cutting room add up to selling diamonds?"

"Remember that over-the-top necklace Nottingham makes twice a year? The one that gets displayed on Celeste Nottingham when they make their trips to Canada?"

"Yes. And I know the diamonds in that necklace get certified before they leave the country."

"Those diamonds, the ones she wears out of the country are real, as I think are the ones that she shows off at the employee dinner in Yellowknife. And I know, because I was there, that when she's not wearing it the necklace stays in a lockbox, and the lockbox stays with Nottingham."

I'd seen him carrying it on the plane on the trip back, at the time confused that he hadn't put it in the hands of one of his security team.

"I think after she shows it off at the dinner he takes it to put it in the lockbox. Then he replaces the real diamonds with similarly shaped cubic zirconia stones. He's an expert diamond cutter, and could easily make two nearly identical sets: one real, and one cubic zirconia. There were two sets like that on the table when I saw him polishing the diamond. After he takes out the real diamonds and replaces them with the fakes, he sells the real ones. Celeste doesn't wear it on the way back and no one ever looks at it again."

"I told you, diamonds are tightly controlled. There's no way he could sell the real diamonds without the provenance."

"He couldn't sell them at their total value. But he could sell them on the black market, if he were willing to take a huge loss. Each of those stones are worth tens of millions of dollars; if he sold them for ten percent of what they're worth that would be—"

"About the same amount of money that was injected into Rykov's accounts," he murmured.

"Check the dates that the cash infusions made it into Rykov's account. I'll bet a lot of them were made within days of Nottingham's trips to Canada."

"Huh. I wonder why Mason didn't say anything about this? He told us everything else."

"I doubt he knew about it. I don't think he was as close to Nottingham as he thought he was. Nottingham used him, just like he used everyone else. So, are we good? Are you going to take care of the Frank Chimen thing?"

"Sure."

I turned to go. I didn't bother asking him if they'd found Gigi. He would have told me if they had.

"Sagarine . . ."

He held out his hand. I pulled the rest of the stones out of my pocket and handed them to him.

I turned away when his phone rung.

"Yes? . . . Great, thank you."

He called after me. "They found Gigi."

I turned to him, then waited for what seemed like an eternity, but was barely seconds, before he added, "She's alive."

THIRTY-SIX

I ran back to the house. Smith had already called Maude, and she was waiting with her keys in her hand. She drove us to the hospital in record time.

When we got to Gigi's room Michael was sitting next to her. She was holding his hand. I noted fresh purple bruises on her face.

"Hey." I leaned over the bed and gave her a hug. "How are you doing?"

"OK," she said, sleepy.

"What happened?"

A question that could mean a million different things, including, "How did you end up here?" Or, "Why did you leave rehab, it seemed like it was going so well?" Or, "Which dirtbag dealer pulled you out of rehab?" Or, "Why the hell didn't you call me?" But I let her choose which one to answer.

She looked down, embarrassed. "I OD'd."

She'd been lucky. Junkies who OD'd on the street didn't often make it to the hospital.

"How did you get here?"

She didn't answer, already nodding off. They'd given her something to prevent withdrawal symptoms for the time being.

"Looks like your boyfriend came through," I said to Maude.

She shook her head. "Jeb's man didn't find her." She pointed to her brother. "Michael did."

He looked away, embarrassed.

"How did you do that?"

"Maude told me you were looking for her. I still have some friends on the street. I asked them to keep an eye out for her. One of them found her at the tent city under the Dan Ryan. It was, uh, one of the places where Sheila used to score. He called me."

Sheila was the homeless addict who'd kidnapped Michael when he was two, and with whom he'd lived with for years. Even though she'd taken him from his family, she'd cared for him, and he had a soft spot for her.

"Gigi was almost dead when he got there," Maude added. "Michael called 911 and they brought her here."

I felt a fresh wave of anger at her dealer, whoever it was. He'd left her on the street like a pile of garbage. And what the hell had Smith's guy been doing? Smith said the tent city was one of the first places he was going to check out.

Michael saw my face, and added, "For what it's worth, Mike Rivers' guy did look there. But they wouldn't have told him anything. They don't trust law enforcement."

I touched Maude's arm and pointed to the hallway. We left Michael there, still holding Gigi's hand. I was weak with relief, and hadn't realized how much I was dreading finding her dead. But I knew what would happen next.

When Maude and I were out of earshot, I said, "They're going to keep her overnight, then she'll be back on the street. How would you feel, if for a little while, we—"

"Sure, she can stay with us."

I looked at her gratefully. We'd talked about her staying with us, but it was always in the context of her successfully completing rehab. So this wasn't a small ask. Maude knew from previous visits what it meant to have an addict in the house. We'd need to lock up anything we didn't want stolen and pawned. Any cash laying around would disappear.

"I was thinking, I might ask Michael to move in, too, if you're OK with that. He's getting a little antsy, staying with Mom and Dad."

I looked back at the room. "Of course. It might be good for her. They seem to have a connection."

"Who knows? Maybe one day we'll be related." Maude gave me a hug.

We stopped at the nurse's station. "How is she doing?"

"She was beat up, and she's detoxing. We're giving her clonidine."

"How long will you keep her here?"

"She's remarkably healthy, all things considered. If nothing changes she'll be discharged in the morning."

"Thanks. I'll be here then to pick her up."

We went back to the room and said goodbye to Michael. Gigi was fast asleep.

"I feel like we should celebrate. How about a drink?" Maude asked as we got in the elevator.

We definitely needed to celebrate. "I have a better idea. Can you drop me off at the restaurant? And I need you to make a few calls."

There were times it was particularly good to be a restaurant owner.

I closed Saga for the day, but asked Stephen and Courtney to come in and put them to work setting up the bar while I got to work in the kitchen.

The last week had been too much. Too much adrenaline, too much worry, too much angst. The best thing for me to calm down, to center myself, was to cook. To make food that I loved to make.

French food was my comfort food, and my go-to when I needed to relax. Early in my culinary career I'd been enamored with French food. Learning the basics of French cooking was a staple of any culinary program, but one of my instructors was French, and he regularly invited his students over for meals at his home, cooked by him and his wife, Dominique. Comforting, elegant, and delicious, the meals were a revelation.

Stephen popped his head in while I was head down at the stove with a sauce. "They're here."

Six hours had gone by in a flash. "Thanks."

Stephen and Courtney had arranged one large table in the center of the bar. Sitting at it were Maude, Smith, Michael, Linda, Tasia, and Zach. Courtney broke out the champagne, a decent Collet. Not Nottingham level, but not bad.

I'd cooked up a storm. Stephen and Courtney helped me carry out steamed haricot verts with butter and sliced almonds, and fennel salad with tangy orange vinaigrette, followed by a massive bowl of beef bourguignon and platters of rich, earthy coq au vin, both served with my secret recipe, extra crisp French fries.

The last thing to make it to the table was one of my specialties, courtesy of Dominique. She and my instructor were from Grenoble, the largest city in what had historically been known as the Dauphiné region of France. No longer existing as an administrative entity, the food culture lived on through its most famous dish, gratin dauphinois—potatoes layered with Gruyère cheese and cream. Dominique made a version of it that used endive instead of potatoes. The slightly bitter endive coupled with rich cream and caramelly Gruyère kicked the dish up to eleven.

Everyone was feeling the same way I was: relieved, exhausted, sleep deprived, and very hungry. The food disappeared quickly.

Even after the food was gone no one was interested in leaving. They lingered, breaking up into small groups, drinking and talking. I joined Tasia at the bar.

"Where's Martin?"

"In rehab."

I raised my eyebrows. "Already?"

She nodded. "He's at the Future Horizons Center."

I gave a low whistle. "That place is pricey." I'd looked into it for Gigi. But even if I could get my dad to pay for one more try at rehab, there was no way he could gather enough cash for that one.

She laughed. "Yes, it is. But it turns out we can afford it. Martin and I own the estate now, and the business."

"So . . . they let him go?" The last time I'd seen Martin he'd been handcuffed to a hospital bed.

"Yes. The DA wasn't all that eager to go after him, especially when I let them know about the phalanx of lawyers I had ready to take them on."

Even if she had an army of high-priced lawyers, the FBI didn't mess around with terrorists. "What did he tell them, about, you know, why he didn't inform the FBI sooner about what his dad was doing?"

"Martin knew that dad was planning something that had

to do with Jardine, but he didn't know any of the details. He had no idea that the city water supply was in jeopardy. He thought it would be fun to give it to the police as a code. I told you, he's just bored, all the time. If he'd known all of what my dad was doing he would have told them right away. He had no idea it was something as bad as that." She shook her head. "And he was honestly surprised it took the police that long to figure it out. He has no idea how much smarter he is than anyone else. Neither of us knew my dad's history. We had no idea we were Russian, for starters. I also made sure they knew about his drug problem. The DA let him go on condition that he go to rehab, which as far as I'm concerned is a great outcome. Do you . . . do you know, did Alan and Celeste know? About my dad?"

"No. That's a question for the FBI."

She shook her head. "No thanks. I've had enough law enforcement to last me a lifetime."

"I don't know, Smith's not that bad." I looked over at him. He was sitting next to Maude, his arm around her shoulders.

"Will you be moving back in? To the estate? Once they're done with it?" The FBI had been going over it with a fine-tooth comb.

"Only until we can find somewhere else. Then we'll sell it. There are too many bad memories there."

"Will you be . . . staying in the city?"

"Yes," she said, leaning forward and kissing me.

I let out the breath I'd been holding. I hadn't realized how much I desperately wanted her to stay.

"We're having my mother moved to Rosehill. There's a service tomorrow, if you want to come."

"Of course.

"Nice to see him," I nodded to Zach, who was being chatted up by Linda.

"We're taking care of him. He'll never have to work again. He was the only one of the security team to look out for Martin. It's the least we can do. Speaking of the least we can do, I understand Gigi's being discharged tomorrow."

"Yeah." My euphoria at Tasia staying in the city disappeared at the thought of Gigi. I wasn't naïve enough to think that staying with me and Maude would be enough to keep her off the streets and away from drugs.

"If it's OK with you, I've booked her a spot at Horizons."

"What?"

"We have more money than we know what to do with. And Horizons has one of the lowest recidivism rates in the country."

She leaned forward and put her arms around me. "Maybe we'll get them both back."

I was stunned. I didn't know what to say, so I just hugged her.

"Can I get in on this?" Linda had left the group and was standing next to us. We broke off our hug.

"Any time," I smiled.

"Actually, Sags, can I talk to you alone for a moment?"

We moved over to take seats at the empty booth.

"I wanted to tell you, personally, that you're officially cleared of Frank Chimen's death."

I tried not to obviously exhale. "That's good to know."

"Yeah. We got some additional information from the FBI that points toward a rival drug dealer."

So Smith had come through. I looked over at him. He nodded.

"Of course, Carter's not happy. For some reason he really has it in for you."

"No kidding."

"Any idea why?"

"It goes back. He thinks I was responsible for Louie Ferrar's murder."

She laughed. "Why would he think that?"

"I have no idea."

EPILOGUE

Gigi and Martin were both at Horizons, two weeks into their programs. They'd be there for a while.

They were well past the painful physical withdrawal period of their recoveries. But the emotional elements of their addictions would need to be addressed before they could leave, and have a shot at staying sober.

It was good, I thought, that they were there at the same time. They'd been through similar childhood trauma, and it helped that they were together, and that they had a connection.

Things were more or less back to normal. Part of me was a little disappointed; they really didn't need me at the restaurant, and I had tons of time on my hands.

I spent a lot of time with Tasia at the estate. It was a big place for her to be in by herself. I helped her clean up the mess the FBI had made, then we went through everything in the house.

We started with her dad's diamond cutting room. We completely dismantled it, taking up the table and emptying out the file cabinets. Once everything was out she noticed a small hook in the cement floor, under where the carpet had been.

The hook pulled up a thin square of cement, under which was embedded a small safe. We used a crowbar to get it out, then I took it to Maude to help us get it open.

"Wow, that was fast," I said, after she'd taken all of ten minutes to open it.

"It's a standard rotary dial, I just used a dial decoder. I'm not sure why someone like Nottingham would use such an archaic safe to keep valuables."

"I don't think he ever expected anyone to find it."

I didn't feel right opening it without Tasia, so took it back to the estate where we could open it together.

Inside was a set of old photos. Faded, black and white pictures, all dated in Cyrillic, of a young man we presumed was Nottingham. Standing next to a mine, sitting at a table in front of primitive cutting equipment, proudly holding up a stone, perhaps the first one he'd cut.

We sat silently and looked over each photo. "His most prized possessions," Tasia said acidly. "What should I do with them?"

"I don't know. I'd hang on to them for now. At least until Martin's had a chance to see them. Then maybe some kind of ritual burning?"

As we went through the house we made a point to have sex in the rooms we cleaned out. Kind of like burning sage, but way more fun.

"I don't know," she said, as we were laying on what had been Alan and Celeste's bed. "Maybe I'll keep the place. It feels a lot happier now."

"It should." By now we'd consummated our relationship in every room of the house. All except Nottingham's master bedroom. She hadn't even opened the door to it.

"I'll need to see how Martin feels about it."

We laid there, entangled, when my phone rang.

It was Smith. "Do you have time to meet today? I can come by."

It was weird, him asking me, rather than demanding. I definitely preferred it.

"Sure. I'm at the estate."

I waited for the sound of the doorbell before I dressed and left Tasia to meet Smith downstairs.

When I opened the door and gestured him in, he said, "Let's take a walk."

I joined him outside, and we wandered around the side of the house on the gravel path.

"We just got word that the plane that was carrying Richard Nottingham, Alan, and Celeste made an emergency landing on their way to Moscow, in Krasnodar. Richard Nottingham died on the plane."

"When?"

"Two weeks ago."

"And you just found out now? You're slipping, Smith."

"It's not like we get instant news from Russia these days."

"Well, it looks like there is some justice in the world."

He continued crunching down the gravel path toward the oak tree, underneath which Tasia's mother had been buried.

"He died of a massive fentanyl overdose. It had apparently been mixed into his milk."

"Kumis."

He stopped and turned to me. "You don't happen to know anything about that, do you?"

"Does it matter?"

"Only for my personal curiosity."

Even if the Russians investigated Nottingham's death, there would be little they could do about it. And it wasn't like anyone in the US would help them with it.

"Let's see," I said, looking up. "Nottingham was a pedophile. He procured and abused little boys, including his own two sons, for decades. He murdered his own wife. He financed and supplied the men for what would have been the largest terrorist attack on the country, ever. One that would have killed, best case, thousands of people in this city, and worst case, millions, and then completely shut it down for the foreseeable future. If I did do something, and I'm not saying I did, I wouldn't feel bad about it. I don't think it's right that someone like that should get to live out his life in luxury. Frankly, I think it's too bad Alan and Celeste will. Even if they weren't directly involved they benefited from his wealth. And they would have had to turn a blind eye to what he was doing. At least the abuse."

"I'm not so sure about that."

"About what?"

"About them living out their lives in luxury. After the three of them left the country, the estate went to Tasia and Martin. The FBI froze all of Richard Nottingham's accounts. The assumption is that Alan and Celeste were complicit in what Nottingham was doing, so their accounts were frozen, too."

I doubted they had any idea about his involvement in the terrorist attack, but it didn't look good that they skipped the country with him.

"I know, but I assume they took a bunch of diamonds with them."

He nodded. "They did. Or, at least, they thought they did."

He waited, a small smile forming on his lips.

"They took the necklaces."

He nodded again, his smile broadening.

Ah. "And they don't know they're fake."

"Doubtful. Nottingham knew they were, but he didn't care. After what he did, the Russian government would have taken care of him for life. But we know he didn't tell anyone about the fake necklaces, even Mason Cooper. I'm guessing Alan and Celeste took them as insurance, thinking wherever they were going they could sell them and live in style on the proceeds. They're going to be in for a rude shock when they try to make a living in Russia on a bunch of cubic zirconia. And it's unlikely the government will be interested in spending any resources making them comfortable. As far as we can tell, they weren't working with Richard on any of this. I doubt they even knew he was Russian."

I felt a little bad, thinking of Celeste, stuck in Russia with Alan and no money. At least she'd have plenty of booze, although her days of diamond-filtered spirits were over.

"Thanks for letting me know. Want to stay for a drink? I think there's some decent vodka in the office."

Acknowledgments

Don't go looking for the Nottinghams' estate in North Edgebrook, as it is fictional, as is the White Wolf Lodge. The Hopleaf Pub is very much real, and I miss it.

Chicago's Jardine Water Treatment Plant is one of the most secure pieces of infrastructure in the country, and in the interest of not having anything to do with making it less so, I left details of it non-specific.

There is no definitive proof that Russia was responsible for the Nord Stream explosion, although they did benefit from it. Russia has claimed it was a false flag operation by Ukraine. In no way was it my intent to imply that either the US or Ukraine was responsible.

I love it when writing gives me an opportunity to connect with creative and talented people. Maggie Hennessy, food writer extraordinaire (https://www.maggiehennessy.com/), allowed me to include a fictional review of Sagarine Pfister's restaurant Saga under her byline. To be clear, I wrote the review myself, and while I endeavored to give it the tone and style of Maggie's, I know it fell well short of her unique style. I urge anyone who's interested in food writing that is fresh, interesting, and well written to look up her articles in places such as *Time Out* and *Bon Appetit*, and follow her on Instagram where you can keep up on her latest content (@edible_words).

As I was researching foods north of the border I came across "birch syrup". I ordered a sampler pack from Crooked Creek Birch (https://crookedcreekbirch.com/) and shared it with friends. All I can say is, if you haven't tried this stuff, you need to. Crooked Creek Birch is family owned and a delight to work with (@crookedcreekbirch).

Ongoing and heartfelt thanks to the team at Severn House. Tina, Laurie, Sianna, Martin and the rest who make sure my books are as good as they can be before going out into the world.

I can't express enough my appreciation to Anna, and to my beta readers and friends Jennifer, Lynn, Stuart, Kristen and Cindy Gaines. Your input and support are priceless.